A Rob Wyllie paperback
First published in Great Britain in 2023 by Rob Wyllie Books,
Derbyshire, United Kingdom

RobWyllie.com

The Maggie Bainbridge Series

Death After Dinner

The Leonardo Murders

The Aphrodite Suicides

The Ardmore Inheritance

Past Sins

Murder on Salisbury Plain

Presumption of Death

The Loch Lomond Murders

The Royal Mile Murders

The

Royal Mile Murders

Rob Wyllie

Prologue

Charlie McCrae took a final puff on his ciggie then tossed it down onto the pavement, stubbing it out with a toe of his boot. It wasn't a bad job this, he reflected, all-in-all. The hours were pretty rubbish, forcing him to drag himself out of bed five days a week at half-two in the morning, and the money wasn't exactly amazing either, but then again, he was pretty much his own boss, which he liked very much. His supervisor, a prickly Welsh twat called Tony Hancock, who definitely didn't share the sense of humour of his famous namesake, had never fancied the stupidly early starts, so it was months since he'd seen the bloke in the flesh. Which was just the way Charlie liked it, although he knew the suspicious bastard checked the CCTV recordings from time to time, just to make sure Charlie had actually turned up for duty. But Edinburgh's Royal Mile was a big beat, with plenty of benches to plonk your backside on if you fancied a snooze or a sly read at the news on your phone anytime during your shift. He had three or four regular facilities to take care of in his role as *Senior Orderly, Public Conveniences*, his official job-title. Or in other words, bog-cleaner, which is how he described himself if any of the guys down the pub asked him what he did for a living. Unless it was some good-looking bird of course, when he said he was a helicopter pilot working on the North Sea rigs.

As was his routine, this morning he would be starting with the big ladies' loo up on Castle Wind, the one not too far from the Castle esplanade, and heavily-used by the tourists that flocked to the city in the summer. At this time of the day of course there were not many people around, bar the occasional drunk mumbling to himself - or herself - as they tried to work out where the hell they were and how they'd got there. But tonight it was all quiet on the western front, which was how Charlie liked it. Although it was just twenty-four hours since his last visit, he knew pretty much the scene that would await him. Ten stalls to be cleaned, with a hundred percent certainty that at least half-a-dozen would be in a disgusting state. He pushed open the main door, trundled in with his trolley, then gave his head a scratch as he considered where he would start this morning. Left to right, or right to left, it really made no odds, although he'd always tended to favour starting from the right for some reason. But what the hell, we'll start on the *left* this morning, he thought, joking to himself. *Live dangerously, eh? Why not? Rock and Roll!* Five stalls in, he was congratulating himself on an inspired choice. There was nothing to worry about in any of them, needing nothing more than a skoosh with the anti-bacterial spray and a quick lick with the mop and that was it, job done.

Until, opening stall six, his luck ran out.

Chapter 1

Yash Patel took a sip from his pint and lolled back in his chair, surveying the scene before him. This was a nice room, no doubt about it, the biggest function suite in Edinburgh's swanky Royal Mile Grampian hotel, the wall-to-ceiling plate-glass windows to his left affording a fine view across the twinkling evening cityscape. And then he gave a wry smile as he recognised the source of the old-fashioned adjective. *Swanky*. Goodness, was he already turning into his dad at the age of thirty-four? Not that that would be a bad thing, but the old boy still contrived to sound like an actor in one of these old forties black-and-white movies. Doing the sums in his head, he estimated there were about a hundred or so tables in the room, each elaborately dressed with stiff white linen table-cloths, the dinner having being served on fine china, although the food itself had been nothing to write home about. Now a small army of waiting staff were clearing away the dessert plates in preparation for the ceremony to begin. It was looking like being a long night, he thought ruefully, with a never-ending succession of obscure and boring awards to sit through before they got to the big one, the only one that mattered. *Story of The Year.* Of course, that was the one that he, Yash Patel, superstar investigative journalist with the *Chronicle*, was up for. And naturally he expected to win, delivering some reward for making the long trek northwards from his sleek Battersea flat. Yeah sure, these were just the *Scottish* Media Awards, so strictly second-division in the overall scheme of things, but every gong helped towards the super-impressive CV he was intent on building. *Yash Patel, Winner of Scottish Story of the Year 2023*. That didn't sound too bad, so he would take it of course. But that wasn't why he was here.

He leant over and smiled at his dinner companion, his paper's recently-appointed Scottish editor, Jimani Shah. He liked Jimani, despite a strong pang of professional jealousy directed at her rapid rise up the career ladder. Annoyingly, she was exactly the same age as himself, almost to the day, but he had consoled himself with the fact that the *Scottish Chronicle* was just the Mickey-Mouse rag when compared with the proper London paper for whom *he* worked. She, it turned out, was up for an award too, *Scottish Editor of the Year*, although given the comically-second-rate nature of the media up here, that wasn't exactly something to shout about. Still, he hoped very much she wouldn't win it, although as both a woman and from a minority culture too, he could - and would - rationalise any win as the awards committee simply wanting to show off their right-on liberal-progressive leanings. Actually, the truth was he didn't just *like* Jimani, but he fancied her something rotten too, and was hopeful that afterwards he might entice her up to his executive room for a post-award celebration. Not something he would share with either of his parents of course, who were still holding out for him to marry a nice girl of their choice, naturally from their own faith. No way was that happening, unless of course they managed to conjure him up a sexy little billionaire's daughter.

'Hey Jimani, all set for the ceremony then?' he said breezily. 'Got your acceptance speech ready? Keep it short is my advice.'

She laughed. 'I don't think I'll win, but if I do, a simple *thank-you* will suffice from me. What about you Yash? Have *you* got something prepared?'

He patted his jacket pocket. 'Yeah, about ten pages or so. Nice and short.'

She laughed again and nodded in the direction of the next table. 'There's your competition. Dominique Tremblay from the *Globe*. She's broken some big stories this year. In fact, I was thinking of asking our Board if we could make a bid for her. We could pay her so much more than she's getting from *that* rag.'

Yeah, he could see what she was doing, trying to wind him up. But he wasn't going to rise to it.

'Her, a winner? I don't think so,' he said dismissively. But now his attention was focussing on the real reason for his trip north. That being the search for his next blockbuster story, and goodness, wasn't there enough of the smelly brown stuff flying around up here in Scotland to fill a month's worth of sensational Yash Patel front-page scoops? He had noted earlier the presence of a bevy of local politicians on the guest list, including golden-boy Jack Urquhart, who just happened to be the partner of the aforementioned Dominique. Good-looking and charismatic, presently he was the Scottish Government's Diversity and Minority Employment minister, whatever the hell that was, but more importantly, he was strongly tipped to win the top job in the upcoming Nationalist leadership election. Present too was Livvy Foden, the Finance Minister and Urquhart's nearest rival, currently batting off allegations that she had siphoned off a cool quarter of a million pounds from the

Western Isles Regeneration fund. That wasn't going to do her leadership campaign any favours, Yash thought, but it certainly made for a great story. And the fact was, there seemed to be a few of those stories around, the local hacks suggesting that this was just the tip of the iceberg, with further juicy revelations to come, including the alleged existence of a senior married minister's love-child. Whatever way you looked at it, he thought, and despite their fervent denials of wrong-doing, the ruling party was in meltdown, with the drip-drip of scandal seeding a feeling amongst the Scottish electorate that their time was up. The economy was a mess, the health and education services were imploding, and the much-loved First Minister Sheila McClelland had stood down with the tantalising prize of independence further away than ever. It wasn't a good look, and nor was it a recipe for election success either.

And into the vacuum had stepped Tommy Taggart and his Scottish Freedom Party. Yash glanced over to Taggart's table, where the man sat with his attractive younger wife Sienna and a couple of muscled goons who looked as if they were about to burst out of their ill-fitting dinner jackets. True to form, Taggart wore a replica Scotland football shirt under his jacket, as did the goons. It had become the trademark of himself and his party, although whether the football authorities approved of this appropriation of their brand was open to question. In contrast, and in deference to the mandatory dress-code so pointedly ignored by her husband, Sienna Taggart wore a vivid red cocktail dress with a plunging neckline that displayed her impressive cleavage to the full. Involuntarily, Patel found himself staring at it, the thought occurring that it was probably surgically-enhanced, but that didn't make it any less alluring. As to her husband, there was no doubting that Taggart was a charismatic figure. Late-forties, powerfully-built, square-jawed, and newly-elected to the Scottish parliament after a contentious by-election, he had come from nowhere to become the man of the moment in Scotland's political landscape. Taggart was lounging back in his chair, a pint in one hand and an arrogant look on his face. Patel took a deep breath, shot Jimani a nervous smile and got to his feet. 'Wish me luck,' he said. He wandered over to Taggart's table, pulled out a conveniently-vacant chair and sat down beside him. Out the corner of one eye, he saw one of the goons beginning to make a move in his direction. 'It's a' right Gav,' Taggart said laconically, raising a restraining hand. Patel withdrew a business card from his pocket and slid it in front of Taggart. 'Yash Patel, the Chronicle. The London edition by the way, not the local comic.'

Taggart gave it a dismissive look. 'Aye, I know who you are. So you're here to write more shite about me and my wee party I suppose?'

'Not at all Mr Taggart,' Patel said smoothly. 'On the contrary. It's a fantastic story, your rise to prominence, both you and your party. It's a story our readers will be hugely interested in, I know that for certain. On both sides of the border.'

'You English don't give a feckin' crap about us up here pal, other than exploiting our natural resources for your own enrichment. And before you say anything about North Sea oil, I'm not talking about that old-school shit. Wind, waves and water, that's what it's all about now. We've got the stuff coming out of our ears. And once we're free from

English colonial oppression, we'll have more money than we know what to do with. It'll be like feckin' Dubai up here.'

Yash smiled to himself. *Colonial oppression*? He knew something of the history, but judged there would be no profit in mentioning that the three-hundred-year-old Act of Union had been mainly instigated by the Scottish Government of the time, who were in deep trouble, having more or less bankrupted the country through ill-starred foreign investments. Instead he gave a nod and said, 'That's a very interesting point of view Mr Taggart, and I don't think anyone's ever argued that Scotland couldn't make a go of it on its own. But that's what I'm offering you. The chance to tell your own story in your own words to the biggest newspaper in the country.' That was a lie of course, because this was going to be a Yash Patel story, not a Tommy Taggart one, but that was a detail that could be dealt with further down the line.

But it seemed that Taggart wasn't going to be taking the bait. 'Nah pal, that's not going to happen. Because if someone's going to tell my story, it'll be a Scottish hack in a Scottish paper. I mean, take a look around this room. There's a hundred desperate bastards here who'd sell their grannies to get a seat at the court of Tommy Taggart. So thanks pal, but no thanks.' Taggart's reaction didn't exactly surprise Patel, but the breathtaking arrogance of his response did, even if he'd half-expected it. But then Sienna Taggart leaned over and squeezed his arm, making sure he got an eyeful of her cleavage. 'There there son, don't get yourself all upset.' She turned to her husband and said condescendingly, 'Tommy darling, can we not give the boy just a *tiny* story? He seems such a nice lad. Even if he is an English Paki bastard.'

Shocked, Patel yanked his arm free. 'So is this what Scotland's going to be like under your *Freedom* Party is it? I'll tell you what, *that's* a story my readers are going to be interested in and make no mistake.'

Tommy Taggart laughed. 'Aye, well that *would* be your mistake pal. Do you think I keep Gav and Malc here on my staff just because they're so good-looking? So if you take my advice, you'll bugger off back to London pronto, if you don't want that pretty face of yours needing some plastic surgery.'

'Is that a *threat* Mr Taggart?' Patel said, astonished. 'Because it sounds very much like it to me.'

Taggart shrugged. 'Take it how you like pal.' He adopted a mocking English accent. 'But just toodle off old boy, and let me and my friends enjoy the rest of the evening. There's a good chap.'

Seething, Patel got to his feet. 'You've not heard the last of this Taggart, believe me.'

'Aye whatever pal,' Taggart said, returning to his menacing Glaswegian vernacular and giving a dismissive wave. He turned his back on Patel and took a swig from his pint, the message obvious. *Conversation over.*

'How did it go then?' Jimani asked him when he got back to their table.

'So-so,' he said, shooting her a wry smile. 'I didn't exactly get his agreement for a story.' Feeling calmer now, he wondered for a moment if he should tell her about the racial slur, but decided against it. It would only upset her, and he didn't want her to be upset, not tonight when he had other plans for the lovely Miss Jimani Shah. Besides which, he didn't want her getting a sniff of what he knew was going to be a *massive* story, bigger than anything he had ever imagined. 'But I'm not too bothered,' he lied. 'I'll probably get some sort of an article out of it at least. Not front page, but it will do.' No *probably* about it, he thought slyly. *Definitely*.

'Ah well,' she said. 'At least you tried. Let's just enjoy the rest of the evening now, shall we?' And then she beamed him a smile, which gave hope that his carnally-focussed *après-ceremony* scheme might indeed come to fruition.

The next hour of the evening seemed to crawl by at a snail's pace, as award after interminable award was announced by the smooth and attractive master of ceremonies, Siobhan Forsyth. Or should that be *mistress*, he mused? It was so easy to say - or in his case, to write - the wrong thing these days, when even the most innocent and innocuous comment could unleash the wrath of the professional offence-seekers who evidently spent their entire waking hours on social media, looking to be offended. Yeah sure, he thought bitterly, it must *really* hurt to be addressed by the wrong pronoun. But try being called a Paki bastard or worse five times a week and see what *that* felt like. Miss Forsyth, whose day-job was a news anchor with Scottish Television, and so presumably was eligible for an award herself, was speaking again. And reading from an autocue too, Patel reflecting somewhat unkindly that she was probably incapable of coherent speech without it.

'And now, ladies and gentlemen, I'm pleased to say we've reached our penultimate award of this wonderful evening, the award for Editor of the Year.' Patel gave a knowing nod in the direction of Jimani, and waited as Forsyth carefully prised open the gold envelope. 'And the winner is... Jimani Shah of the Scottish Chronicle.' He forced a smile as warm applause reverberated round the room, then watched as she made her way up to the stage to collect her award. Big fish, small pond, he thought in way of consolation, and anyway, the award, deserved or otherwise, was bound to put Jimani in a good mood. He knew too she wasn't a strict follower of her culture's traditions, so would probably be more than happy to celebrate her success with a couple of glasses of champagne. Smiling, he leaned back in his chair and imagined the pleasures to come. True to her word, she accepted the award with a smile and a simple *thank you*, and was now making her way back to their table. He stood up and applauded her arrival, rather more enthusiastically than he felt inside. 'Bloody well done,' he said, leaning over to kiss her cheek, an action that somehow now seemed perfectly appropriate. 'Thank you Yash,' she said, and for a long moment their eyes met. *Promising.*

Momentarily distracted, he noticed that Siobhan Forsyth was speaking again. 'And now, ladies and gentlemen, to our final award of the evening.' With her eyes locked onto the transparent autocue monitor, it was evident there was to be a scripted preamble before the award was handed over. 'So, I think we can say without fear of contradiction that this year has been a seismic one in the life of our proud nation.'

Too bloody right, Patel thought. *My Lomond Tower story was the biggest thing to happen here in a hundred years. Never mind story of the year, it should be story of the bloody century.* 'The two biggest stories of course,' Forsyth continued, 'were our men's football team beating Spain and our Rugby boys finishing second to Ireland in the Six Nations.' Forsyth paused - this too almost certainly scripted - for the laughter that duly arrived. 'But on a more sombre note, the people of Scotland were shocked and saddened to learn of the scandalous events surrounding the Lomond Tower tragedy, unmasked by the fantastic work of Yash Patel of the Chronicle.' He raised a hand to acknowledge the ripple of applause that broke out, though faintly embarrassed by the thought that the people of Scotland really ought to be thanking Maggie Bainbridge, not him. 'But in more recent months, the people of Scotland have been equally shocked by Dominique Tremblay's fearless exposure of scandal at the very heart of our government.' Patel scanned the room until his eyes fell upon the table hosting the delegation from the Scottish government. Finance Minister Foden, Justice Minister Rhona Black and Health Minister Hughie Smith, they were all here tonight, in a collective show of defiance, continuing to strenuously deny the string of allegations that Tremblay had published in the *Globe*. It took some balls just to turn up, that was for sure, when the love the Scottish people formerly held for the ruling party had turned to outright disdain, and when they seemed now to be prepared to put their faith in an unsavoury chancer like Tommy Taggart. This was the story of the moment, and with a sinking feeling, Patel realised that *his* story, although a mere nine months old, was now old news, only fit for wrapping up fish suppers, if they still did that. And, it turned out, he wasn't wrong.

'And the winner is...' This time it seemed to take an age for Forsyth to rip open the damned envelope. 'The winner is... Dominique Tremblay of the *Globe*.' He knew the TV cameras would be on him, so for the second time that evening he tried hard to force a smile. But not that hard, because actually, *so what?* It was only a second-rate award anyway, and there was every hope that a pitying Jimani would be keen to help him forget his disappointment when they shared his bed later in the evening. But as his brain continued with its rationalisation process, a thought suddenly struck him, a thought that made him forget both his loss, and momentarily at least, his upcoming assignation with Miss Shah. It was something that Maggie Bainbridge's cop pal DI Frank Stewart had said to him once, in the context of murder on that occasion, but it applied to any situation. *When two similar things happen, I can just about buy that as a coincidence. But when there's three, then that's a conspiracy. Def-in-itely.*

How *convenient* that the Mickey-Mouse government up here had suddenly been afflicted with not two, but *three* scandals, each one exposed by the Globe, and with the sickeningly self-satisfied Miss Dominique Tremblay hinting there were more to come. Now *that* was a story worth digging into.

Chapter 2

For Maggie, it was the strangest of days, a day she had been dreading ever since her associate Jimmy Stewart had given her his shocking and unexpected news a month or so back. And now here she was, plonked at her desk on a wet Glasgow Monday morning, in the tiny Byers Road office of Bainbridge Associates. *Alone*. Even the name of her firm, recently sign-written above the front door of the premises, conveyed a melancholy sadness, because by rights it should have said *Bainbridge & Stewart.* They were to have been full business partners, but Jimmy had decided, for reasons that she understood but did not pretend to like, that he must follow his own path. Now he had moved up to the Cairngorm Mountains, to his own little premises in Braemar, where he had set up his outward-bound school with an old mate from his army days. Yes, she understood his reasons, but God how she was missing him, and she knew she would continue to do so for a long time to come. But then again, it wasn't as if Jimmy was going to be out of her life forever. In fact quite the opposite, for in just five-and-a-half months' time she was to marry his lovely brother Frank. The date, delayed for reasons of logistics rather than any reluctance on the part of either party, was now set for the third weekend in October, to take place in her home county of Yorkshire, in the beautiful Dales town of Grassington. Or was it a village, she wasn't quite sure. Whatever its designated status, there was no denying its charm, and she was naturally looking forward to it very much. Jimmy was to be his brother's best man, and the two Stewarts had decided on full kilted Highland dress for the occasion. She, on the other hand, had not yet determined what she would wear. She reasoned it was often a dilemma for a bride second time around, the choice being whether to go for the traditional white wedding gown, or to settle for something more sober. Frank, bless him, and entirely in keeping with his divine character, had made no demands, nor even expressed the slightest preference. In fact, when she had casually brought up the subject one evening not that long ago, he had given her an answer she would never forget. *Maggie, I love you and you can turn up in a bin-bag. Just as long as you turn up.* And then she'd remembered how he'd been stood up at the altar all those years ago, an experience that had left a deep scar, and explained why he'd studiously avoided intimate relationships until he had fallen for her a year ago. And thank God he had.

Allowing her mind to drift onto the wedding had the effect of improving her spirits immeasurably, and glancing at her watch, she saw that her appointment with what might turn out to be the first client of the post-Jimmy era was imminent. She wondered if she might just have time to dash the two doors down to pick up a takeaway americano from the Bikini Baristas cafe, but then thought better of it. The *Bikini* employed a delightful but garrulous waitress named Lori, and experience had taught Maggie that it was impossible to make the purchase of any beverage in much less than ten minutes if Lori was in charge of the transaction. More than that, with the current absence of an assistant, she would have to shut up shop, and even if she was only out for ten minutes, that might mean she could miss a valuable walk-in client. Really, she needed to find an hour or two to go through the applications that had come in following her recent on-line job advert. But the thought of that filled her with dread, because how could she ever hope to replace Jimmy? With a sigh, she turned to her laptop and clicked on the document where she had recorded a few notes about her impending visitor. Jack Urquhart, that was his name, a guy who had recently become important enough to merit his own Wikipedia entry, albeit a sketchy four-paragraph job with several *citation required* tags. Thirty-nine years of age, born in Perth, took a Business Studies degree at Abertay University in Dundee. First job as a syndicated technology reporter for a local newspaper group, before switching to political journalism, where evidently he had failed to make much of an impression. But then, about four years ago, a sudden switch to politics, riding the wave of Nationalist popularity to get himself elected to the Scottish Parliament. A year or two back, First Minister Sheila McClelland had made him a Junior Minister, and now it seemed he was strongly tipped for the top job following her imminent departure from the political frontline. Scanning down the article, she saw he was living with another journalist, one Dominique Tremblay. The bitter break-up of his marriage, not long after the start of his political career, had briefly made the headlines it seemed, he having callously dumped the woman he had met at University and with whom he'd had two daughters. However, it was not just his sudden rise to political prominence that was making the front pages today. The Scottish edition of the Chronicle had recently ran a story that he was having an affair with a junior civil servant in his department, a woman fifteen years younger than him, and just one year into her public-sector career. Both had come out and denied it, and it didn't seem to have inhibited his rise, but Maggie wondered if it might be used in the future by his opponents to damage him, the old saying about no smoke without fire coming to mind. She wondered too what his current partner Miss Tremblay might think about the affair.

With that in mind, Maggie clicked on the link to take her to Tremblay's Wikipedia profile, this one an altogether more comprehensive affair than his own. It seemed that Dominique Tremblay - a Canadian, a fact that for some reason surprised Maggie - was currently the superstar of the relationship, although it might not stay that way for long if her partner's star continued to rise in the way that the media pundits were predicting. She was the political editor of the *Scottish Globe*, and evidently a serial award-winner too, the last just a few days earlier when she'd picked up a prestigious *Story of the Year* award at some big media shindig over in Edinburgh. She was an extremely attractive woman too, just a couple of years younger than Maggie herself, but on an annoyingly-different level in the glamour stakes. She clicked back on the link taking her to Jack Urquhart's page, featuring an obviously-posed photograph of its subject. *Good looking guy*, she thought, then reproached herself before giving a short laugh. Getting married didn't mean she would stop noticing attractive men, nature for some reason not working that way. After all, that was why the traditional marriage vows had been framed so severely, with all that stuff about being faithful and promising to forsake others. But for her, there was only Frank, vow or no vow, and it would always be that way. That she knew for certain.

For the first time it struck her how curious it was that a man with the growing public prominence of Urquhart should decide to cross the city to meet with a private investigator. Still, she wouldn't have to wait long to find out why. On cue, the old-fashioned bell above the door tinkled and Jack Urquhart strode in. He was wearing a dark navy suit, light blue Oxford shirt with a button-down collar and no tie. She estimated he was just under six foot, slim-hipped and broad-shouldered, with a shock of slightly greying hair which was brushed back from his forehead, falling into an unfashionable centre parting. And yes, he *was* pretty good-looking, if anything more so in the flesh than in his pictures. Shooting her a smile he said, 'Miss Bainbridge I presume?'

'That's me,' she said, getting up from her desk and extending a hand. 'Call me Maggie, please.' She gestured to a chair on the other side of her desk. 'Here, take a seat Mr Urquhart.'

He shot her another smile, this one, to Maggie's mild disconcertment, causing her heart to skip the tiniest beat. 'And I'm Jack.' He pulled the chair back and sat down. 'I hope you can help me.'

'That's what we're here for,' she said breezily, wondering for a moment if her casual use of *we* was breaking some arcane trade descriptions law. 'And I'm so sorry Jack, but I can't offer you a hot drink. We're between assistants at the moment and recruitment is such a nightmare in this part of the city.' There it was again, the *we* word. It was only a harmless white lie, she tried to convince herself, but it made her realise she needed to get off her backside and do something about recruiting a new assistant, and sharpish too.

'That's not a problem,' he said, smiling that smile again. 'I grabbed a takeaway americano before I jumped on the

Underground, and I downed a couple before I left home too. I'm caffeined up to the max now.'

She laughed. 'Good to know. So Jack, if you don't mind, can we get straight to the matter in hand? What is it you would like our help with?'

He gave her *another* bloody smile, still attractive but this one rather rueful. 'It's the old old thing and I'm sure it probably makes up half your work. You see, it's my partner. I'm pretty sure she's having an affair and I want you to find out if my suspicions are right. Because it's really doing my head in. The not knowing I mean. The whole thing's really got to me.'

'Okay,' she said slowly, processing what he had told her. 'Actually, I've read a little bit about your partner. She's a journalist isn't she? Dominique Tremblay. Writes for the Scottish edition of the *Globe* I believe.'

'Oh yes, darling Dominique's a journalist alright,' he said, making no attempt to hide his bitterness. 'She's the darling of Scotland's chattering classes, and a cheating cow to boot.'

Maggie remembered how she'd felt when she'd discovered her late husband Phillip was having an affair with that tarty Latin bitch who was his so-called *associate*. She'd had her suspicions for months, but it didn't make it any easier when one afternoon she had caught them *in flagrante*. So she could easily sympathise with what Jack Urquhart was going through. There were always two sides to every story of course, but for now, she would be on the side of her potential client.

'It's always a very distressing situation,' she said, in what she hoped was a sympathetic tone. 'So Jack, I know this might be difficult, but do you have any evidence to support your suspicions? Or in fact, do you know the name of the man you think she is involved with?'

He shook his head. 'I've no actual *evidence*, not as such. It's just she's become... well, *different*. And cold too, if you know what I'm getting at.'

'And how long have you been together?' Maggie asked delicately.

'Not long,' he said, shrugging. 'Two and a half years. I was married at the time.' He paused for a moment. 'I left my wife for Dominique.' The way he said it made Maggie think it was something he now regretted.

'Okay,' she nodded. 'And these... *difficulties*, if I can call them that? How long have they been going on, if you don't mind me asking?'

He gave an ironic laugh. 'Yeah, for about two and a half years. No, that's unfair. But I learned pretty soon who came first in our relationship.'

'And who was that?' Maggie asked.

'The bloody *Globe*, that's who. All she thinks about is her damn career.'

Maggie nodded. 'Yes, well I'm afraid that's something that happens in a lot of relationships, unfortunately.' Including in her own doomed marriage to Philip Brooks, late father of her beloved son Ollie. The contrast was stark. He had been the famous human-rights lawyer, friend of Prime Ministers and Presidents, she was the sad failed barrister, resigned to defending a succession of low-lifes for minimum fee. Except Philip hadn't been just devoting all those absent hours building his career. He'd spent plenty of these hours screwing around too.

'But I guess you must have known that when you got together?' she said. 'That her career was very important to her?'

'I've got a career too, and if I say so myself, politics is a bloody sight more important than being a bloody newspaper hack.' He spat out the words, sounding like a child denied another piece of birthday cake. 'Not that she gives a damn about me or what I want out of life. It's all about *her* in this relationship, one-way traffic. And now she thinks she can just throw me away now that she's tired of me.' *Rather like you threw away your wife and shattered the lives of your two lovely daughters,* Maggie thought, although of course she didn't voice it out loud.

'Well I'm sure she doesn't think that way,' Maggie said, trying to sound sympathetic, whilst at the same time hoping her growing irritation wasn't starting to show. The whining and self-pity were at odds with his confident good looks, although it perhaps explained why Dominique Tremblay was in search of pastures new. She wondered too what the electorate of Scotland would make of it if they knew the man tipped to be their new First Minister harboured such insecurities. But she was a private detective, not a political analyst nor a bloody marriage guidance councillor. As if she was in any way qualified for *that* latter line of work.

'Look, have you actually confronted her with your suspicions?' Maggie asked. 'Asked her straight out I mean? After all, you want to know, don't you?'

'Hell no,' he said dismissively. 'She wouldn't admit it anyway, and I don't want her to know I'm on to her sordid little trysts. And of course in my current position, with so much at stake...' He hesitated for a moment, then lowering his voice said, 'Well, let's just say, I can't afford there to be another...' He hesitated again. 'What I mean is, I can't afford there to be any scandal.'

Maggie smiled to herself. What he meant was *there's so much at stake for me personally, with the big prize tantalisingly within reach, I don't want another scandal like when I dumped my wife*. She said, 'Yes, I can understand that, and of course we would be very discreet should we take on your matter. But as to whether you should confront her or not, well I guess you know best in that regard.' Dialling in the sympathy once again she continued, 'Jack, I'm sorry I can't help you with your relationship, but I might be able to either confirm your suspicions or put your mind at rest. So why don't you email me a few details to get me started? The address of her place of work, any gym or club memberships she's got, any regular social events she attends, you know, like after-work drinks with friends or colleagues. Routine stuff like that. And I'll need you and your partner's home address too of course. Then just give me a couple of weeks or so and I'll report back to you. How does that sound?'

He gave a thumbs-up, then got up and took a step towards the door. 'Yeah, that's sounds great Maggie, thank you so much. And listen, I'm sorry I came over as such a wuss before. It's not like me, honestly. It's just that this whole thing has really got to me.' He gave a short laugh. 'But I think I said that earlier.'

She smiled. 'Don't worry about that. I understand what you're going through.'

As he reached the door, he turned then paused for a moment.

'Thank you again,' he said. 'I appreciate it. And actually -and I hope you don't mind me saying it - you're rather lovely. Would it be okay if I gave you a call sometime?'

***

The question had been as disconcerting as it was unexpected, so much so that she had to immediately shut up shop, hastily flipping over the *'Gone to Lunch'* sign and then heading the two doors down to the Bikini Baristas Cafe. Fortunately - or was it unfortunately, she wasn't quite sure - Lori was on duty.

'Hi there Maggie,' the young waitress said brightly. 'What can I get you? Oh aye, and before I forget, there's something I've been meaning to talk to you about.'

'Oh yes sure Lori,' Maggie said, still distracted. 'Just get me an americano, and as fast as you can. Black, and with a double shot. No actually, make that a triple and I'll have cream with it too.'

'Coming right up.' Lori sped off to the counter and passed on Maggie's order to Stevie, who was the owner and evidently in sole charge of barista-ing this morning. Turning on her heel, she returned to Maggie's table, pulled out a chair and sat down.

'So what's up?' she said. 'I know there's something. I can *detect* that just from your face. I'm good at detecting so I am.'

Maggie laughed. 'Well actually Lori, I think a man just made a move on me.'

'Is *that* all?' Lori said, sounding disappointed. 'Aye, well I suppose you're not *that* old. It's bound to happen occasionally, so it is. Even at your age.'

'Well thanks a *lot*,' Maggie said, struggling to suppress another laugh. 'Actually, he was quite hot, if you must know. At least, I think that's the expression one uses nowadays.'

'One uses nowadays?' Lori said, in a passable imitation of Maggie's Yorkshire accent. 'What, are you my old granny or something? Anyway, did this hot guy ask for your phone number? And did you give it to him, that's what I want to know?'

'My phone number's up above the door of my shop, painted in foot-high letters. So it's there if he wants it. But as you well know, I'm a nearly-married woman. I don't want hot guys giving me their phone numbers or anything else besides.'

'But it's still nice though, isn't it?' Lori said. 'To be noticed I mean. Me, I never turn down an opportunity if it comes along. Because you never know who might turn out to be the one.'

'I've already found the *one*,' Maggie said, and it was true. For her, it was Frank, only Frank and nothing but Frank. The sudden appearance of Jack Urquhart in her life had been briefly unsettling, but now she recognised her reaction for what it was. It was nothing but shallow vanity, and that just wasn't who she was.

'Actually, I thought I'd already found the one for me too,' she heard Lori saying, in a sad tone. 'It was your guy, Jimmy. But I don't think the feeling was two-way. That's what happens, isn't it? And now he's gone off somewhere and I'll probably never see him again. Although I know he was way out of my league,' she added. 'I'm not *totally* stupid.'

Maggie gave her a sympathetic smile. 'You're not stupid at all Lori, far from it. But Jimmy's got issues at the moment. He's getting over a break-up. In fact, he's getting over *two* break-ups. So I don't think he's looking for a relationship at the moment.'

Lori's eyes lit up. 'So there's still hope then, is there?'

It was an awkward question, and for a moment, Maggie didn't quite know how to respond. She shrugged and said gently, 'I don't know Lori. Perhaps the age gap might be too much. He's what, ten years older than you? I expect he's probably looking for someone more his own age.'

That seemed to satisfy her, because the young waitress said, quite brightly, 'Aye, I suppose you're right. Oh well, not the end of the world, plenty of fish in the sea, that's what they say isn't it? But anyway, I told you there was something I wanted to talk to you about. You see, I saw your job advert online and I want to apply.'

Her request took Maggie completely by surprise, and for the second time in less than a minute, she was unsure how to answer. Finally she said, 'Well okay Lori, but I have to be honest that you weren't *quite* what I had in mind. I was looking for someone with...well, with a bit more direct experience in the field. In fact, I was actually hoping to take on a junior lawyer, so that the firm could start doing regular legal work again.'

Lori nodded vigorously. 'I know, I know, I read all that stuff you said about having legal training or a police background and all that. And I know I haven't got any of that. But there's other things I've got that people like that don't have.'

'I'm sure that's true Lori...' Maggie paused for a moment, wondering how best to put what she was about to say. 'But well... look, I'm sorry, but you're just not at all what I had in...'

'Okay, okay, I get that Maggie, of course I do, ' Lori interrupted. 'I'm not what you had in mind. But just take a moment to look at me, and tell me what you see. Go on, tell me. I won't be offended.'

Maggie gave her a puzzled look. 'I'm not quite sure where you're going with this Lori.'

'Bear with me, bear with me, please, ' the young waitress said earnestly, her words gushing out and tumbling over one another. 'Go on, tell me what you see. Tell me.'

'Well okay. So first of all, I see a young woman bubbling with enthusiasm. And quite loud too, if you don't mind me saying so.'

'Good, good start,' Lori said. 'But what would you see if I switched off my mouth for a minute?'

Maggie laughed. 'Can you do that Lori?'

'Of course, if I want to. But go on, tell me what you see. I told you before, I won't be offended. Honestly.'

'Well okay then.' God, this was going to be *really* difficult, and despite Lori claiming she wouldn't be offended, there was every chance she would be. But luckily, Maggie didn't get the chance to prove that one way or the other.

'See, I *knew* you wouldn't do it,' Lori said, jumping in, 'because you're *way* too nice. So I'll answer for you. I'm slightly below average height, my hair is sort of mousy brown or maybe a dark blonde, I'm a few pounds heavier than I should be but I'm not fat, I'm not stand-out pretty but I'm not stand-out plain either. I'm little Miss Slightly-Below-Average. No-one turns their head when I walk into a room, and just so you know, I'm perfectly happy with that.'

Maggie shook her head, whilst suppressing a grin. 'I think you're being very hard on yourself Lori. You're a very nice girl.'

'Aye, I know I am,' she said, smiling. 'And by the way, I'm not dumb either. I've got five Highers and the only reason I didn't go to Uni was I had to look after my sick mum. But you see, I don't stand out, whereas you do. You're English for a start, and you're nice-looking, and you often speak in posh lawyer-speak even if you don't realise it. No offence by the way, but you do.'

'Do I? Yes, I suppose I do sometimes.'

'You see that's the whole point. If you took me on as your trainee, I'd be amazing for any undercover stuff you have to do. I just melt into the background, you see. No-one gives me a second glance. And I'd be cheap as well. Stevie gives me three quid above minimum wage here and I'd come for the same money. And I'd do all your admin and answer your phone and run your office, no problem at all. I'd be a right bargain. Oh aye, and I make great coffee too. *Obviously.*'

Maggie paused for a moment. 'Well, it's a very interesting proposition Lori, I must say. But as I said, you weren't exactly what I was looking for. And I've had quite a lot of applications, I really need to take a look at them before I make any decision. I'm sure you understand that.'

Lori shrugged. 'They'll all be rubbish. And *I* can start next Monday. Oh aye, and there's just one other thing.'

'What's that?' Maggie asked, now seriously amused.

'When I'm your *associate*, I'll be using my full name, and that's Lorilynn by the way. *Lorilynn Logan, Investigator.* That's what I'll be having on my business card.'

Chapter 3

'Have you heard about these killings sir, on the Royal Mile? It's all pretty bizarre, that's what I've been hearing from a couple of the murder-squad boys who are on the case over there.'

DCI Frank Stewart and DC Lexy McDonald were in the canteen of New Gorbals police station in Glasgow, a duo of full Scottish breakfasts in front of them, both as yet untouched. It had become somewhat of a daily routine for the pair, a routine that for Frank was having a slightly concerning effect on his waistline. Concerning, because in just a few months' time he would need to be slipping into that made-to-measure kilt, in preparation for his wedding to the lovely Miss Maggie Bainbridge. With a sigh of disappointment, he gave the third of the sausages on his plate a wistful look then said,

'No more than what I read in the paper Lexy. Two men found dead by a bog-cleaner at four in the morning apparently. In one of the stalls of the ladies' loo. The poor bloke nearly had a heart-attack, hardly surprising given the state the bodies were in.' He stretched over to grab the recently-discarded free newspaper which he'd been skimming before Lexy arrived. *'Royal Mile Murders: Police Scotland believe the men, who were both thought to be in their twenties, were members of the night-time economy.* What's that all about?'

Lexy laughed. 'I think it means they were part of the gay scene sir. Apparently they were found hand-cuffed together, wearing tight leather shorts and those vests that show off their muscles. And with the knives still sticking out of their chests too. Bloody gruesome by all accounts. And this is the third gay murder in six months you know. That community's getting seriously worried.'

Frank nodded. 'Aye, I can well understand that. But I'm glad it wasn't me that found them, that's all I can say.'

'They're saying they might have been pole-dancers at one of those Edinburgh gay clubs,' Lexy continued. 'A place called Harley-Dee's apparently. You know, named after one of those big American motorbikes. Harley-Davison. It's just off the Royal Mile, not far from where the bodies were found.'

He forked a plump mushroom and stuffed it into his mouth. 'I have heard of the iconic motorcycle brand, yes, but you speak as if I should know all about these establishments too, and this Harley-Dee one in particular. Which of course I don't, being not actually gay as witnessed by the fact I'm about to be betrothed to a very lovely woman. But anyway, how come you know so much about the crime? The bodies were only discovered the night before last.'

She gave him a sheepish look. 'There's a WhatsApp group. Me and some of the guys I was on the DC's course with over at Tulliallen HQ.'

'Oh aye?' Frank said, his eyes narrowing. 'Well you need to be careful about what gets passed around on these things, because they can be bloody dangerous. But I see in the paper our Edinburgh colleagues are appealing for any eye-witnesses to come forward. Haven't they got CCTV, for God's sake? These tourist areas are stuffed with cameras, with the full facial recognition software and the whole works.'

'The system was down sir. A cyber attack is what I'm hearing on the grapevine. Down since about one o'clock on the day of the murder and still not back up and running yet.'

Interesting, Frank thought, wondering immediately if his wee forensic mate Eleanor Campbell might be working on that matter right now, back at his old Atlee House base in London. Later, he would give her a call and find out. But right now, he'd better get stuck into his breakfast or he wouldn't finish in time for his meeting with the Assistant Chief Constable. He mused that he might even have to leave that third sausage untouched, which would be a minor tragedy given how more-ish they were.

'Pretty convenient for the murderers then, eh, that outage,' he said, as he demolished a compensatory slice of black pudding.

'Murderers plural sir? So are you thinking there was more than one of them?'

Frank shrugged. 'Can't be certain of course, but it wouldn't have been easy to take care of two fit young guys single-handed, would it? But I guess we'll know more when the Scene-of-Crime guys and gals have done their work. I expect the place is swarming with them right now.'

She nodded. 'Yes it is sir. According to my WhatsApp mate, they've taped off the whole area and closed it to all tourists, which is causing a fair amount of disruption to the traders in that part of the Mile.'

'Poor dears,' he said sardonically. 'But not as much disruption as those two lads suffered. Anyway Lexy, I need to stop gassing for a while and push on with this feast. I'm seeing the ACC in about six-and-a-half minutes' time and I don't want to be strolling in with a chunk of bacon stuck in my teeth and brown sauce dribbling down my chin.'

Although *why* he was seeing the ACC he couldn't say, the arrangements for the meeting coming by email and containing little more than place and time, save for making it clear that non-attendance wasn't an option. The fact was, when an Assistant Chief Constable said *jump*, you simply said *how high* and left it at that, but that didn't stop you being curious. As far as he understood, ACC Natalie Young had an organisation-wide remit across Police Scotland, a sort of Assistant Chief without portfolio, not sitting at the head of a regionally-focussed pyramid like most of the other brass who operated at her level. He knew that she'd been in charge of the security operation when the King had invited a bevy of world leaders to Balmoral for one of his hopeless climate conferences a month or two back, and she'd also been Officer in Command when Tommy Taggart's SFP yobbos had been marching along Princes Street last year during the Festival and smashing windows as they went. She had led from the front too on that occasion, and as a result had earned the respect of the rank-and-file. That alone was enough to make her pretty unique amongst the brass.

Respected though she was, she was also notoriously short of *bonhomie* when it came to her dealings with the lower ranks or in fact anyone, or so it was reputed. So he made a mental note to dial down his out-of-the box flippancy for the duration of the meeting - or at least, he would try, because he knew enough about himself to know that the stuff just had a habit of coming out, despite his best intentions. Someone would say something, he would see the funny or ridiculous side of it, and involuntarily, he would make some smart-arsed quip. That's how it worked, and it had got him into a load of trouble in the past, but today, he vowed, would be different. The location for the meeting was a top-floor corner office until recently occupied by Detective Superintendent Peter Sweeney, who was now enjoying a radically different experience of the Scottish Criminal Justice System from the inside of a Barlinnie Prison cell. With mild trepidation, he stopped outside the closed door, then wrapped gently on it with what he hoped was a respectful cadence.

'Come.' Hearing the muffled reply, he twisted the handle, pushed open the door and went in. There were two women in the room, the uniformed ACC and another woman in plain clothes whom he didn't recognise.

'Morning ma'am, DCI Frank Stewart.' They had in fact met once before, or at least he had been in the room when she had been doing one of those 'all hands' communication sessions that big organisations were so fond of nowadays. And he'd asked a question from the floor that day, he remembered with a mild sinking feeling. Because to be more accurate, what he'd *actually* done was make a sarcastic remark, something about the stupid new hate crimes procedure that was about to be implemented at the time. He wondered if she might remember his intervention. Evidently, she did.

'Yes, I know you,' she said, with just enough reproachfulness in her tone for him to understand he'd *really* better watch what he said today. She was, he guessed, about his own age, slim and quite tall, with high cheek-bones and dark deep-set eyes. And quite attractive he thought, particularly if you were into the dominatrix type of woman. He tried hard to suppress a smile as, involuntarily, that idea began to develop in his head. She'd be pretty handy with a whip and a set of manacles, probably owned a set already, with a fully-equipped dungeon set-up in her smart Edinburgh flat in the place where the home gym would normally go. *See, there it is again*, he thought ruefully. *You're letting your sense of the ridiculous get the better of you. Not a smart move.*

'This is Carrie-Anne Fisher,' the ACC said, thankfully interrupting his thoughts as she nodded in the direction of the other woman. 'Carrie-Anne's with the security services.' He gave her a brief smile of acknowledgement but made no comment. 'Take a seat Frank.'

'Thanks ma'am,' he said. He sat down as instructed and suppressing a powerful instinct to make his usual mood-lifting remark, waited for her to continue.

'As I said, Carrie-Anne's with the security services, but the specific matter we need your help with Frank is very much within police jurisdiction.' She said it as if to give him reassurance, which immediately set him wondering why he might need it, and this early in the meeting too. 'Frank, you'll have heard of Tommy Taggart and his Scottish Freedom Party I assume. The SFP'. He wasn't sure if it was a question or a statement so he hedged his bets by restricting his response to an almost-inaudible grunt. 'So,' she continued, 'there's a whole raft of things surrounding the SFP and Mr Taggart in particular that are causing alarm at the moment.' And evidently causing enough alarm to attract the attention of the spooks, he thought, giving Carrie-Anne Fisher the once-over out of the corner of one eye. She looked a bit like a plain-clothes version of the ACC, being similarly slim and athletic, and with a thin drawn face that had an austere look about it. But she too was attractive, although he speculated she might not exactly be a bundle of fun on a night out. But she was a spy, and he supposed that being inscrutable was probably part of their training, along with the ability to give away nothing but name and number under enemy interrogation. Into his head came a vision of the pretty spook trussed up in ACC Young's Stockbridge dungeon, glazed-eyed and a trickle of blood running down from a corner of her mouth. And this time, he couldn't suppress the smile. Which then, unfortunately, evolved into a short laugh.

'Finding something funny?' ACC Young said sharply. Frank, thinking fast, shook his head. 'No ma'am, sorry. I was just thinking about your man Taggart, that's all. He's a bit of a ridiculous figure in my opinion.'

Fisher spoke for the first time. In an American accent. 'Actually, we think he's dangerous. Both him and his wife.'

'Hey, you're American,' Frank blurted out, the phrase *stating the bleeding obvious* instantly and embarrassingly coming to mind. He raised a hand in apology. 'Sorry, it was just unexpected that's all. I thought you would be MI5 or MI6, and they're mostly posh Oxford or Cambridge types.'

She gave a tight smile. 'I'm on secondment. London often requests input from us on homeland security matters. And it's two-way traffic by the way. There's a ton of you Brits working for the CIA on the other side of the pond. We think we can learn from each other, in the way we each operate, and other matters too. It's a sort of cultural exchange if you will.' Aye, but *you've* still got a bit to learn culture-wise, he thought with amusement. Try using the *you Brits* thing in a pub in Glasgow on a Saturday night and see where that gets you.

'Aye, but getting back to Taggart,' he continued. 'I suppose he is a bit dangerous when I think about it. He certainly causes enough disruption on the streets with those rallies of his.'

'Exactly,' Fisher said. 'Tommy Taggart may come over as the populist rebel-rouser, but beneath the surface we know that he's running a slick and well-organised operation. And a well-funded one too, which raises the spectre of foreign actors being involved. Which is why I'm here.'

'Foreign actors?' Frank said, genuinely surprised. 'What, are we talking about the Chinese or something?'

'Yes them, very possibly,' she said, nodding. 'Or Russia or Iran or North Korea and plenty of others besides. There's no shortage of potential enemies out there. In fact, after Brexit you Brits don't actually have many friends at all.' The comment surprised him, he having always assumed that spooks, especially foreign ones, were meant to keep their political opinions to themselves. But it was probably a reasonable bellwether as to how the people in power - and our American so-called allies too - continued to view the whole Brexit affair. And given the toxic nature of the debate even seven years after the referendum, it wasn't something he intended to get involved with himself.

'Aye, well I wouldn't know about that, that's way above my pay grade,' he said disarmingly. 'But isn't the elephant in the room the fact that Taggart was actually *elected* to the Scottish Parliament, all fair and square? See, that's the tiny problem with democracy, isn't it? That not everyone gets the outcome they would like.'

ACC Young gave him a wry look. 'It's interesting that you should say that Frank, because actually, that's one of the things we'll be wanting you to take a look at. But we'll get onto that later. What I wanted to clarify first is the boundary between the police operation and Carrie-Anne's area of responsibility.' This will be good, Frank thought, having had some past experience of how these spooks worked. Basically, *they* had an access-all-areas backstage pass and could do things and go places where no policeman could. It wasn't quite a licence to kill, but it wasn't far off.

'Yes, that's right,' Fisher said. Unexpectedly she stood up, stretching her arms above her, whilst suppressing an obvious yawn. 'Sorry Frank, it's the damn jet-lag. I just got in to Glasgow yesterday morning on a red-eye from Washington and I haven't caught up yet.' The move allowed him to get a better look at her, and much to his consternation, he rather liked what he saw. She wore a light green round-necked sweater which he thought might be cashmere, over a navy pencil skirt that stopped a couple of inches above the knee, highlighting long slim legs. Her hair was auburn and luxuriant, gathered in a French plait and draped over one shoulder. There was something of the forties movie-star about her, he thought, and briefly he imagined himself as Raymond Chandler's Phillip Marlowe, cruising down Sunset Strip in a battered Pontiac convertible, gaping admiringly at the women making their way to the clubs and restaurants just as the sun was going down. *A broad with curves in all the right places.* That's how Marlow would surely have described Miss Carrie-Anne Fisher. You couldn't say that sort of stuff nowadays of course, and quite right too, but that didn't mean it wasn't true.

'You get jag-lag when you come up here from London on the train,' he said, deciding a lightening of the mood was called for, despite his resolution to play it straight. 'Or culture-lag more like. The beer's terrible but the cakes are a *lot* better. And the jokes too.' And to his surprise, it made her smile.

'Sure, I love Scotland, or at least what little I've seen of it. And as you say, you guys have got *such* a sense of humour.'

'Aye, and you bloody need it too, believe me.' Out of the corner of an eye he saw the ACC shooting him a disapproving look. Getting the message he said, 'But sorry Carrie-Anne, I'm digressing. Carry on, please.'

'Sure,' she said again. 'So, *our* role in this affair is to look out for any potential activity which could be the responsibility of foreign actors. Because as I said, there are plenty of bad guys out there who are loving the political turmoil that's happening up here at the moment.'

'And you think there's some big bad Russians or Chinese behind some or all of it?' he asked. 'Stoking the fires if you will?'

'You sound sceptical,' Fisher said primly. 'But I can assure you that it's not just something that happens in the movies. In real life, that's their modus operandi. Misinformation campaigns on social media is the usual start point, but they're not above making direct interventions in the field where there's the opportunity and where they see potential profit.'

Frank frowned. 'And you think there's some of this stuff going on in *Scotland*? You mean *right now*?'

ACC Young stepped in. 'We've reasonable grounds for suspicion let's say. That's one of the reasons our security services asked for some input from our American friends.'

'Yes, or more specifically, from our Langley cyber warfare facility,' Fisher added. 'You guys have got some awesome capability at your GCHQ, but our guys in Virginia take it to the next level.'

Frank grinned to himself as he thought of his mate Eleanor Campbell wetting herself when he told her he was on a case featuring next-level cyber capability. *Next-level.* It was a phrase he'd heard her use often, evidently a favourite in geek-land, with its never-ending worship of the latest shiny baubles of technology.

'Interesting,' Frank said, because it was. 'So what exactly are you planning to focus this next-level stuff on? Taggart's crappy Scottish Freedom Party I'm assuming? And the man himself I guess?'

She nodded. 'Yes that, but we have a wider remit too. Let's just say we're looking at the whole Scottish political canvas, from soup to nuts.'

He gave a puzzled look, realising he had no idea what she was talking about, and was about to say exactly that until he thought better of it. Instead he said, 'Aye, right, sure, that makes sense.' Then he paused for a moment before speaking again. 'So whilst you spook guys are doing the next-level soup-to-nuts stuff, what is it you want *me* to do?'

'Some good old-fashioned police work,' ACC Young said. 'We have two specific but separate matters that we would like you and your team to look into.'

'Let me stop you there ma'am,' he said, in what he hoped was a respectful tone. 'Just so you know, I don't actually *have* a team up here. My Department 12B reprobates are all based down south, so all I've got in this neck of the woods is about two hours a week from a smart little DC called Lexy McDonald, and I only get *her* through some weapons-grade grovelling on my part. So if you think this job of yours might need a ton of resources, you'll need to make some arrangements to ship some folks in.'

She nodded. 'Understood. We'll arrange whatever resources you need.'

'Thank you ma'am,' he replied, when what he really meant was *aye, I'll believe that when I see it.* Although in actual fact he wasn't too worried, knowing as he did that a call to his old gaffer DCI Jill Smart down at the Met would instantly expedite the shipment northwards of the slow-moving lump of lard known as DC Ronnie French. That assumed of course that Frenchie wasn't currently busy on a case, an unlikely scenario given the sloth-like DC's world-class ability to dodge anything that looked like hard work. Or any kind of work in fact, hard or otherwise.

'The first case is an allegation of electoral malpractice in respect of the election of Tommy Taggart to the Scottish Parliament,' Young continued. 'The sitting Nationalist MSP was a gentleman called Dr Donnie Morrison, and you may have seen he was forced to resign his seat over a sexual scandal. He denied everything, but it was all very unsavoury and of course the party then had to select a new candidate to contest the bye-election. Which they promptly lost to Taggart and his Scottish Freedom Party.'

'Aye, I vaguely remember that ma'am,' Frank said, furrowing his brow, 'although I was still down in London then so didn't really follow the detail.'

She nodded. 'That's understandable. But afterwards, the defeated candidate, Kelly Prentice, alleged a catalogue of malpractice by the SFP, including voter intimidation at the polling stations and some serious fraud with the postal voting system. And there was enough hint of suspicion for the Electoral Commission to get interested. Their investigation was blocked at every turn by Taggart and his party officials but despite that, the Commission has concluded that there might be a case to answer.'

'And electoral fraud is a criminal offence,' Frank said. 'Which is where we come in I guess?'

'Exactly. And that's case number one for you. Dig into that ballot and see what you can find out.'

'So I'm guessing we're looking for links back to Taggart and his party of nut-cases?'

The ACC nodded. 'Well, of course, we will have to see where your investigation leads, but if there was indeed malpractice, then there's really no-one else who would have a motive.'

He shrugged. 'Unless it was just sour grapes on the part of the loser of course.'

'Yes, well there is that,' she conceded. 'But remember, the Electoral Commission believe there's sufficient evidence to justify the police being called in. They did quite a thorough study before coming to that conclusion.'

'Fair enough,' Frank said. 'I'll take a look. So case number two. What's that all about?'

Young smiled. 'It's actually related to case one, quite directly in fact. You see, the Nationalist party MSP who had to stand down from the seat maintains he was framed. That he was set up in some elaborate conspiracy that he doesn't understand.'

'This is the Dr Morrison guy we're talkin about?' Frank asked.

'That's right. He was photographed in a bar in his constituency, apparently inebriated and making inappropriate advances to an attractive woman.'

Frank gave her a knowing look. 'Oh aye, I remember who he is now. He's the guy who's the Wee Free minister isn't he? All fire and brimstone and threats that you'll go to hell if you're a homosexual, or have sex outside marriage, or you over-indulge in the demon drink, all that sort of archaic stuff.'

Young nodded. 'That's the one.'

'So it's a tricky situation on a whole lot of levels ma'am, isn't it? Very embarrassing for him to say the least, and it wouldn't have helped his party win the seat either.'

She nodded again. 'Indeed. Except Dr Morrison maintains he was set up. Yes, he admits to being at the bar that night, but he says it was simply to meet a constituent. He's adamant that nothing else happened. According to him, he was drinking only coke, and that it was the woman who was all over him, not the other way round.'

'Well he would say that, wouldn't he?' Frank said, 'As I recall, he's being saying that from day one, but everyone thought he was lying to cover his arse. So why are we just getting round to looking at it now?'

'Let me try and answer that one Frank,' Carrie-Anne Fisher said. 'The fact is, in the course of our initial cyber investigations we've uncovered credible evidence that deep-fake operations may be being conducted here in Scotland by a party or parties unknown.'

'Deep what?' Frank said, his puzzlement genuine. 'What's that when it's at home?'

'Video and image manipulation, but taken to the next level so that it looks just like real life.'

Unable to help himself, he laughed. 'It's that next-level stuff again. It seems to be everywhere. But sorry, you'll need to explain it in plain English for a dunderhead like me.'

'You may remember there was an incident at Waverley Station back in February, at the time of the Scotland-

England rugby match?' ACC Young said. 'When a group of English supporters brutally attacked two young Scotland fans on the concourse. And of course as you would expect nowadays, it was caught on video by someone's smart phone and soon it was all over the media. It caused considerable outrage up here.'

'Oh aye, I remember that,' Frank said. 'The papers up here made a right who-ha over it, didn't they?'

'Not just the papers,' Fisher said. 'So did Taggart and the SFP. It was a perfect opportunity for them to drum up more anti-English feeling.'

'And it doesn't take much for them to do that, does it? They just love stoking up hatred.'

'Yes they do.' Fisher said, then paused for a moment. 'Except we don't think the incident actually happened.'

'What?' he said, astonished.

'That's right,' Young said. 'Naturally we investigated the attack in response to the public outrage, but despite intensive enquiries, we found absolutely nothing. The station's CCTV had no record of the incident, nor could we track down the two boys who had been attacked.'

He shrugged. 'Well, the CCTV around the city's not exactly reliable from what I've been hearing, but surely the two boys would have come forward after a public appeal or something like that?'

The ACC nodded. 'Exactly, you would have thought so. But they didn't.'

'So what are we saying?' he said, frowning. 'Because everybody saw that video.'

'Your GCHQ guys looked at the video more closely,' Fisher

said, 'and got in touch with us for corroboration. And we both came to the same conclusion.'

'Which was?'

Fisher smiled. 'That it was a fake. A clever fake, but a fake nonetheless.'

Frank nodded, suddenly comprehending. 'So *that's* your deep fake stuff then is it? But *why*? What's the point of it?'

'Why, and *who*,' Fisher said. 'Like any crime, motive and means and opportunity need to be considered. Luckily, there are not too many parties who have the technological means, which narrows it down a lot as far as that aspect is concerned.'

'And Russia or China would be top of the list I suppose.' Shaking his head he said, 'But this is just tiny wee Scotland and we aren't in a bloody Bourne movie either. To be honest, this whole thing sounds absolutely ridiculous, if you don't mind me saying so.'

'I would agree if it wasn't for the fact we have reasonable evidence it's actually happening,' she said. 'Or at least it's happened on *one* occasion to be more accurate. But you don't have to worry about that for now Frank. We have a team on it, back in the States. We're all over it, I can assure you.'

He smiled. 'Good to know.' Turning to the ACC, he said, 'So ma'am, I'm to look into this election stuff, that's my mission is it? Find out if there's any dodgy business been going on, both before and after?'

For the first time, she allowed herself a smile, then nodded. 'Yes, I guess that's it in a nutshell.' Gathering up her notebook, she got up and made for the door. 'Okay, we'll schedule a follow-up in a week or two. But must dash, I have another meeting. There's *always* another meeting.'

He got up too, moving aside so he didn't impede her exit. 'Okay then ma'am, I think that's pretty clear. I'll get to it forthwith,' he shouted after her as she disappeared up the corridor. And then with a distinct feeling of disquiet, he realised that it was just Carrie-Anne and himself in the room. Then he noticed she was smiling at him. And evidently about to speak.

'It's been great meeting you Frank,' she said, before pausing for a moment. And then she said, 'You know, maybe we could meet up for a drink sometime, and you can tell me all about that famous Scottish sense of humour. And perhaps show me the sights since I'm new in town. What do you think?'

Taken by surprise, he heard himself saying the words but it was as if he was watching a play and someone else was speaking the lines.

'Aye, that would be nice,' he mumbled, his face reddening as he made a bee-line for the door.

***

Afterwards, he felt as if he needed a stiff drink, but that option not being available to him at New Gorbals Police Station at ten-thirty-nine in the morning, he made his way back to the canteen for a stiff dose of caffeine instead. *Aye, that would be nice. And you can meet my Maggie at the same time. We're getting married in a few months. You'll like her. Everybody likes her. She's bloody amazing.* That's what he *should* have said and that's what he *meant* to say, but somehow the words just didn't come out. And now he felt sick and ashamed and a bit confused too. Thank God he was going to be seeing his brother this evening, Jimmy being back in the city for a couple of days for some unspecified reason connected to his outdoor activities business. His brother, being blessed with ridiculous good looks and being eight years younger to boot, was always being propositioned by women, yet never had much trouble in dealing with any suitor, no matter how alluring or persistent. So it would be nice to talk this troubling occurrence through with him, see what he had to say about it.

Feeling better, he picked up his phone and swiped through his contacts. *E Campbell, Maida Vale Labs*. He'd set up her details before he'd really got to know her properly, and before she'd started spending most of her working hours at his Atlee House offices, hence the formality of the label. Now that he had got to know her, he often reflected that *Wee Eleanor, Right Pain in the Arse* would be a more appropriate description, if perhaps slightly unkind. Maybe one day he would work out how to change it to that, just for a laugh. Or, better still, he would ask Maggie's fantastic little boy Ollie to do it for him tonight when he got home.

She picked up on the first ring, making him think she hadn't glanced at her screen to see it was him.

'Hello.' The tone was terse but that didn't mean anything. Eleanor's tone was generally terse right out of the box.

'Hello yourself. It's Frank here, in case you don't recognise my sweet voice.'

'What do you want? I'm busy.'

He grinned. 'Wouldn't expect anything else. And as for why I'm calling, it's just a social call, that's all. To see how you've been doing since I've been away.'

'You're not my boss. You don't like have to do all that human resources thing.'

'Aye, I'm maybe not human resources but I'm a human

being,' he said, laughing, 'and it's what us humans do. We call our friends from time to time, to make sure they're okay.'

'You want something. I know you do.'

'You're a very cynical woman,' he said affectionately. 'As it happens, I was only calling to tip you off on a situation that's occurring which I thought you might find quite interesting. But don't worry, if you're too busy, I'll get one of the local geeky lassies up here to take a look at it instead.' He felt a pang of guilt as he said the words, recognising that after accusing her of cynicism, he was doing exactly the same thing. Cynically pushing all her buttons that was, because more than anything in the world, Eleanor Campbell hated the thought that there might be any rival contenders for her crown as queen of IT Forensics. And she hated it even more if any of these contenders might be another woman.

'What's the situation then?' With some satisfaction, he noted a softening in tone.

'It's called Scotland.'

'That's not a situation, it's a district.'

'It's a country actually, if we're being strictly accurate. But the fact is, there seems to be a pile of cyber-trickery going on up here, and I wondered firstly if you were aware of it already, and secondly, if not, whether you might want to add it to your to-do list. I mean, to take a quick look at.'

'Cyber-trickery?' she said, making no attempt to disguise her disdain. *'Like what's that?'*

He laughed. 'Aye, I know it's my own description, but it pretty much nails what's going on up here. Firstly, there was an attack on the CCTV systems at Waverley Station. That's in Edinburgh, just so you know, and a station is a place where the trains come in. Secondly, the Scottish police have got a CIA agent from some place called Langley Virginia on secondment and she says...'

'You mean there's Langley guys working here in the UK?' she interrupted. *'That's like awesome.'*

'It's a guy singular, and the guy's actually a girl, if I'm allowed to say that, and to be absolutely pedantic, she's assigned only to Scotland not the UK, but yes, we are honoured by the presence of a CIA spook in our midst.' He gave a gulp as he remembered his disconcerting and involuntary reaction to his first sight of Carrie-Anne Fisher, then shoved it to the back of his mind, where he very much hoped it would stay. 'So anyway young Eleanor, tell me what you know about deep fakery. If indeed you have heard of it at all.'

'Deep fake ops?' she said, a discernible note of excitement in her tone. *'Is that what this is all about?'*

'Might be, might be,' he said, teasing her. 'So you obviously know all about the stuff then?'

'We're like world leaders in that technology,' she said with obvious pride. *'Zak got me some awesome beta software which I've got on my laptop. It's off-the-scale cool.'* Frank knew of this Zak, a shady backroom figure at MI5 or GCHQ or one of these other acronymic organisations, whom he believed also ran his own ethical hacking firm on the side. *'I could actually make a fake Frank Stewart if I wanted to. That would be cool.'*

He laughed. 'You think so? Actually, I think that would be a step too far for the world. But it's good that you know all about this stuff. I think it might come in very handy in the near-ish future.'

'For like what?' she said suspiciously.

'Nothing specific. It's just that it might be useful in one of my investigations, but it's early days yet. Anyway, I just wanted to touch base, to see that you're alright. I'll leave you in peace now. Cheerio.'

'Wait,' she said sharply before he could hang up. *'Is that all?'*

He laughed again. 'I thought you were too busy to talk to me? Yes, that's all. I'll be in touch. Bye for now.' He heard a *grump* as he ended the call. *Mission accomplished then.* Of course, he wasn't involved in the investigation into the horrible murder of these two poor gay lads, nor was that suspiciously coincidental CCTV outage on the Royal Mile connected to either of the two cases he had been given. It was just that with all the talk about foreign actors and deep fake operations, he had a gut feel that he would be needing the impressive skills of Eleanor sooner rather than later. So the call was a kind of place-holder, to whet her appetite for some yet-to-be-specified but vital duties in the future.

Job done, he could turn his mind to what was really bothering him. Which was, the sudden appearance of Carrie-Anne Fisher on the scene, and whether he should mention her to Maggie. Because his reaction to the American woman, involuntarily though it was, seemed to merit a confession and perhaps even an apology.

The only issue now was finding exactly the right moment to do it.

Chapter 5

They had gathered for their traditional after-work Thursday night drink, which, since their move north of the border, now took place in an old-school Glasgow corner bar on the Great Western Road, just a couple of streets up from the Byers Road office of Bainbridge Associates. The Horseshoe Bar was half the size and ten times more down-market compared with their former London watering-hole, but its convivial atmosphere made it no less welcoming. And this particular Thursday was a red-letter day, or was it a red-letter night, because for the first time since he had left the employ of her little firm and moved to Braemar, Jimmy was going to be there. Maggie had been looking forward to seeing him for several days now.

He had already arrived when she turned up, supping a pint, leaning against the bar and chatting to Frank, who, from the fullness of his glass, looked as if he was already onto his second beer. And was it her imagination, she had wondered, but were they both wearing rather earnest expressions, as if they had been discussing some matter of great concern to one or both of them? Whatever the case, the seriousness had melted when they spotted her arrival, Jimmy beaming a beguiling smile and wrapping her in a warm embrace. Jokingly, Frank had pushed him to one side and planted a huge kiss on her lips, which struck her as quite odd, since he was generally fairly reserved when it came to public shows of affection. Still, she wasn't complaining, that was for sure.

'By the way, Yash Patel from the Chronicle's up here for some awards ceremony and he said he might drop in for a chin-wag,' Frank said, smiling. 'That's why I've put the drinks on a tab. He's always a generous lad with his paper's expense account.' He stretched out an arm and patted his brother on the back. 'Anyway, isn't it great to have this big guy here back in town for a while?'

She laughed. 'Yes it is. We've missed you terribly Jimmy, both of us, and my little Ollie is missing his Uncle Jimmy too. The place just isn't the same without you.'

He shrugged. 'Aye, well it's nice to be back, but to be honest, I'm loving it up in the Cairngorms. It's absolutely beautiful up there, although I have to confess, Stew is doing my head in a bit.'

She gave him a rueful smile. Stew Edwards was Jimmy's partner in his new outdoor adventure business, an old pal from his army days. 'Well I guess it's a bit like a marriage, having a new business partner I mean. It can take a while to settle into a comfortable day-to-day routine. I'm sure it'll all work out fine if you give it time.'

He nodded. 'You're probably right, and to be fair he's working his socks off for the firm. And he's brilliant at the old sales and marketing chat, so we've got no shortage of potential customers, which is great for a new business like ours. Anyway, I'm obviously interested to know how the old outfit is doing. Have you managed to find a replacement for me yet? Although I guess I'm actually irreplaceable and the place is going to wrack and ruin already.'

'Yes you are, but no it's not,' she said, laughing. 'In fact, we've just taken on a very interesting client. But as to your replacement, I'm afraid no-one yet has met your ridiculously high standards, at least not in any of the online applications I've looked at so far.' She wondered if she should mention Lori's cheeky application, which much to her own surprise, she was actually giving serious consideration to. He guessed he would find it hilarious, but she would also value his opinion on what would be a very unconventional and probably risky appointment. But before she could bring it up with him, Yash Patel appeared, impeccably turned out as usual, wearing a grey suit with a dazzling white shirt and red silk tie, the suit obviously and expensively made-to-measure to perfectly fit his slim frame. If you had to pick one word to describe Yash, she thought, there could only be one, and one alone. *Smooth*.

'Hi guys, good to see you all again,' he chirped, stretching out his arms. 'Anyone ready for another? What can I get you guys?'

Frank grinned. 'You never let us down young Yash, and as it happens, we *are* running low and there's already a tab behind the bar with your name on it. But I also know that you're generally expecting something in return, is that not so?'

Patel shook his head. 'Nah, not this time Frank, not really. I just thought it would be nice to catch up with you guys whilst I'm in town. Chew the fat, see how you're all doing before I fly back to London.'

'So are you on a story Yash?' Maggie said, instantly realising what a daft question it was, because Yash was *always* on a story. 'What I mean is, on a story up here in Scotland?'

He nodded. 'Well it's not exactly a story yet, but I think there's every chance it might become one. It's all this stuff that's being happening to the government. You know, Livvy Foden allegedly siphoning off all that island development money, and the guy who had to give up his seat over the sexual shenanigans with that woman. And my sources are telling me there's another huge scandal about to break, another one of those cocaine-and-sex ones involving a married minister.'

Frank laughed. 'Don't you think it's just our politicians showing their true colours? I mean, *Politician sensationally found to be honest*, now *that* would be a headline that would sell some papers.'

Yash grinned. 'You may well laugh Frank, but the whole thing stinks in my opinion. And don't forget it was you that told me that thing about coincidences and connections, and it's stuck in my mind ever since.'

'Well that's good to know, but I think we're just witnessing the death throes of a dying and corrupt administration, that's all, and anyway, it's all old news son. I thought you might be more interested in these two Royal Mile murders. Now *there's* a case that's dripping with tons of sleaze, and that's what you guys normally like to salivate over, isn't it? In fact, I thought you might already have been down at that Harley-Dee's place, interviewing the punters.'

'I've left that one to my *Scottish* colleagues,' he said. There was no disguising the dismissive tone, prompting Maggie to shoot Frank an amused look, knowing exactly what he'd be thinking. *Actually, some stupid provincial murder isn't big enough for a journalist superstar like me to waste my time on.*

'I'm not on that one either,' Frank said. *'Actually,* I'm not sure I'm supposed to reveal this, but I've been lined up to take a look-see into the affairs of that Tommy Taggart guy, or to be more specific, at the circumstances of his election to the Scottish parliament. You'll have heard of him I'm sure.'

'Heard of him?' Patel said. 'I've just met the guy, yesterday. Nasty piece of work, and his wife's ten times worse.'

'Hang on, are we talking about the SFP bloke?' Jimmy said, interjecting.

Frank nodded. 'That's the guy bruv.'

Jimmy frowned. 'It just that they've approached us to run a mountain endurance event for all their MSPs and all their prospective MSPs too. They've asked us to set up something really hard-core, a three-day trek in deepest February or something along these lines. They want it to be really tough and dangerous, which believe me, is no problem in a Cairngorm winter. But it was something I was going to run past you guys actually. Stew's really up for doing it, but I'm a bit worried it might damage our business to be so closely associated with the SFP.'

Maggie saw Patel's eyes suddenly light up with excitement. 'No no, go for it Jimmy, please,' he gushed. 'I mean, this has got bloody blockbuster written all over it, I can just see the headline now. *Scotland's far-right talisman leads troops in paramilitary-style mountain manoeuvres.* God, this one would be off the scale. So yeah, go for it Jimmy, and let me tag along, please.'

'I'm not so sure Jimmy,' Maggie said, giving her former colleague a concerned look. 'I think you're right, that it may damage your brand to be associated with these thugs. I wouldn't, if I was you.'

'I can fix that.' Patel shot out the words in a staccato burst. 'The Chronicle will underwrite it. We'll say we were behind it, to expose the truth about the SFP, and that we hired you as part of our investigation. And think of the publicity for your firm. It'll be absolutely huge.'

'Aye, but maybe not in a good way,' Frank said, frowning. 'I'm with Maggie, I wouldn't rush into it if I was you. Even if young Yash here is bribing you with a thousand pieces of silver.'

Suddenly, Maggie broke into a smile. 'I tell you what *would* be funny Jimmy. If you could get all the political leaders to take part in some sort of mountain race, a bit like that reality show you took part in a year or so ago.'

'Aye, and the winner gets to be First Minister,' Frank said. 'Now *that* would be a laugh. But I don't see many of them agreeing to it. Unfortunately.'

'I'm serious,' Patel said, sticking to his guns. 'You should do it Jimmy. My paper will underwrite it, and besides, you'd be doing your country a favour, by exposing what a bunch of sad losers Taggart's pathetic followers are.'

Jimmy gave him an uncertain look. 'I'll talk it through with Stew, but I think I'm in Maggie and Frank's camp at the moment. But we'll see. And besides, we've got another big client lined up and this one's not so controversial. In fact, that's why I'm back in Glasgow, to meet up with them and flesh out their programme.'

'And who's this outfit when they're at home?' Frank asked.

'Ah, if I told you, I'd have to kill you,' Jimmy said, causing Maggie to laugh again as she recognised one of Frank's favourite sayings.

'Fair enough,' Frank said, shrugging. 'Anyway, these lovely get-togethers always end up with us talking shop when we're supposed to be relaxing. Let's talk about what we're watching on the telly at the moment or where we're going on our holidays shall we? Just for a change?'

Everybody laughed, and the evening settled into that effortless bonhomie that Maggie had valued so much from the very first day she had met the Stewart brothers. It seemed too that whatever had been concerning them earlier in the evening was now forgotten. She eavesdropped with affection as they argued over which minor-league football club they should support now that they were living in Scotland, and Jimmy suggested that it would do Frank's fitness a power of good to try out one of his mountain adventures himself sometime. Yes, she reflected, Jimmy was back, even if only for one night, and everything was good with the world once again.

But the evening was ticking on, and she would soon have to catch the train back to Milngavie to relieve Ollie's baby-sitter. Glancing at her phone to check the exact time, she saw she had received a text. It was from Jack Urquhart, her latest client. Surely he wasn't looking for a progress report already? She prodded the icon to open it. And then her heart gave an involuntary start as she read it.

Dinner? Then let's see where it leads :-) x

Chapter 6

Maggie sat forlornly behind her desk in her Byers Road office, with a sheet of paper in front of her, blank save for its underlined title. *The Jack Urquhart Case*. It had been amazing to see Jimmy again the previous night, but now, this morning, the sense of isolation was almost overwhelming. Not that she was lonely of course, because how could she be now that she and Frank and lovely Ollie were living together in the smart rented bungalow in leafy Milngavie? No, this sense of isolation was professional, not personal, but that didn't make her feel any better about it. As she thought about Frank, she remembered the text from Jack Urquhart. Presumptuous, and bloody rude too, and she would tell Urquhart that, politely but in a way that left no doubt, when they next met. But somewhat shamefully, she had admitted to feeling a hint of pleasure too. The fact was, at approaching forty-four years of age it was nice to be fancied, but it was nice to have the luxury of saying a firm *thanks but no thanks* too. The only problem was, she should have thought of all that before she sent that *stupid* off-the-cuff response. *What kind of woman do you think I am? :-) x*. That *bloody* kiss. What the hell had she been thinking? It was meant as a joke, but maybe it wasn't the smartest thing she had ever done.

Pulling herself up sharp, she reminded herself again she had a case to deal with and she needed to be getting on with it, and pretty damn quickly too. But with no-one with whom to mull over the options, getting on with it was proving a lot more difficult than it looked on paper. What would Jimmy do, she kept asking herself? Maybe put a tail on Dominique Tremblay, to see what she was getting up to in her spare time? Or maybe he would go and meet with the woman, flirt with her even, test if she was a loyal partner or if she was open to a bit of extra-curricular sexual activity? Listlessly, she picked up her ballpoint and scrawled a few bullet-points on the blank sheet.

- *Follow her?*
- *Why not just call her and ask her straight out?*
- *Speak to some of her work-mates?*

It wasn't much of a start, but it was a start nonetheless. The second option had the merit of directness and simplicity, but of course Jack Urquhart himself could quite easily have asked his partner straight out whether she was having an affair, and he had been adamant that he didn't want to do that. Maybe she could try and talk to some people at the *Globe*, but that wouldn't be so easy, given she had absolutely no contacts in the organisation. But that's what detectives did, wasn't it? Poked their noses into places where they weren't wanted. The thing was, as was the case for so much in life, it was just a hundred times easier when there were two of you. With that thought, she shot to her feet and strode purposefully to the door, flipping over the 'Gone to Lunch' sign behind her, even though it was only just past nine-thirty. Thirty seconds later, she was back in the Bikini Barista Cafe and heading for her favourite window seat. Spotting her arrival, Stevie the proprietor looked up from behind the counter, put down the cup he was drying, and shouted over to her.

'Morning Maggie, what can we get you? The usual? And how about a nice square sausage on a Morton's crusty roll?

Set you up for the day so it will, and we've just had them fresh in. They're pure magic.'

She laughed. 'You know what Stevie, I think I'll take you up on that offer. But I was actually looking for Lori. Is she due in today?'

'Oh aye, she's just out the back, checking in some deliveries. I'll send her through in a minute, once your order's ready.'

From the knowing look he gave her, Maggie wondered if Lori had already provided Stevie with a heads-up about her desire to become a private investigator. The fact was, she now knew she needed someone desperately, if only so that she could leave the office for more than five minutes without having to put up that stupid little sign every time. And when she thought about it some more, what did she really have to lose? If Lori didn't work out, she would simply look for someone else and she would be no worse off than she was at the moment. Perhaps she *would* take the girl on, but just on a part-time basis at first, maybe twenty-five hours a week, which would also allow her to work a few shifts here at the Bikini Cafe too. They could agree a probationary period of say three months, which would be long enough for both of them to assess whether the arrangement suited them.

As if on cue, Lori emerged from the storeroom, smoothed down her apron with her hands, then picked up the tray that Stevie had just loaded up with Maggie's order.

'Here you go Maggie,' the girl said brightly as she arrived at the table. 'I see you've gone for the roll-and-sausage too, and with brown sauce as well. Highly recommended, but maybe not so much if you want to squeeze into that slinky wedding outfit in a few months' time.'

'Yes I know,' Maggie said, giving a rueful smile, 'but they're just so tempting, aren't they?' She glanced around the room and noted with some satisfaction that she was presently the only customer. 'Lori, can you come and sit down for a moment. I'd like to run something past you. A little proposal, to see what you think.'

'Oh yes!' the girl exclaimed as she pulled out a chair. 'So are you going to give me a chance Maggie? Are you? That's pure brilliant so it is.'

Maggie laughed. 'Well, as a matter of fact, I am. It would only be part-time at first, and we would have to agree a trial period, but yes, I would like to give you a chance.'

Lori punched the air in triumph. 'Yes yes!' she shouted again. 'Maggie, I won't let you down, honest I won't, and I'll work any hours you want me to and I'll listen and learn from everything you do, and I'll do everything you tell me to and...'

'Yes, I'm sure you'll do all of that and more besides,' Maggie said, laughing again. 'So let's shake hands on it and we'll agree the finer details later. How does that sound?'

Lori shot out a hand. 'Deal. And you won't regret this Maggie, honest you won't.'

Maggie was just about to answer when the bell above the entrance door rang. Involuntarily, she glanced up to see who had just entered, then gave an astonished double-take. The woman was dressed in a grey tailored business suit, a white silk blouse and patent leather heels. Slim and elegant, she wore an expression that radiated supreme self-assurance, the self-assurance that came so easily to those blessed with good looks and a hugely successful career. Stevie was evidently a follower of the Scottish political scene because, like Maggie, he had recognised her immediately, and was now staring at her, open-mouthed.

'Miss Tremblay, welcome to the Bikini Barista Cafe,' he said, rather too obsequiously in Maggie's opinion. 'Please, take a seat and we'll be with you in a jiffy.' She was only a bloody political journalist after all, even if she was always on the telly and looked like a super-model too. Or to be more accurate - and Maggie had just noticed this - even if she looked like an upmarket call-girl.

Tremblay didn't reply, but gave a tight-lipped smile before conducting a rapid survey of the room, finally plumping for a table towards the back, more or less alongside the serving counter. Lori got up to serve her, then sat down again as she saw her boss was already on the case.

'So what brings you to Byers Road and our cosy establishment?' Stevie said, notebook in hand and pencil poised to take her order. 'This is your first visit, I think?'

'Yes it is,' she said, her Canadian accent somewhat jarring in the West End of Glasgow. 'I was hoping to see that Bainbridge investigator woman who has an office just two doors along, but it seems she's closed for the day and she doesn't seem to answer her phone or emails either. I think I've probably had a wasted journey.'

Bloody hell, Maggie thought, her original astonishment in seeing Tremblay walk in amplified by a factor of ten, *she was coming to see me? She must have found out that her partner's engaged me and is going to kick up a fuss.* And she had to face it too, Dominique Tremblay's complaint was fully justified - she was miles behind *looking* at the messages in her inbox, never mind answering them, another reason why she *so* needed an assistant. But really, there was nothing for it but to grab the bull by the horns. She stood up and walked slowly over to the journalist's table.

'Miss Tremblay, I'm sorry but I couldn't help overhearing,' she said, with what she hoped was an apologetic smile. 'Actually, *I'm* Maggie Bainbridge. From Bainbridge Associates.'

'You're a hard woman to get a hold of,' the woman said, in a tone that was lighter than Maggie was expecting. 'I suppose that means you must be quite good at what you do.'

Maggie smiled. 'Well I'm not sure about that Miss Tremblay. What it actually means is I'm a bit short-staffed at the moment. We only relocated from London a few months ago and I must confess we've found recruiting the right team rather difficult. And Brexit and the Pandemic haven't exactly helped.' She'd heard a lot of business folks citing this as the source of a myriad of woes in the last year or two, and it always sounded plausible, whether it was true or not. 'But I'm pleased to say, I've made a little progress on that front just today.'

Tremblay shrugged. 'Well, that's your business. Anyway, the reason I'm here is I want to know why my partner is consulting with you.'

Her statement took Maggie by surprise. 'Sorry?' she blurted out. 'I mean, what makes you think that he is?'

'So you're confirming it are you? You can hardly deny it, given that he visited you the other day and has your number on his speed-dial. I looked, you see. I always look at his phone when he leaves it lying about on the coffee-table.'

Slowly, it began to dawn on Maggie. Evidently this woman was tracking her partner's movements, using *Find My Phone* or something like it she guessed. Involuntarily she let out a smile. So he was worried that *she* was cheating, whilst meanwhile his partner was using the wonders of modern technology to check up on *him*. Really, you couldn't make it up.

'I'm afraid that's confidential between Mr Urquhart and myself,' she said. 'I can't deny he was here of course, but you'll understand that I'm not able to reveal what we discussed.'

Tremblay gave her a disapproving look. 'You're quite pretty I suppose, but I wouldn't have thought you would do for him. You're a little old for a start, and it's all about sex for Jack you see.' She reached out a hand, and to Maggie's astonishment, ran her hand through her hair and then, more slowly, traced a finger across Maggie's cheek. 'Yes, quite pretty, but quite frankly you look like the type who just lies back and thinks of England. He prefers someone a little more let's say, *imaginative*.'

'What, do you think I'm having an *affair* with your partner?' Maggie said, unable to hide her amazement at how this bizarre encounter was unfolding. 'I'm sorry Miss Tremblay but that's ridiculous. He came here to ask for my help about a confidential matter and that was it. It's a purely professional relationship, nothing else, I can assure you of that.'

'So you say. But he has form of course, you must know that?'

Maggie leaned back, folding her arms and frowning. 'Actually, I don't.'

'He left his wife for me. She was devastated of course, but we fell completely head over heels in love, and it's *so* important to follow your heart don't you think?' She didn't wait for an answer. 'But now it seems he's tired of me and his eye has started to roam again. Well, when you see him, you can tell him that's not going to happen. I simply won't allow that, do I make myself clear?' She stood up, giving Maggie a withering look. 'I don't expect we'll meet again Miss Bainbridge, unless of course you decide not to take my advice. That, believe me, would be a mistake. Good bye.'

***

Lori looked at her open-mouthed, whilst valiantly attempting but failing to suppress a grin. 'Well, she was a right piece of work wasn't she? I couldn't *totally* hear what she was saying, but I think she was basically accusing you of shagging her partner. And let's face it, that would have been pretty quick work, since you've only met him once. Although I know you'd quite fancy it.'

The waitress had joined Maggie at her table, arriving pre-armed with an americano fortified with a triple shot of espresso.

'I'm still shaking to be honest,' Maggie said, taking a gulp of the coffee, 'and I'll ignore that last remark of yours if you don't mind. But yes, she's bloody scary. And the way she *touched* me. *Yuk*. It gave me the creeps.'

Lori nodded. 'Yeah, it's weird. And yet he thinks *she* is having an affair. The whole thing's pretty mental Maggie, don't you think? But interesting.'

'Yes, both of the above.' Goodness, Maggie thought, wasn't it great to have someone to talk things through with again, even if that someone was as cheeky and disrespectful as young Miss Lorilynn Logan?

'But does that performance mean she's *not* having an affair?' Lori said. 'Or is that all it was, a performance for our benefit? Like a smoke-screen, to put us off the scent?'

That amused Maggie quite a bit. *To put us off the scent. Us.* The way she said that short word, it was as if Lori had worked for her firm for five years rather than just five minutes. It appeared that the girl's feet were already firmly under the table, to coin a phrase, and at that moment, she knew it was all going to turn out just fine.

'So, that's for *us* to find out Lori,' she said, smiling. 'Me and you. And tomorrow we start the surveillance, eight-thirty prompt outside the offices of the Globe. And wear dark clothing.'

That settled, she could turn her attention to Jack Urquhart's impertinent and presumptuous text. But what to do about it, that was the question.

Chapter 7

It had been great to see his brother again, and he was pleased that Jimmy's new outdoor adventure business up in the Cairngorms seem to be taking off. Frank had always believed that the magnificent mountain scenery and the abundance of fresh air was exactly what the boy needed to get his head straight again, and he was delighted that it seemed to be working out as he had expected. And the chat they'd had about the Carrie-Anne Fisher incident had been super-valuable too. Jimmy had been dismissive when Frank had told him about his guilt over his reaction to the American's surprise proposal of a drink. *You were put on the spot and you said yes when you meant no,* was his brother's assessment of the situation, *so what's the big deal?* And Jimmy had been right of course. He had meant *no*, firmly and unequivocally, but now he had another thing to worry about. What if Miss Carrie-Anne-bloody-Fisher wouldn't take no for an answer, and somehow Maggie found out about that and got the wrong end of the stick? Nah, he was being stupid, he reflected. Carrie-Anne-bloody-Fisher hadn't been in contact - and he was mightily relieved about that, make no mistake - so the chances were she had totally forgotten about it herself, and the whole thing would blow over, as if it had never happened in the first place. Aye, the more he thought about it, the more he realised he was worrying about absolutely nothing at all.

Having half-settled that matter in his head, he could now give his full attention to his new case, or to be more accurate, the two new cases. So the question now was, where to start? Analysing it in his mind, he saw there were probably three or four threads he could follow to get the thing up and running. There was that Wee Free guy who had been forced to give up the seat, what was his name again? Donnie Morrison, that was it. Morrison's embarrassing demise had gifted Tommy Taggart the opening he was looking for, a bye-election in a mainly working-class constituency that might prove susceptible to his prejudicial anti-English rants. But the guy Morrison was a non-entity, making the claim that he had been the victim of some shady conspiracy faintly ludicrous. Sure, it had been a handy turn of events for Taggart, but if he'd been prepared simply to sit tight for another eighteen months until the general election, he would almost certainly have won the seat anyway.

Then there was the claim by the replacement Nationalist candidate Kelly Prentice that the election itself had been rigged, a claim that had been serious enough to prompt the Electoral Commission's Scottish office to fire up an investigation. This, Frank thought, was an area of more promise. The tide of public opinion may have been turning against the Nationalist government and in favour of the populist upstart Taggart, but prior to the by-election, the opinion polls had been predicting a close-run thing. It was entirely possible that Taggart and some of his hard-nut followers had indulged in a spot of polling-booth intimidation, and there were suggestions of dodgy business with the postal votes too. So, definitely, all of this would need to be investigated. He would assign DC Lexy McDonald to do the initial digging, perhaps to have a chat with the Electoral Commission guys to see what evidence, if any, they had turned up. Then if anything interesting emerged, he would take a look at it himself. Because the thing was, free and fair elections were the bedrock of any democracy, and anything that threatened them needed to be taken very seriously.

So that left one rather more appealing tactic, which was of course to go and have a chat with Mr Tommy Taggart himself, or to be more accurate, to have a chat with Taggart and his missus as well. Because if the critical media reports were to be believed, Mrs Sienna Taggart was the actual power behind the throne, a Lady Macbeth of uncertain age, with a Barbie-Doll figure and Botoxed to within an inch of her life. Never short of a provocative quote, Sienna Taggart had become tabloid gold, as much due to her fashion sense- which was definitely more porn-star than *haute couture* - than her frequent political pronouncements. Given her prominence, the papers had done a bit of digging into her background, and had discovered her given name was Agnes Lomond, and she'd grown up in care in the working-class town of Renton, by coincidence not far from the shores of Loch Lomond itself. After a torrid schooling untroubled by the gain of any qualifications, she had gone to work as a holiday rep for a leading tour company and in that regard had lived on Cyprus for many years, before returning to Scotland five or six years ago. When asked about her name change, she had simply answered *who wants to be a f**king Agnes?*, this brazenness adding to her growing legend.

Frank, unlike his lovely Maggie, wasn't a great fan of TV crime drama, considering them absurdly unrealistic and nothing like the dull monotony of real-life police work, but he had always retained a soft spot for *Columbo,* and not just because he shared the fictional detective's scruffy deportment. The LA detective's trademark was to identify his prime suspect nice and early, then get right in their faces, turning up unannounced day after day with another seemingly innocuous question, drip-drip-dripping like Chinese torture. The effect and intention was to unsettle the suspect until they made some stupid mistake that gave the game away, and of course on the telly, it always worked. Here in the real-life world of UK policing the practice was frowned upon, not least because the criminal justice system took a dim view of what it saw as intimidatory behaviour. But as far as Frank was concerned, it was a tool in the armoury that could sometimes prove effective, especially when the suspects were a couple of slippery customers like the Taggarts. If - and it was a big if, he conceded - if the Taggarts were implicated in either Morrison's misfortune or the allegations of shady deeds concerning the election, it was unlikely that, figuratively speaking, their personal fingerprints would be on either of the crimes. No, from what he had seen of them, they would have been way too smart for that.

By good luck, it turned out that Taggart and his Scottish Freedom Party were due to speak the next day at one of their risibly-titled 'Freedom Rallies' on Glasgow Green. The next day being a Saturday, it would be an unwelcome intrusion into one of the idyllic weekends he loved to spend with Maggie and her little boy Ollie. It was a shame, but at least the event wasn't kicking off until 2pm so they would still have time to visit their favourite cafe in the square, where he would have the full Scottish fry-up and the wee lad would load up with pancakes and maple syrup topped off with a swoosh of whipped cream from an aerosol. Now all that was required was to track down Lexy to see if she fancied a bit of weekend overtime.

***

By some quirk of meteorology, the May weather was often fair and sunny in the West of Scotland, but this Saturday was turning out to be one of these frequent exceptions that proved the rule. Frank had checked the forecast before leaving their Milngavie bungalow that morning. *Mild, with a light drizzle and a moderate breeze.* As he stood waiting for Lexy, he wondered ruefully if the tentacles of the Scottish government's spin-doctoring machine had enveloped the national weather forecasting service too, because it was bloody freezing, the rain was coming down in stair-rods and it was blowing a howling gale. The mini-umbrella that Maggie had insisted he take with him had proved to be not up to the task and now hung, crumpled and forlorn, at his side. Still, surveying the size of the gathering in front of him, it seemed the weather had not discouraged either the army of Taggart supporters nor the contingent of protesters, smaller in number but considerably more vocal. Probably, they'd been guided - or misguided- by the same weather forecast that he'd seen. More worrying for Frank, the policing arrangements seemed to be distinctly low-key, with just a small handful of uniformed officers dotted around, a few of whom he recognised as being from his own New Gorbals nick.

He felt a tap on the arm. 'Morning sir, sorry I'm a bit late. Hit some traffic on the expressway. Not literally, obviously.'

It was DC McDonald, clad in sturdy boots and a heavy-duty walking jacket with the hood up and drawn tight against her head. 'Aye, well you must have got a better weather report than me Lexy,' he said, laughing. 'Is it actually you in there?'

She smiled. 'It is, definitely me. So what's the plan sir?'

He shrugged. 'Not really got one. I thought we'd just listen to the Taggarts ranting on and then we'd sidle up afterwards and have a chat with them.'

She nodded towards a crowd standing a few yards in front of them, holding aloft a banner that read *Taggarts Don't Speak For Scotland*. 'Students do you think sir?'

'Aye, probably, the poor flowers. But I'm more worried about these other guys.' He pointed in the direction of the stage. 'The Taggart Boot-Boys, is that what the press are calling them?' There were about two dozen of them, each equipped with a walkie-talkie. Young, male and shaven-headed, they projected an air of effortless menace in their uniform of jeans, Doc Martins, leather jackets and replica Scotland football shirts. Back in the seventies they would have been called skinheads, proving once again that there was nothing really new in fashion. On a normal Saturday they would be at the football, getting tanked up before the match and looking for a fight after it. But this was the end of May and the season had just finished, which on reflection was probably why Taggart had chosen this date for his stupid rally.

'So do you think there might be trouble sir?' Lexy asked, with a relish that suggested she might welcome it.

Frank gave a rueful shrug. 'I bloody hope not. The last time I was at one of these events, I got my head well and truly booted in. *Not* an experience I'm particularly keen to repeat, as you can imagine. So if it does kick off here, we'll leave it to the uniforms, okay? But to be honest, I don't think that student lot will fancy it much, so we should be alright I think.' He glanced at his watch. 'Should be starting in a minute. I wonder if they've got a warm-up act?'

As if in answer to his question, a youngish guy holding a large wireless microphone bounded onto the stage, a guy he vaguely recognised as someone off the telly, although he couldn't quite put his finger on the exact genre. Was he a soap actor, or was he one of these alternative comedians, *alternative* being a synonym for *not funny*? And then it came to him. Johnny Pallas, that was the name, one of these reality show stars, if star was the right word, having appeared on a bizarre gay version of *Love Island* that he remembered had caused a tabloid storm for a brief period the previous year. 'Hello *Scotland,'* he bellowed, in that over-familiar tone favoured by Radio Two DJs and similarly second-division entertainers. 'Welcome to the *future*! Welcome to *Taggart-land*.'

Frank turned to Lexy and gave her a raised-eyebrow look. 'We need a banner that says *not my future*, don't we? And Taggart-land? What the hell is that all about, for God's sake? Although sorry, I don't suppose I should be speaking for you.'

'Are you serious sir?' she said, laughing. 'Do you think I would give these bam-pots my vote?'

'I never presume,' he said, 'but, no I didn't, and thank God I was right.' He focussed back on the stage, where it appeared the fake-tanned Lothario was approaching the end of his sloganeering. 'Freedom for Scotland,' he bellowed randomly, 'and now I'm pleased to introduce the couple who are going to deliver it for youse all. Ladies and gentlemen, please give it up for Tommy and Sienna Taggart!' To raucous cheers and applause, the pair strolled onto the platform, Tommy Taggart in leather jacket and football shirt, his wife in her trademark cheap-tart outfit of stilettos and a short low-cut, figure-hugging navy dress.

A male student, evidently well-refreshed, thrust aloft a half-litre bottle of San Miguel and shouted, 'Hey Sienna, get your tits oot for the lads!' Another shouted, 'Aye, even if they're fakes', causing his mates to collapse into gales of laughter. Over by the stage, the Taggart's minders spun their heads around, intent on seeking out the offenders, who wisely had melted back into the crowd. Up on the platform, Sienna Taggart gave a serene smile and waved, Frank suspecting she would see the barb as a compliment. After all, if you dressed the way she did, what could you expect, he thought, a dinosaur-like opinion he knew would get him into serious trouble if he ever decided to voice it in public.

'*Hello Scotland,*' Tommy Taggart roared, thrusting his arms aloft, 'and welcome to our big Freedom Rally. Power to the people!'

Frank gave Lexy a wry look. 'Did he actually just say that? What next, wear a flower in your hair? He's like a bloody sixties or seventies tribute act.'

'I wasn't around then sir,' she said, smiling. 'I wasn't born until nineteen ninety-five.'

He laughed. 'Aye, alright, alright, no need to rub it in. But just so you know, I wasn't around back then either. Or at least, I would have only been a tiny baby and my mum wouldn't have let me go on one of these protest march thingies. Anyway, let's have a listen to what this pair of eejits have got to say for themselves.'

What followed was half an hour of vitriol directed at a long list of supposed enemies of Scotland, starting with the ruling nationalist party, moving through dark-skinned immigrants who supposedly didn't share the values of the indigenous Scottish people, to finally, of course, the English. But whereas the Nationalists generally cloaked their overtly racist anti-English rhetoric by insisting it was only Tories they hated, Taggart made no such distinction. From him, the message was stark and simple - he just didn't like them, irrespective of political hue. After twenty minutes, he handed over the platform to his wife, to great cheers from their supporters. By this point, their gang of thugs had dispersed through the crowd, and this time the pneumatic Mrs Taggart attracted no hecklers.

Frank had heard Sienna Taggart speak before, and there was just something slightly odd about the way she talked that he couldn't quite put his finger on. Whatever the case, her rage was directed chiefly at the country's South Asian community, and how Scotland's political landscape and been dominated by *these kind of people* over the last twenty years. Frank couldn't help smiling at the irony of her words, it evidently being lost to her that the reason for the success of that community was that they worked hard, brought up their children to respect their elders and valued a good education above all else - exactly the values that had once served to define the Scots, but was now in danger of being lost. Undisguisedly racist no matter how you looked at it, he was ashamed that so many of his countrymen seemed to be in thrall to the Taggarts' twisted creed.

Finally the performance was over, the Taggarts bounding off the stage holding hands, arms aloft like a rock band leaving in triumph after a rapturous encore. Aptly enough, they were to be followed by a concert from Black Diamond, one of Scotland's best-known if fading rock combos. Frank quite liked the Diamonds, an old-school outfit who looked and sounded like a pound-shop Rolling Stones, but he mused that associating themselves with Taggart's neo-fascists would surely put the final nail in the coffin of their fast-dying career.

He tapped Lexy on the arm. 'Right, better get our skates on before Mr and Mrs Taggart scoot off. Follow me.' Earlier, he had spotted it parked behind the stage, the hundred-grand luxury motorhome that the Taggarts had bought with donations from ordinary party members, to be used, they claimed, as their personal election battle-bus. 'You see it, over there?' he said, pointing in the vehicle's direction.

'I'd forgotten about the motor-caravan thing,' Lexy said, grinning. 'It caused quite a stink at the time, didn't it? I wonder what they get up to in there. It looks like a right passion-wagon.'

Frank raised an eyebrow. 'Well you never know, we might be unlucky enough to catch them at it. But anyway, let's get a sprint on so we don't miss them.'

It took a bit of doing to thread their way through the dense crowd, but finally they reached the door of the motorhome. The retractable steps were down, signifying that the owners were indeed in residence. Frank winked at Lexy then rapped on the door.

'Mr and Mrs Taggart. It's DCI Frank Stewart with Police Scotland. We'd like a word if you've both got a minute.' After a few seconds, the top half of the door was pushed open and Tommy Taggart's head appeared through the opening.

'Aye, what do you lot want?' he said, giving them a suspicious look.

'Can we come in for a minute Mr Taggart?' Frank said pleasantly. 'There's a couple of questions we want to ask you. We'll be out of your hair in no time, I promise.'

Taggart said nothing for a moment, then shouted back into the van. 'Hey Sienna doll, get your arse out here, the cops want to have a word. Are you decent?' Frank couldn't make out the reply, but it must have been in the affirmative, because a second later, Taggart kicked open the bottom half of the door and nodded for them to enter.

'Swish place,' Frank said, as he took in the plush decor, all polished hardwood panelling and soft velour furnishings. 'Must have cost a packet eh? Although I know, it's rude to ask. But it's a natural question, isn't it?'

'It's a legitimate political expense,' Taggart answered, giving a shrug that plainly said *I don't give a f**k what you think.* 'Anyway, the lovely Sienna's through here in the dining area. Come through and grab a seat.' He pushed open a door and led them through to a small area located just behind the front driver's cabin. Two well-upholstered benches were set at either side of a generous-sized wood-laminate table. At one end sat Sienna Taggart, wrapped in a towel having evidently showered after their performance.

'What did you make of our big show?' she said with an air of conceit. 'Don't you think I do very fine acting?'

'Aye, very polished, and you made a lot of sense to me,' Frank said, nodding. 'All good stuff as far as I'm concerned. Every word of it. Like you said, there's just far too many of these kind of people in our country.' He caught the look of absolute horror on Lexy's face and wondered if he should have told her of his *Columbo* strategy in advance. That was what you needed to do, of course, ingratiate yourself with the suspects so that they drop their guard. It was all part of the plan, but that didn't stop the words seriously sticking in his throat.

Tommy Taggart gave an expansive smile. 'You should take out a membership of our party DCI Stewart. It's dead easy to join, all done in seconds on our web-site and just thirty quid a year. In actual fact we've got loads of you cops on board already, which is going to be very handy come the revolution. But anyway, what is it you want to ask us? Because we're busy people.'

Frank nodded. 'Of course you are, and as I said, we won't take up too much of your time. In fact, the whole thing's just a tick-the-box exercise, something that I quite frankly can't be arsed with if I'm being honest. But my gaffer plays everything by the book, so we need to go through the formalities, you know what it's like.'

'So?' Sienna said, impatience bubbling to the surface.

'Aye well, it's the whole thing about your husband's election. There's a bunch of nosey-parkers at the Edinburgh branch of the Electoral Commission who're suggesting that your party might have breached a few rules here and there. And the Nationalist's candidate said the same.'

She gave a smug smile. 'Kelly Prentice? Have you seen her? I mean, they don't call her Mrs Shrek for nothing, and she had nothing to do with the constituency either. She was one of Mrs McClelland's old pals from Edinburgh. They just shipped her in and thought the locals would fall for it. But they didn't.'

Frank gave a half-smile, but didn't immediately respond. Yes, it was true that Ms. Prentice might not win any beauty contests, but since when did that matter in politics? Show-business for ugly people, wasn't that what they called it. The trouble was, when a charismatic chancer like Tommy Taggart came on the scene, the normal rules didn't apply.

'You see the thing is,' he said finally, 'they're suggesting there might have been some intimidation outside of polling stations, courtesy of your private army of football hooligans. Of course it all sounds like a lot of bollocks myself, but my gaffer's insisting that me and DC McDonald here look into it. So we'll be popping down to your constituency and asking a few questions here and there. Strictly routine you understand.'

'Of course Chief Inspector, you need to do that, quite right,' Tommy Taggart said smoothly. 'But you'll find there's nothing to see, nothing at all. It's all part of the establishment witch-hunt. Everybody hates us and we don't care. And on the subject, I don't much like the language you're using to describe my loyal followers.'

Frank laughed. 'It was just a joke. I'm sure they're all

perfectly law-abiding citizens.' He gave Lexy a look that signalled he thought anything but. 'Anyway, just for the record, are you saying there's nothing in these allegations?'

Taggart smiled. 'Nothing. Nothing at all. As I said, the establishment hate us, and it sticks in their throats that the ordinary people of Scotland don't feel the same way.'

'Aye, well you're probably right,' Frank sighed. 'But I've got my orders.'

'So is that it?' Sienna Taggart said. 'Because I have very big list to get on with.'

'Aye, I think we're about done here Mrs Taggart, and sorry for taking up so much of your time,' Frank said, raising his hand in apology. He smiled at Lexy. 'What about you DC McDonald? Anything to add?'

She shook her head. 'No sir, I think you've covered about everything for now.'

'Okay, that's great. So Mr and Mrs Taggart, we'll head off now,' he said, getting to his feet. 'And you probably won't hear from us again, but best of luck with your project.' He followed Lexy to the door and down the steps, squelching onto muddy grass. 'Bloody weather eh? Typical Scottish summer's day.'

'I'll not come out, if you don't mind,' Taggart said. 'But thanks for your visit.'

Frank shrugged. 'No bother.' He was silent for a moment then said. 'Oh aye, there was just one thing I'd forgotten to mention. Did you or your wife have anything to do with that business in that Paisley pub? Because old Dr Donnie Morrison says he was set up and he never touched that woman.'

***

'I don't think he liked that question sir,' Lexy said as they made their way back to his car. 'There was a definite hesitation before he answered, as if he was having to work out what to say.'

'Aye, I thought that too. Which surprised me a bit, because the whole fakery thing seems a bit implausible to me.'

'I suppose it could be true though sir,' she said, frowning. 'I think the Taggarts would be well capable of paying some tart to come on to Morrison in that pub.'

He nodded. 'Aye, I suppose if there was any skulduggery involved, then that's the most likely explanation. I'm guessing we know who the floozy was, do we?'

'I don't know off the top of my head sir, but I'm sure we can easily find out. I'll get onto it as soon as we get back to the station.'

'Great stuff. And I'll try and figure out what to do next.'

She gave him a curious look. 'And sir, is it true what you told the Taggarts? That they probably won't hear from us again?'

He grinned. 'You need to get onto that YouTube thingy and watch a few episodes of Columbo, to see how he works. Believe me, he's a right pain in the butt, and me and you are going to be *exactly* the same. A few weeks of us annoying the arse out of them, and Mr and Mrs Taggart will be putting their fancy big house up for sale just to get away from us.'

Chapter 8

Today was day one of a new chapter in the illustrious history of Maggie Bainbridge's little firm, and despite some justifiable reservations, the proprietor of the eponymous Investigation Agency was looking forward to it very much. As Frank had said to her over breakfast, there really was nothing much lost if the gregarious Miss Lorilynn Logan didn't work out, and anyway, from what little he had seen of her, he thought the chances of that were pretty small. *She seems a smart wee lassie* was his verdict, a description that seemed to sum up the girl perfectly. But actually, that wasn't the only thing Frank had said over breakfast, and it was the other thing he had said that had occupied quite a bit of her thoughts as she was travelling into the office. Because for about the third or fourth time this week, he had dropped the name of some American woman he was working with into the conversation. Carrie-Anne, that was her name, and it was the way that he seemed to be already on easy first-name terms with this woman that had caused her some mild alarm. She was probably being stupid of course, but she remembered the way her late husband used to casually mention his associate Angelique Perez as if she was just someone he worked with, whilst all the time carrying on with the bitch behind her back. Probably she *was* being stupid, but that didn't mean she wasn't going to take a good look at this woman for herself. However, that would have to wait for another day.

Lori was waiting for Maggie as arranged, in a little coffee-shop handily situated opposite the main entrance of the *Globe* newspaper on West Nile Street. With only a few tiny stool-height tables squeezed in along one wall, the place clearly catered mainly for the take-away trade, and on this chilly late May morning it was doing steady business. Her new associate had been here some time it seemed, as evidenced by the drained cappuccino and half-eaten roll-and-sausage in front of her.

'So here we are,' Maggie said brightly, slipping her bag off her shoulder and placing it on the floor. 'Your first day. Excited?'

'Bloody right I am,' Lori burbled. 'I didn't sleep a wink last night as a matter of fact. Oh, and by the way, I've ordered for you already. The barista lad will bring it straight over as soon as I give him the nod.'

Maggie laughed. 'Such efficiency, thank you! Well I'm afraid today is going to be a bit boring, but that's just the nature of surveillance operations. A lot of sitting about doing nothing and then hopefully, some action.'

'I don't mind. I'm a very patient person. And here, I've brought my driving licence like you asked.' She slid the credit-card-sized item across the table. 'And it's nearly clean. Just six points for speeding last year, nothing else. And I was only doing ninety.'

'Oh dear, that's going to bump up our insurance quite a bit,' Maggie said, suddenly wondering if Miss Logan's employment might turn out to be a bit more problematic than she had been hoping.

'You can't hang about when you're a detective,' Lori said seriously. 'Foot to the floor, it's the only way.'

'You were a waitress,' Maggie said, giving her a look of mild amusement. 'Anyway, my Golf's in the multi-storey over there in case we need it. I think Dominique normally takes the train in but her partner gave me her car's registration number and said he'll tell us if she's using her car on any particular day. And it won't be hard to spot, because she apparently drives a bright-yellow Porsche sports car with a personalised number-plate.'

'She didn't drive in today,' Lori said, 'because I saw her go through the front door about twenty minutes ago, and she was walking up from the direction of the station.'

'So you've been here *that* long?' Maggie said, surprised and impressed at the same time.

'Yeah, I checked the train timetable. I guessed she would catch it from Patterton Station. That's the nearest to their house, and I knew if she wanted to get in before eight she would have to catch the 7.05.'

'Ah, clever. So anyway, about today...'

'And there was something else I was thinking about too,' Lori interrupted, the words tumbling out at a speed of about Mach Two. 'So there's a very good chance that if Miss Tremblay is *really* shagging someone else, then it might be some guy she works with, don't you agree?' She didn't wait for Maggie to answer. 'So I was talking to the barista guy over there - his name's Shug by the way, I think he quite fancies me - and it turns out he's got a good mate called Nathan who works for the paper. So I thought that maybe we could ask this Nathan guy if there are any rumours kicking about the place, you know, about Dominique.

Anyway, I got Shug to ask his mate to pop over to see us mid-morning, and after that, I thought we could ask his mate to keep an eye out for us on an ongoing basis, to be our inside man if you like, although of course we need to check him out first to make sure he's not a complete dipstick. Because he works in IT, so I expect he probably will be. He'll be one of these spotty-faced floppy-haired dweebs that can't look you in the eye.'

'I think I got *most* of that,' Maggie said, struggling to keep up. 'But that's good work Lori, really good work.'

'Nae bother,' she said, with a hint of embarrassment. 'So what's the plan boss? Going forward I mean?'

Maggie laughed. 'Well today was meant to be a training day, with me working alongside you to show you the ropes. But actually, I think you're already way ahead of me. So the plan is just to hang around here and see if Dominique emerges at any time during the day. I would have thought she would slip out for lunch at some point, and we can follow her and see if she meets up with anyone. Same thing after work. These journalists are very fond of an after-work drink, so maybe we can track her to her favourite pub and see if she's getting too cosy with anyone. I'm afraid it's going to be a long day and a bit boring too. No exciting car chases or anything like that. No, we just need to keep our eyes peeled on that revolving door across the street and hope that she pops out at some point.'

And it was true, that they would be facing a few days comprising of mainly tedious inactivity, but it was something that was just part of the job, and at least they had the meeting with Shug's mate Nathan to look forward to. Helpfully Lori had explained that 'Shug' was the Glasgow argot for 'Hugh', and that basically everyone in the city christened with the latter was known by the former. In a similar vein, since moving up from London Maggie had come to realise there were two flavours of the local accent. The first was the mellifluous lilting tones much in demand by broadcasters and call-centres, perhaps best epitomised by the two lovely Kirsties, the Misses Wark and Young of the British Broadcasting Corporation. The other was rather more rough and ready, more prevalent too, and completely impenetrable to outsiders like herself. This was the accent that came naturally to Lorilynn Logan, and to the rabble-rouser Tommy Taggart, and, it turned out, to Nathan Duke too. She guessed he was no more than about twenty, and as Lori had expertly predicted, floppy-haired, spotty, and tall and awkward-looking in faded jeans and a vermillion hoodie. The interview, conducted entirely by her new assistant in her role of interpreter, yielded no immediately useful information about their target, save that Dominique wasn't exactly popular with her colleagues. However, the youth had, with little persuasion, agreed to act as their informer going forward. It was a risk of course, because as Lori had so eloquently put it, he might turn out to be a complete dipstick, but in Maggie's opinion it was a risk worth taking. And the good thing was, it was something concrete, something they could report back to their client Jack Urquhart as evidence of progress. Which made her remember she owed him a phone call, a phone call that might turn out to put a bit of frost on company-client relations. But that could wait until a little later. Right now, she had come to a decision.

'You know Lori, I think I'm feeling that I could easily leave you to do this job on your own. I know you've only just started, and you must tell me if you wouldn't be happy about it, but I actually think it would be best for the investigation.'

Lori smiled. 'Aye, I was thinking that too, and, no, it's not because I believe I'm brilliant or anything like that, honestly it's not. But the thing is, Dominique knows you, doesn't she? So if she was to walk in here right now and see you sitting there, then that would screw the whole thing up, wouldn't it? And she might do that, it's very possible, since she only works across the street. Whereas although I was at the Bikini too that day, she just looked straight through me, as if I wasn't there. That's my USP you see. I fade into the background.'

Maggie had heard of people using this mysterious USP phrase before, but had to confess she hadn't a clue what it meant. Still, she couldn't help but agree with Lori's analysis of the situation.

'Okay then, let's go with it. And please, if you need my help on anything, just give me a call and I'll be right there. We're only fifteen minutes from the office here.'

'Right boss.'

'And Lori, there's just one more thing?'

'What's that boss?'

'Try and make sure I get my car back in one piece. That little car and me have been through a lot together and I wouldn't want to lose him just yet.'

***

Having pledged her Golf to Lori for the duration of the surveillance exercise, Maggie was faced with the short walk to St Enoch's Square to grab a subway train back to her Byers Road office. Or to be more accurate, to *their* Byers Road office, a more precise description now that Lori had joined the staff and was already looking like becoming a permanent fixture. On the walk down, she decided to give her client a call.

'Hey Maggie,' he said, after answering on the second ring. *'Is it a quickie? Because I'm in a Select Committee meeting right now and getting a right grilling from that bunch of rottweilers I call my colleagues. We're just having a five-minute tea-break before I'm thrown to the lions again.'* Maggie vaguely knew about the Select Committee system, where Government Ministers were quizzed by back-benchers on policy matters pertinent to their department. Somehow, she couldn't imagine that a smooth operator like Jack Urquhart would have much trouble in dealing with anything they could throw at him. But then again, people didn't always like smoothies.

'Just a couple of quick points. First, just to let you know we've got the surveillance operation up and running. My associate Lorilynn is assigned full-time and that means twenty-four-by-seven if needs must. Right now she's set up camp right opposite the offices of the Globe.'

'That's great. And I know it might sound odd, but of course I'm hoping it's all in vain and she doesn't find anything.'

'That would be great, naturally,' Maggie said, but her gut was already telling her that was unlikely. 'And we've also found an inside agent, just in case she is close to someone on the paper. But whatever the case, we'll keep you fully up to speed with developments.' She hesitated for a moment before continuing. Now it was time to bring up the prime reason for her call.

'Jack, about your invitation to dinner, and...well, that other thing. I suppose I should regard it as flattering, but the fact is, I wasn't very happy about it. You see, I'm crazily in love with an amazing guy and I'm getting married in a few months.'

'I guessed you would be with someone,' he said, sounding wistful. *'All the loveliest ladies are. But I've just been feeling so inadequate given the situation with Dominique, and I had this overwhelming craving to prove that I'm not totally unattractive. Plus, if you don't mind me being vulgar, it's weeks since I've had..well, you know what I mean... and that's not good for a man.'*

Maggie gulped. 'Jack, I think that can be safely filed under the heading *way too much information*. But look, you're *quite* an attractive man, and if it ever goes wrong with Frank and me, you *might* just manage to squeeze in to my top ten list of possibles. Now, hadn't you better get back to your exciting committee meeting? There's a country to be governed, I believe.'

She heard him chuckle. *'Yes, you're right Maggie, and I'd be very honoured to make your top ten should the situation arise. Anyway, thanks for the progress update, and I hope I haven't offended you.'*

'You haven't,' she said as he was hanging up. But even as she was saying it, and even although the whole thing was a joke, she could feel a wave of fear and melancholy overcoming her. Because the fact was, if it ever went wrong for Frank and her, she doubted if she would be able to carry on at all, no matter who might be on the shortlist.

Chapter 9

Much as he had hated to admit it, Frank had rather enjoyed winding up the Taggarts, Columbo-style. They were a nasty pair and dangerous with it, that was his opinion, promoting an insular version of Scottishness that was alien to the natural outward-looking *mien* he had always ascribed to his fellow countrymen. Look back through history, anywhere in the world, and you would find a feisty and determined Jock at the heart of things. It was Scots who had tamed the vast expanses of Canada for civilization; their fingerprints were all over imperial India; and he had been interested to learn that it was one of his compatriots who'd built the first electric power-station in Scandinavia, erected to power a paper mill somewhere in deepest Finland. But there had been plenty of baddies too of course, for example a really dreadful guy called Joannes Wyllie who had made a small fortune running guns to the Confederates during the American Civil War. The latter excepted, the Taggarts couldn't hold a candle to any of these illustrious predecessors, and he was determined that their growing and malignant influence should be nipped in the bud. But that of course depended on them having actually committed a crime, and right now the inconvenient truth was that their rise to prominence had, on the face of it, been entirely legitimate.

So there were two angles to explore. Firstly, had there been, as the Electoral Commission had alleged, either intimidation of voters at the polling booths or funny business with the postal voting, or indeed both? And secondly, had the Taggarts somehow been involved in the scandal that had forced the incumbent Donnie Morrison to resign? Of the two, Frank reckoned it was the first that was the more likely to bear fruit, and maybe a bit easier to prove too. It would depend on tracking down a few constituents who had been coerced by threat of violence to vote for Tommy Taggart, or - and this had just occurred to him - had been bribed to do so. Although this latter point he suspected would be well-nigh impossible to prove, on the grounds that it would be hard to find anyone prepared to admit to having accepted a sly twenty-quid note to place their 'X' in the box marked *Taggart*. As for intimidation, that might be easier, because if they found anyone prepared to admit to it, the police could guarantee anonymity in return for their witness statement, and no need to make a personal appearance in court. That might just be enough to persuade someone to talk. All of this was the subject of discussion as once again he and Lexy set about an attack on another three-sausage Full Scottish breakfast in the canteen of New Gorbals nick.

'I see we've got *two* fried eggs today Lexy,' he beamed, pointing to one of the exhibits with his knife. 'A right red-letter day, eh? And they look nice and runny too.'

'There's a new chef sir. I think she's trying to make a good impression.'

'Aye, well it's working with me. This is lovely.'

Lexy laughed. 'And what about that kilt you'll be squeezing into in a few months' time sir? I thought you said you were practising restraint.'

He gave her a wry look. 'That's the great thing about kilts. You wrap them round yourself, so they're fully adjustable.

Anyway, we're here to talk work, not discuss my wedding plans or my waistline. So, we're off down to Paisley to see Dr Donnie Morrison in about an hour's time. That should be interesting I think.'

'Definitely sir. And I've been thinking about the other stuff, you know, the electoral fraud business. I think our best option would be to do a door-to-door in one of the posher areas of Taggart's constituency.'

'It's Paisley. Are there such areas?' he laughed.

'A few sir. And it's mainly elderly residents in these districts, who might have been easier to intimidate. But there was something else I've been worrying about too.' She lowered her voice then quickly glanced around the room, as if checking for eavesdroppers. 'You see, I'm not sure who we can trust around here. To do the interviewing I mean. Because they're a right bunch of racist misogynist bastards in this nick. I bet at least half of them are Taggart supporters, if not more.'

Frank nodded. 'Funnily enough, I had the same fears, much as it pains me to say it. But luckily I think I've got a solution to that one. Or rather, a big fat ball-of-lard solution.'

Lexy laughed. 'I don't think you're allowed to say that sort of stuff about your colleagues anymore sir. But I assume you're talking about DC French.'

'That's the man. I'm sure Ronnie would love another holiday up here, before he hands in his warrant card and heads off into glorious retirement. He loves the old expenses-paid away-days in the Premier Inn.'

'I like him. He's funny, in a sort of dinosaur from a different age sort of way. And I love the way he talks. He sounds like an extra from East Enders. *Know what I mean me old china?*' The last phrase was rendered in her attempt at a Cockney accent, which Frank, a bit unkindly, thought was best filed under the heading *needs some work*.

He smiled. 'Aye he does. It'll be interesting to see what the good burgers of Paisley make of him, that's for sure. If they can work out what the hell he's saying of course. Anyway, we'd better get our skates on and polish off our breakfasts. Don't want to be late for the Reverend, else he might get us sent to hell. He speaks to Jesus every day apparently.'

***

It turned out the Morrisons lived in one of the elegant nineteen-twenties-built bungalows that were such an architectural characteristic of the posher suburbs of Glasgow, this one set, as they all were, in a pleasant leafy street of identical homes. But what immediately set this home apart from the others, Frank observed as he pulled their car up outside, was the notably dishevelled state of the front garden.

'Look at this,' he nodded to Lexy, 'they'll be getting a letter from the residents' committee soon if they don't get that sorted out pretty sharpish.'

She laughed. 'I expect he's got other things on his mind. But I imagine we'll soon find out.'

The door was answered by Morrison's wife Rose. Frank guessed she was late fifties or early sixties, a large woman of plain appearance, with grey hair pulled back from her forehead and tied in a bun. She wore navy leggings and a shapeless purple cardigan, neither of which did her any favours. He thought back to the incriminating shots showing Donnie Morrison with his hand half-way up the leg of that sexy temptress. The woman had done a couple of photo-shoots for the *Globe* after the story broke, posing in a micro-mini dress that barely reached half-way down her arse, obviously surgically-enhanced breasts thrust out in front of her, her eyes surrounded by a half-inch of black mascara and her hair a giant mass of vivid red curls, one strand of which she held between her lips as she stared lewdly at the camera. You couldn't excuse it of course, and Morrison had paid a heavy price for his indiscretion, but maybe you could understand it. After all, wasn't the firebrand Minister himself always banging on about the flesh being weak and all that sort of stuff? It seemed that *his* flesh had been definitely on the weak side, that was for sure.

'Come through please,' she said, in a quiet voice. There was a definite softness to the accent, the origin of which DC Lexy McDonald would doubtless be able to identify, being from the Western Isles herself. 'I've made tea and coffee.' And this being Scotland, Frank thought, there's bound to be cake and chocolate biscuits too. *Excellent*.

Donnie Morrison was standing in the bay of the lounge when they entered, hands in pockets and staring out of the window. He turned to greet them, revealing that under his grey cardigan he was wearing a black shirt with dog-collar. *The Reverend Dr Donald Morrison, Minister of the Free Church of Scotland.* When the scandal was at its height, that

Tremblay woman with the Globe had been sniffing around the University of Glasgow archives and had questioned whether the good Rev had actually been awarded a doctorate, and in fact whether he had actually been properly ordained in the first place. But that had apparently not come to anything, the newspaper's readership preferring to wallow in the details of the Reverend's sex scandal.

'DCI Stewart I presume?' he said. 'And your colleague?'

'I'm DC McDonald sir,' she answered. 'From New Gorbals police station.'

Morrison smiled. 'Ah, so a fellow islander I detect from your accent. Welcome both of you to our home. Please, take a seat.' He nodded towards a large sofa, one of two laid out around a walnut coffee table, formally if somewhat old-fashionedly set with what Frank assumed was the best china. But then Morrison was himself a curiously old-fashioned figure, pedalling a creed that had few takers in twenty-first century Scotland. 'But you, DCI Stewart, are from the *Metropolitan* Police I believe?'

'Aye that's right sir. My gaffers thought it best to bring in an independent resource from another force to investigate this matter. So here I am.' It wasn't quite the truth, but it was near enough so as to make no difference.

'Well I'm pleased about that,' Morrison said, 'and about time too.'

'We're not doing a very good job of looking after our guests,' his wife interrupted, sharpness in her tone. 'Would you like tea or coffee Chief Inspector?' Even in the few minutes he had been in the room, Frank had detected there was a definite atmosphere between the married couple. He doubted if their relationship was in good shape, given all that had happened in the past twelve months. But then again, perhaps it hadn't been much good even before Donnie had tried it on with that barmaid cum porn-star. It had become a cliché that political wives always supported their husbands in public after they had been caught being unfaithful, smiling through clenched teeth for the cameras. Perhaps Rose Morrison was different.

'Coffee would be great please,' he said, smiling, 'and you don't mind if I help myself to one of these lovely fairy cakes?' He didn't wait for an answer, picking up a tea-plate and sliding a garish pink confection onto it. 'Smashing.'

'So what's changed?' Morrison said plaintively. 'Why have the police finally decided to take my complaints seriously? Because you know we've been through hell, Rose and I. Pure hell.' For the first time, Frank looked at the man properly. He knew he was sixty-three, but he looked at least ten years older, his skin grey and pallid, strands of dandruffed hair forlornly combed over a balding pate, his eyes dull and watery. Whatever the truth of the allegations against him, the matter had taken its toll on his appearance, of that there was no doubt.

Frank shrugged. 'Let's just say there's been a few *developments* that made my gaffers think they should take another look.' He wasn't going to mention the involvement of the security services, especially the fact that a beautiful

CIA agent was now on the case, and actually, he wasn't sure if he was allowed to say anything anyway.

'I'm totally innocent. Of everything. It was all a pack of lies. All of it.' There was a desperation to the message, as if after repeating it a thousand times or more he no longer believed it himself.

'Well, maybe that will all come out in the wash,' Frank said. 'Anyway, we need to go over it all again I'm afraid, to make sure that me and DC McDonald have got our facts straight. So the DC will run us through what we know, and you can correct us as we go along. Is that ok sir?'

Morrison nodded his assent.

'Okay then sir,' Lexy said, removing a small notebook from a back pocket. Frank knew it was basically a prop, because Lexy would have been all over the details of the case, thoroughness of preparation being just one of many professional characteristics he admired in her. And one of many that surely destined her for greater things. He could see her going all the way, to ACC or even beyond. *Chief Constable Alexa McDonald.* It had a certain ring to it he thought. She continued,

'The woman in question is one Jade Niven, thirty-seven years of age, occupation barmaid and part-time exotic dancer, and a single mum with one boy aged eleven. According to the statement you gave to the police at the time, she got in contact with you because her private landlord was trying to evict them from their flat in the Seedhill district of the town for no good reason, and she wanted you to help her. Is that correct Dr Morrison?'

'Aye, that's right,' he agreed. 'Exactly that.'

Lexy nodded. 'So you arranged to meet her at a pub called the Greenock Tavern on the estate where she lived, to discuss the matter. Is that also right sir?'

Frank interjected before Morrison could answer.

'Bit of a strange place to meet sir, if you don't mind me saying so. I would have thought a matter like that would have been better handled in your constituency office.'

'Jade had been working a few shifts at the Tavern,' Morrison said. 'She knocked off at half-nine on a Wednesday so that was the time we agreed. It was convenient for both of us.'

'But you must see how that looks Dr Morrison,' Frank said. 'You slipping out late in the evening to meet up with a very attractive lady in a seedy pub.'

'I like to get out and about in the constituency,' he said primly. 'That's what you need to do if you're a good MSP. Man of the people and all that. It's important to be seen.'

'Fair enough,' Frank said, just managing to suppress a smirk. He didn't like pompous arses, and Morrison was giving every indication that he was a fine example of the breed. 'Carry on DC McDonald, please.'

'Okay sir. So to cut to the chase Dr Morrison, it appears that both of you had a couple of drinks, and then according to Miss Niven, you started to get a bit forward with her. She said, and I quote, that you were like an octopus with your tentacles all over her.'

Morrison shook his head violently. 'That's an absolute lie. Total fiction. I never laid a finger on that woman, I swear to God.'

Frank gave a wry smile. 'And yet someone took a wee video didn't they, with you two sitting together and you sliding your hand half-way up her leg. How do you explain that sir?'

'I don't know,' he exploded. 'I said it over and over again to the police at the time. I don't know how they got that video, but I never touched that girl.'

Lexy looked down at her notebook again. 'According to the case notes, the videos were taken by a friend of Miss Niven's, by the name of Kylie Gilmour. She worked at the Greenock Tavern too apparently.'

Frank nodded. 'Okay, got that. So Dr Morrison, you claim you never touched the woman, but you have to admit the evidence suggests otherwise. But we'll park that for now shall we? DC McDonald, what's next?'

'Right sir,' she said, flipping over a page, 'so we're now onto the matter of the council house. Apparently what Jade Niven actually wanted her MSP to do for her was to get her shooting right to the top of the council house waiting list. She was desperate for a nice flat for herself and her boy.'

Frank nodded. 'I can well understand that. So what happened then?'

She glanced down at her notebook. 'According to Miss Niven, Dr Morrison said he would use his considerable influence with the council in return for sex.' She hesitated for a moment, giving an apologetic glance at his wife. 'Or to be specific, in return for oral sex.'

'No no no!' Morrison was now shouting, his voice rising to a crescendo. 'That's rubbish, total rubbish! We talked about getting her priority on the housing list for sure, but there was no mention of sex. Look, I talk to about a hundred constituents a month about this. There's a big shortage of housing stock and so there's loads of people who're desperate to get on the list. It's what I do, day-in, day-out. It's my job. No, more than that. It's my *calling*.'

Frank paused for a moment, taking it all in. He'd interviewed thousands of suspects in his time and nine times out of ten you could tell when they were lying. But in this case he was struggling to make up his mind. Morrison was certainly persuasive, but then again he'd had thirty years in the pulpit successfully convincing his flock that despite the absence of any credible supporting evidence, there really was a God. But here, the evidence was stacked against him. And as the final nail in the coffin, there was that other video. He said,

'The CCTV in Jade's building caught you leaving her flat at approximately twelve minutes to eleven on the night in question. On leaving, you were seen looking around in a furtive manner as if anxious to avoid detection. I guess you remember seeing that video sir?' It was the stills from that video, carried on the front page of every newspaper in Scotland, that more than anything had hastened the end of Donnie Morrison's political career. It was unlikely he would have forgotten, however much he might want to.

'It...never...happened.' He spelled out the words, the tone more plaintive than angry, and for a moment, Frank wondered if he should feel sorry for the man. Because if Morrison had been the victim of an injustice as he was claiming, it had been a monumentally elaborate one. The whole thing was just too crazy to contemplate. Just crazy enough in fact to warrant a phone call to Carrie-Anne Fisher of the CIA. But then Rose Morrison cut in, breaking his train of thought, her anger undisguised.

'He says it never happened, but I just don't believe him. You see, my sanctimonious husband can never keep his grubby hands off anything with a skirt. *That*'s his calling.'

'That's utter rubbish and you know it,' her husband said, shaking his head, but somehow it wasn't convincing. 'Just ignore her, Chief Inspector. She's not been herself since our boy cut off contact.'

'And whose fault is that?' She spat out the words, each one enveloped in a bitterness she didn't try to hide. 'You drove him away, you sick hypocrite, with all this sordid business.'

Aye, Frank's instinct had been right. Things evidently weren't too clever in the Morrison marriage, and experience told him he needed to hear more. He spoke softly.

'Look, I'm really sorry to hear about your boy. What's his name Mrs Morrison?'

'Rory. He's called Rory. And *he* drove him away. Because our boy is gay, but his father here won't accept it.' Now the woman began to cry, quiet sobs at first then breaking into a dreadful wail that made Frank shiver.

Morrison gave a condescending smile, making no effort to comfort his wife. 'Rory's just not found the right girl yet, I keep telling her that, but she won't listen.' His pleading was evidently directed at Frank and Lexy, but it sounded as if it was himself he was trying to convince. And it definitely hadn't convinced his wife.

'You pathetic old fool,' she said, her voice dripping with bitterness, 'he's *never* going to find the right girl. Because he doesn't like girls. He likes *men*. He likes *men* and he has *sex* with men. Oh yes, what would your stupid God make of that? Rory Morrison, son of the manse, is a raving homosexual who likes to bugger and be buggered.'

Goaded, Morrison leapt to his feet, turning to face his wife who was still sitting on the sofa. He slapped her hard on the cheek, causing her head to snap back. Then he leaned over and, snatching a handful of her hair, pulled her head back up so her face was just an inch from his own. 'You're a blaspheming witch,' he whispered menacingly, 'and you'll burn in hell for what you just said. Believe me, I'll make sure you do.'

Frank, taken by surprise, took a step towards the disgraced politician, intent on restraining him, but Lexy got there first. She yanked Morrison's arm up his back then shoved him face down onto the sofa. 'Now now sir, we won't be having any of this behaviour, will we? Domestic violence is a serious offence and we've already seen enough to charge you.'

'That wasn't very nice sir, was it?' Frank said, his tone more emollient than he felt. 'I think we're going to have to take a trip down the station afterwards I'm afraid. But let's just try and calm everything down for now. Mrs Morrison, why don't you get us all another cup of coffee and you can tell us about your boy.'

***

And so they'd stayed an extra half hour in the neat bungalow, amongst the crumbling marriage of Donnie and Rose Morrison, to hear the life story of their much-loved son Rory. He was a notably good-looking boy, that was clearly evident from the photographs that his mother proudly passed round. After a journalism degree at the Caledonian University, and following an internship gained courtesy of the influence of his father, he had bagged a job as a trainee correspondent with the Globe. The paper had moved him to Edinburgh to cover the political scene, where he had shared a nice flat in Leith and enjoyed a very full social life, if his frequent postings on Instagram were to believed. Rose had always known, she said, that her son was gay and was perfectly relaxed about it, but his father remained in denial. And then, when all the sordid business with Jade Niven had emerged, there had been a huge family bust-up, with the son accusing the father of monumental hypocrisy, happy to shag around and betray his mother whilst deriding his son's lifestyle choice. Words were said, that's what Rose had told them, cruel and hurtful words that were impossible to take back. Worse than that, it had been the last time they had seen or spoken to their son.

And then, out of the blue, Rory had announced on his social media platforms that he was leaving his job with the paper and moving to Ibiza to try his luck as a dance DJ. For about the first two months, there had been a constant stream of postings. Rory doing a headline set at the prestigious Club Macarana; a suntanned Rory on a sun-kissed terrace, having dinner with glamorous friends; Rory water-skiing on a shimmering sea.

And then one day, nothing.

It was the suddenness and completeness of the shut down that had convinced Frank that something stunk about the whole business. Sure, you might blank your parents for a series of slights, real or imagined, but a party animal like Rory Morrison surely was never going to abandon his addiction to posting the tedious minutiae of his life on his socials. Which is why Frank had raised the possibility, as gently and tactfully as he could, that perhaps Rory hadn't just decided to sever all contact with his parents, and that instead he might possibly be in some trouble.

And which is why he found himself suggesting to the Morrisons that they should engage the services of an excellent little firm called Bainbridge Associates to find out what had really happened to their boy.

Chapter 10

It was bloody fortunate that Miss Lorilynn Logan had shaped up so well, Maggie thought as she wandered up Byers Road en-route to the Horseshoe Bar, even if the girl was only four days into her employment with Bainbridge Associates. Otherwise they wouldn't have been able to take on this Rory Morrison investigation that Frank had brought her, and what a seriously interesting case that looked like becoming. For a start, there was a massive serendipity or overlap, whatever the word was, with the Urquhart case. The boy had been a cub political correspondent on the Globe, which probably meant that he'd worked either for or with Dominique Tremblay. And as a reporter of the political scene, he had probably bumped into her client, the up-and-coming Jack Urquhart, on more than one occasion too. At the very least, it gave her a start point, and in particular, it gave her a very powerful excuse to speak to Miss Tremblay again. Speaking of which, she was expecting an update from Lori when they met up in a few minutes' time - that was, if the surveillance exercise hadn't taken the girl elsewhere.

A ding from her phone broke into her thoughts. She slipped it out of her bag and glanced at the message. It was from Frank, apologising that he was going to be ten minutes late. But it being Frank, even the simplest correspondence couldn't be made without him trying to make her laugh. *The boss's ambushed me in my office and she's covering all the exits*. It was just one of the many things about him she loved, causing her to break into a huge grin as she turned the corner into the Great Western Road.

The pub was fairly quiet, just a couple of groups of lads enjoying a pint or two after a hard day's work on the building site. She took a vacant stool at the bar and ordered a Chardonnay.

'Thought we might find you guys here.' Maggie instantly spun round on hearing that familiar and lovely voice. 'Mind if we join you?'

'Jimmy!' She jumped down from her stool and wrapped him in a warm embrace.

'It's brilliant to see you Maggie,' he said, beaming a smile. 'Do you remember my nutcase business partner Stew? I think you two have met once before?'

That made Maggie laugh. Stew Edwards wasn't a man that was easy to forget, especially if you were a woman. He was a good three inches shorter than Jimmy, but in all other respects was the match of her former colleague as far as attractiveness to the opposite sex was concerned. But whereas Jimmy was quiet and diffident and sweetly unaware of the effect he had on women, Edwards knew he drove them crazy, and acted like he enjoyed every minute of it. He was exactly like the bad boy in the romantic novels her mother consumed by the dozen, the guy the sweet heroine fell head over heels for, before seeing sense and hooking up with the town's doctor or school-master or carpenter. Mind you, Maggie had skimmed a few of her mum's latest volumes on her infrequent visits back to her Yorkshire home, and was surprised to find that today's romantic pulp fiction was a thousand times steamier than it was when she herself read the genre as a teenager. Nowadays a rogue like Stew Edwards would have the heroine in bed on the second date and she would, against her better judgement, slip on the handcuffs and succumb to the pleasures of wild sex- often blushingly and graphically described. Until of course, as they all did, she saw through Mr Bad-Guy's shallowness and settled down instead to a life of two-point-four children with Mr Steady, whilst continuing to flourish in her wonderful career.

'God Maggie, I'd forgotten how sensational you look,' Stew said. He smiled at Jimmy. 'Your brother's one lucky fella Jimmy-boy.'

'Ignore him,' Jimmy said, raising an ironic eyebrow. 'He goes into autopilot when he sees a beautiful woman.'

She laughed. 'I'll take that as a compliment. From both of you. Anyway, you didn't tell me you were back in Glasgow.'

'We've been on another sales trip,' Stew explained. 'And I think it's turned out pretty successful, don't you think Jimmy?'

'You've not been talking to Tommy Taggart again have you?' she interjected, slightly alarmed.

Jimmy shook his head. 'Nah, we took your advice on that one. Way too controversial. This one's much more sensible.'

'And are you able to tell me the customer is?'

He grinned. 'You'll find out in a few minutes. When Frank turns up.'

Which he duly did, and a few minutes ahead of schedule too. And whilst he evidently expected his brother to be present, he didn't seem that pleased to see him. He kissed

Maggie on the cheek then said indignantly, 'Team building? Team building in the bloody Cairngorms? Whose bloody bright idea was that, as if I need ask?'

Jimmy laughed. 'Your ACC thought it was a brilliant idea. Test the mettle of her senior ranks whilst they're under pressure and all that. Challenge them, get them working together, mould them into a high-performing team.'

Frank shot his brother a withering look. 'Aye, I've read the bollocks in your brochure and funnily enough, the ACC herself has just been telling me how brilliant she thinks the whole idea is. I tell you what bruv, you're going to pay for this. And anyway, I'm only on secondment up here. I'm sure I can duck out on a technicality.'

Maggie snuggled up to him, putting an arm around his waist. 'But don't you want to be in top shape for our wedding darling? And especially for our wedding night.' God, where had *that* come from, she thought, as her face began to turn crimson. But she knew what it was, it was thinking about all these bloody bodice-ripping books of her mother's. Thank goodness Major Edwards had headed off to the bar, or no doubt he would have made some stupid crack.

Frank gave her a fond smile, seemingly unembarrassed. 'Of course I do. But I don't need to be cavorting about the mountains like a bloody Boy Scout to do it.'

'Lexy WhatsApp'd me about your breakfasts,' she said mischievously. He shuffled uncomfortably, guilt written all over his face.

'Well, I'm in the strength-building phase at the moment. Loading up with protein's crucially important as part of any well-balanced conditioning routine. Everybody knows that.'

Jimmy laughed. 'And you accuse *me* of talking bollocks.'

They were interrupted by the arrival of Lorilynn, looking flustered.

'Sorry I'm a bit late,' she said breathlessly. 'I followed Dominique to her usual pub again. That's every night she's gone there so far this week. She was still there when I skipped out. Normally she stays to about half-seven then goes for her train. I followed her all the way to the station last night just to make sure.'

'And no surreptitious assignations with men so far?' Maggie asked.

'What?'

'She hasn't met with anyone I mean?' She smiled to herself, remembering what Lori had said at her interview, about her over-use of posh lawyer-speak. *Touché.*

'Nope, not yet. And she hasn't been out of the office this week, work-wise I mean. But she goes to the gym at lunchtime. Although I've not actually gone in to the place yet because obviously I don't have a membership. They do a month's trial though, and I was going to ask you if it was okay for me to get one. It's forty-five quid.'

'Yes, sure. It'll all go on our client's bill anyway. He won't mind if it gets a result.'

Evidently Stew had been listening in to *this* conversation.

'Now *there's* the perfect place for a bit of extra-curricular rumpy-pumpy,' he said, shooting Lori his crooked smile. 'All those hot women in their gym-kit. Oh, by the way, I don't think we've had the pleasure.' He extended a hand to the girl. 'Stew Edwards. Major Edwards to my friends.'

'Hi yah,' she said, in a tone that to Maggie sounded distinctly dismissive. Had the easy charm of Edwards this time hit a stone wall, a sensation he must have found as perplexing as it was unprecedented? But the reason was quite clear. Lori evidently still only had eyes for Jimmy, no matter how impossible the chances were of it ever coming to anything. But then again, wasn't that a storyline that was also popular in the romantic genre, stretching all the way back to *Jane Eyre*, the tale of the plain but clever girl who improbably won the heart of the handsome hero? It wouldn't be Jimmy, but Maggie hoped that sometime soon the lovely Lori would find and win her own Rochester - although without any houses having to be burned down in the process of course.

Breaking into a smile, she stretched up and planted a kiss on Frank's forehead. For she recognised she was the heroine of her own romantic novel, except she had skipped the hot-sex-with-the-dangerous-charmer bit and gone straight to being totally besotted with her own wonderful Mr Steady.

Not that she would call him that within his earshot.

***

Maggie hadn't really been looking forward to meeting with her new clients after what Frank had told them about the state of their marriage, but in the event the matter had resolved itself when it emerged that Dr Morrison was refusing to have anything to do with her assignment. Furthermore, he had refused to even have Maggie in his home, which is why that Friday morning she was meeting with Mrs Rose Morrison in a cosy corner of the Bikini Barista cafe, two doors down from her office. Frank had, slightly unkindly, described her as plain and a bit overweight, but this morning she appeared to have made a special effort. Her hair had been freshly washed, held back by a smart jade head-band, and she was wearing make-up, quite expertly applied Maggie thought. Something had changed, there was no doubt about that. It was as if the woman had been dramatically set free from the austere constraints of a doctrine which frowned on any kind of frivolity. And it turned out that Maggie's speculations were accurate.

'Lovely to meet you Maggie,' Rose said, taking a seat at the small table. 'And just to let you know, I told Donnie last night that I wanted a divorce. It's something that I should have done years ago to be honest.'

'Had he been unfaithful to you before? Because I know what that feels like. My late husband was like that.'

'Oh no,' Rose said, her answer surprising Maggie. 'Donnie has always been so *smarmy* around women, but let's face it, he's not exactly Brad Pitt is he? All talk and no action, that's my Donnie. It's just that he's so *boring*. I'm sixty-two. I've got plenty of good years left and I want to do something with them. But I can't do that until I find Rory.'

'It must have been awful for you these past six months,' Maggie said. 'Not hearing from your son I mean. But did you really think he just wanted nothing more to do with you and your husband?'

'I did at first, after the horrible things that were said. But I know he loves me, so after three months or so I began to worry, really worry. But Donnie was too pig-headed to let me do anything about it. I wanted to go to the police but he wouldn't have it. He said he didn't need any more scandal interfering with his political come-back. As if he has any chance of *that*,' she added bitterly.

'But now you've come to me instead.'

'Yes,' Rose said softly. 'DCI Stewart said you would do everything you could to find my boy. And I read all about what you did in the Juliet McClelland case. That was wonderful.'

Maggie nodded. 'We were very pleased that we were able to find out what had happened to poor Juliet. And yes, believe me, we'll try everything in our power to track down Rory too.'

'So you think he may still be alive?' she said, her voice so quiet as to be almost inaudible. 'Because you know about these things, don't you?'

Maggie looked at her enquiringly. 'Do *you* think he's still alive?' It was a difficult question, the most difficult one of all, but one she knew had to be asked.

Rose hesitated for a moment. 'I don't know. I change my mind a hundred times a day. But I have this great hope that he's met a man out there, the sort of man that he thinks we would see as unsuitable, and can't bring himself to tell us about.'

'What do you mean by unsuitable?' Maggie asked, although she thought she already knew the answer to that.

'I secretly followed his social media, when he was living in Edinburgh. I didn't tell Donnie of course. But the men Rory were with...they were wild, promiscuous, what I would call in-your-face gay. I have to admit I started to think like his father, hoping against hope that one day he would tire of the bad boys and settle down with some quiet civil servant or school-teacher or someone normal. But he was...what's the word? Yes, a hedonist, spending his nights in these gay bars and wearing these horrible tight leather outfits and so on. There was one particular place he used to favour, it was called Harvey Dee's or Harley Dee's or something like that. He was there a lot. It's little wonder his father couldn't stomach it, not that I have any sympathy for *him*.'

Gay bars and tight leather outfits? It couldn't help but bring to mind these two poor guys who had been found murdered in the toilets just off the Royal Mile a few weeks ago. Maggie wondered if Rose Morrison had read the story. She must have, given it had been all over the media. But until four months ago her son Rory had been in Ibiza, living the high life. If anything horrible had happened to him, it was out there where they needed to start looking. Which then made her wonder why the Morrisons hadn't already tried that.

'Didn't you think to take a trip out there to look for him?' she asked, trying not to sound too much like an admonishing school-mistress.

Rose was silent for a moment, then said, 'Donnie took my passport from me. He wouldn't give me it back. And yes I know, it's pathetic as a grown woman that I was prepared to put up with that. In fact, I've put up with it for more than thirty years.'

Bloody hell, Maggie thought, so the oh-so-holy Reverend Dr Donnie Morrison was an even worse hypocrite than she had imagined. This poor woman who sat opposite her had evidently suffered a lifetime of being made to feel worthless, but now thankfully, it seemed the worm had turned.

'Well, I think we'll be starting our enquiries there. We probably don't actually have to go to the island initially. In the first instance we'll do some desk research here and we'll get in touch with the British Consul too. I would imagine that would bear fruit quite quickly.' *One way or another,* Maggie thought, but she wasn't going to say that to Mrs Morrison right now. In her head, she did the calculation. It was exactly four months and nine days since Rory Morrison's last posting on Instagram, in which he gave no hint of the emergence of a Mr Right - or should it be a Mr Wrong - in his life. From that moment on, there had been total radio silence. That didn't auger well.

Because as much as she hoped otherwise, in her gut Maggie knew that if and when they eventually flew out to Ibiza, it would be to identify the body.

Chapter 11

Naturally DC Ronnie French had claimed, much to Frank's amusement, that he was run off his feet pursuing a bevy of unspecified but important cases for his new gaffer DCI Jill Smart, who had taken temporary if reluctant charge of the Met's Department 12B whilst Frank was seconded to Scotland. Nonetheless here was Frenchie, barely forty-eight hours after receiving the call, standing with Frank outside the plush Newton Mearns home of Tommy and Sienna Taggart. Many locals would claim that the suburb was the poshest in the Greater Glasgow area, at least those with an interest in maintaining its sky-high property prices. Whatever the truth of the matter, the Taggart place had evidently started life as the same sort of identikit bungalow as that occupied by Donnie and Rose Morrison, but then had been the subject of such a program of 'improvements' as to be rendered unrecognisable. According to the local evening paper, no fan of the Taggarts it had to be said, the couple had spent in excess of six hundred grand in transforming the former modest bungalow into a fabulous two-storey villa, said to include a swimming pool and fitness suite in the basement, and taking advantage of the generous plot, a separate three-car garage with games room above. There had been plenty of speculation as to where the money had come from to effect such a transformation, and Frank had already resolved to get Eleanor digging into the finances of the couple to answer that question once and for all. But today, he was in full Columbo mode, with no specific objective from the meeting other than getting right up Tommy Taggart's nose. Aided and abetted of course by Ronnie, who as well as being full-on English, had a natural talent for getting up people's noses. Although having said there was nothing specific on the agenda, Frank did have one development to bring up, one that was guaranteed to wind up Tommy Taggart big-time.

'So what do you want me to do guv?' French asked as they sauntered up to the door.

Frank laughed. 'Just be your own sweet self Ronnie. Tell them how much you're enjoying your visit to the colonies, say that Scottish beer is nothing but watery piss, and mention how crap our national team is compared with England if the subject of football comes up.'

'Right-oh guv.'

He hadn't bothered to make an appointment, but Frank had taken the trouble to get the local Special Constable to swing past an hour before his visit to confirm that the Taggart's up-market motors were on the drive. He rang the bell and waited. A few seconds later, the door was opened by a noticeably good-looking young man, perhaps just into his twenties, wearing a tight-fitting black T-shirt emblazoned with the image of a motor-cycle. Frank did a double-take, because the guy, though muscular and sporting a sleeve of tattoos on both arms, didn't look like your typical biker, being too clean-cut for that in his opinion. But then, as he looked more closely, he realised he had been mistaken. The tee wasn't advertising a motorbike, it was advertising that Edinburgh club he'd heard Lexy talking about. Harley-Dee's, that was the name.

'Aye, whit do you want?' The accent was broad Glasgow, the tone was petulant, but there was no disguising the definite hint of camp either. He saw Ronnie give him a look, and hoped the DC wouldn't say anything.

'We're here to see Mr Taggart,' Frank said. 'We're the police. And who are you?'

'Ah work for Mr and Mrs Taggart. Ah'm his assistant. Jimmy Petrie. I manage his diary.'

Frank raised an eyebrow. 'Really? That's nice. So Jimmy-boy, toddle along and tell Mr Taggart that DCI Stewart and DC French are here to have a chat with him. Or we'll have an audience with Mrs Taggart, if the main man's not in.'

The youth gave them a suspicious look, then said, 'Aye, alright. Wait here. And don't youse come in until you're told, okay?'

'Thanks for the warm welcome son,' Frank shouted after the boy as he set off on his mission. A minute or so later, Taggart appeared at the door. He didn't look pleased to see them.

'What the hell do you want? I told you before I was a busy man.'

'Of course you are,' Frank said, smiling. 'That's why we're going to be out of your hair before you even know we're in it. Can we come in? Oh and by the way, this is a colleague of mine from the Met, DC French. He's a West Ham supporter but we all have our crosses to bear.'

'Yeah, but at least our manager is from Jock-land,' French said guilelessly. 'Although he's crap.'

Taggart made an indistinct grunt and motioned with his head. He led them through to the kitchen, which as Frank expected, was huge and expensively-appointed.

'Right, this better be quick, because I'm due up the golf course in half an hour,' Taggart said.

French gave a low whistle. 'Nice gaff this mate,' he said in his best Cockney. 'Didn't think they had pads like this up here to be honest. So where do you get the dosh to kit out a place like this? I expect you're a property developer or something like that? Am I right mate? Or is it drugs?'

Taggart didn't answer. Instead he said, 'Look, can we quit this fannying about and get to the point?'

Frank smiled. 'Aye, of course sir. All it is is a courtesy visit to inform you that DC French here is going to be going door-to-door in Ralston over the next couple of days to check out those allegations of electoral fraud. It's a shame that we've had to import one of my guys all the way up from London and at great expense to the taxpayer, but quite frankly I don't trust any of my dozy colleagues from New Gorbals nick to do a proper job.'

'You won't find anything,' Taggart said smugly. 'You shouldn't believe the shite you read in the papers.'

'Never read them myself Mr Taggart. But I expect you're right. As I told you before, this is just a box-ticking exercise to keep my brass happy. A couple of days up here and then DC French will bugger off back down south and that'll be the end of it. Job done and everybody will be happy.'

'Aye well, the sooner he buggers off the better,' Taggart said, giving a leering smile.

'I'm sure he feels exactly the same sir,' Frank said. 'Actually he was surprised they had electric light and hot and cold running water in his hotel. But aye, once he's done the door-to-door, there'll be just one more thing and he'll be off.'

'What's that?' Taggart said suspiciously.

'I've asked him to drop into the main sorting office in the town before he goes and have a chat with the lads there. Because you'll remember there was that allegation of some hanky-panky going on with the postal votes, and we just want to take a quick look at that. You know, just another tick in the box for my gaffers.'

This time, Frank thought interestingly, Taggart didn't seem quite so sure of himself. The man seemed to hesitate for a moment then said,

'You won't be able to do that without talking to the Union. Try and pull a stunt like that and they'll have everybody out.'

'I doubt that Mr Taggart. All we're going to do is ask a few of them if they saw anything suspicious and if they say no they didn't, as I expect they will, that'll be it. I can't see the whole thing taking more than an hour to tell the truth.' He didn't wait for a reaction. 'Anyway, I promised we'd be out of your hair in no time, and that's us finished. So thank you for your time Mr Taggart, you've been a great help. Come on DC French, let's disappear.'

'I'll see you out,' Taggart said sourly. 'It's this way.' He ushered them down the wide hallway to the front door and opened it.

'Aye, well thanks again,' Frank said as they stepped out onto the drive. And now it was the moment he had been looking forward to all morning, the ultimate Columbo tribute, where he would pause, stroke his chin, swivel on his heels and say *there's just one last thing sir*.

'There's just one last thing Mr Taggart,' he said, opting for a scratch of the head instead. 'Did you happen to see this morning's opinion poll in the *Chronicle*? They're saying that Jack Urquhart guy is a shoo-in for the leadership of the Nationalists, and that if he wins he's going to batter you and your party in the general election. What do you make to that? Makes interesting reading you've got to agree? Anyway, cheerio Mr Taggart. It's been nice seeing you again.' He didn't wait for a reply and to be honest he wasn't really interested in what the guy made of it. It was all about keeping the pressure on, about making the cocky Mr Tommy Taggart a lot less sure of himself.

Because, in Frank's experience, when that happened, that was when the bad guys started to make mistakes.

Chapter 12

It had taken a couple of days and upwards of half-a-dozen voicemail messages to get any sort of response from the British Consulate in Ibiza Town, or be exact, from that institution's bloody annoying automated telephone answering system. *We are always particularly busy in the summer months and so we ask for your patience. Please understand your call is important to us blah-bloody-blah.....* Eventually Maggie got a call back from a woman who identified herself as Jasmine. And only Jasmine, until Maggie insisted that the woman provided her surname. At least Miss Wright, for that was her name, prefaced the call with a perfunctory apology for the delay in getting back to her, explaining that the combination of excess sun and alcohol often led to what she called *incidents*, which took up much of the time of the Consulate staff at this time of year. Maggie could well imagine the nature of these affairs, the staple of the tabloid press on quiet news days. The girl on the hen party from Barnsley deciding to get into the spirit of things by having sex on the beach with a guy from Manchester she'd met just five minutes earlier. The lads from Wakefield who ended up in A&E after having bitten off more than they could chew bating a group of locals. This shameful behaviour wasn't of course exclusive to visitors from her home county, but she imagined, with a faintly embarrassing feeling of warped pride, that if there were a league table, her Yorkshire compatriots wouldn't be far from the top. Just behind the Glaswegians in fact, whom, she'd come to learn in her short time living in the city, liked both a drink and an argument to go with it. As for Rory Morrison, Jasmine Wright listened patiently whilst Maggie explained the background. Without promising anything, the woman said they would try to make some enquiries over the next few days and they would get back to her if anything turned up. It wasn't hugely encouraging, but it would have to do for the time being.

That settled, there were now three strands of enquiry Maggie wished to pursue. Firstly, she wanted to get some insight into Rory's state of mind leading up to his decision to up sticks and move to Ibiza, which is why in around thirty minutes or so she was going to pick up the phone and call Dominique Tremblay, who may have been his boss, or at least would have worked closely with the cub reporter. Secondly, she wanted to construct a timeline from the point Rory had stepped on the plane at Edinburgh airport, building up a picture through his social media postings about what he had been doing following his arrival on the island. Specifically, she hoped to track down the identities of any friends he may have made out there, friends who might be able to give some clue to his disappearance. And thirdly, she needed to let the world know that Rory Morrison was missing, and for that she had a plan. A plan that went by the name of Yash Patel of the Chronicle.

But before all that, she needed to catch up on the latest from Lori, still tracking the movements of Tremblay from her base in the cafe opposite the offices of the Globe. Maggie swiped down through her recent calls and selected her number.

'Hi Lori it's me.'

'*Oh hi boss*,' Lori answered, '*Morning*.' Except what Maggie heard was only about every second syllable.

'Are you in a dungeon or something?'

'The underground car park,' Lori said. *'There's been a development you see.'* At least, that's what Maggie thought she said.

'What sort of development? And can you speak slowly, 'cos you're breaking up.'

'She came to work in her car this morning, that yellow sports car. That was the first time in nine days. So I thought I'd better be ready when she heads out.'

'Makes sense,' Maggie said, 'but I'm afraid it'll probably be just something boring to do with her work. Some meeting or other in connection with the latest story she's working on.'

Lori seemed unconcerned. *'Aye it might be. But that's our job isn't it? Patient and methodical detective work. Chip away until you find that tiny thing that opens up the case.'*

Goodness, this girl was an absolute gem, Maggie thought. 'And you're okay with all of that are you?' she said anxiously. 'Because I did tell you most of our work is a hundred times less exciting than what you see on the telly cop shows.'

Lori laughed. *'Do you think serving coffees was exciting? Nah, I'm loving my new job so I am. Besides, there's going to be a massive big car chase later. And I'll be in your Golf.'*

***

It was probably a forlorn hope, but Maggie was crossing her fingers that this change to Dominique Tremblay's routine might provide the breakthrough they were looking for. Because the fact was, their quarry's behaviour was showing all the signs of someone who was simply work-obsessed, a feeling amplified by the fact that Miss Tremblay had gone into the office on both days of the past weekend too. Which meant of course that Maggie had had to ask Lori if she could continue with her surveillance, a task the girl had accepted without complaint. Now they were nine days in to the investigation, and thus far there was nothing suspicious to report to her client. If Dominique was involved in some wild passionate affair, then she was showing remarkable fortitude in resisting her desires and staying away from her lover. More likely, she had simply fallen out of love with her partner and was putting in all these hours at work to minimise the time she had to spend at home. So they would give it another eight or nine days max, Maggie decided, and then they would advise Jack Urquhart to call the whole thing off. She suspected that deep down, he already knew the truth of the matter, and had been clinging to the existence of this probably-imaginary affair to make some sort of sense of his rejection. Of course, given that she was just about to call the woman, she could simply ask her straight out. *Just wanted to ask you Dominique, and forgive me if this is a bit blunt, but are you having a steamy affair?* But if the journalist denied it, which she almost certainly would, then where would that get them? No further forward, that's where. So she would park that idea for now, and concentrate on finding out what Tremblay knew about Rory Morrison.

Maggie hadn't been sure whether Dominique would take her call, but in the event she answered on the third or fourth ring.

'*Tremblay.*' The word was fired out, the tone conveying an unequivocal message. *Why are you interrupting someone as important as me?*

'Hi, it's Maggie Bainbridge. Look, please tell me if this is a bad time for you, but I wanted to ask you a few questions concerning Rory Morrison. I'm acting for his parents. Well, for his mother actually. She's worried that she hasn't heard from him for a few months and has asked my firm to try and track him down. I'm guessing you knew him?'

Dominique hesitated for two or three seconds, as if she was trying to work out how she should answer what was surely the simplest of questions. A hesitation which Maggie registered and tucked away in her mind for future consideration.

'He was just a junior reporter. But yes, of course I knew him.'

'And you were both political correspondents, I know that. So I guess you were his boss. Am I right in that assumption?'

'I wasn't his boss,' she said, with more than a hint of condescension. *'I'm chief political correspondent, not some sort of middle-management apparatchik. As I said, Rory was a junior, way down the food chain. I had very little to do with him on a day-to-day basis.'*

'But you knew him.'

'*Well of course I knew him, I said that. But not well. I doubt if I spoke to him more than a couple of times a month.*'

'So would you have discussed the stories you were both working on?' Maggie asked.

Tremblay laughed. *'You don't work on stories at his level. All he did was the arse-numbing boring stuff, you know, what's being discussed in Parliament today or which foreign dignitaries are visiting. So no, we didn't discuss our stories. Although of course if you listened to Rory talking, you would have thought he was some sort of Ernest Hemingway.'*

It was an unkind comment, causing Maggie to remember what the paper's IT geek had said to her and Lori about Tremblay not being popular at work, and thinking it wasn't hard to see why. Nor was it difficult to see why her relationship was heading down the plug-hole too if she spoke to her partner the same way.

'Okay,' she said cautiously. 'Well perhaps I may be wasting your time, if you didn't know him very well, and if that's the case I apologise. But maybe I could just raise a couple of quick points and then I'll let you get on with your day.'

'Sure,' Tremblay said dismissively. *'Just get on with it.'*

'I will. And I think in fact I've only got one question. So can I ask, did Rory ever mention to you that he was thinking of resigning and going off to Ibiza to be a DJ?'

Her reply surprised Maggie. *'Well actually he did. Several times. In fact, I would go as far as to say he was rather consumed by the idea.'*

'Okay,' Maggie said again. 'And what was your reaction, if indeed you had one?'

'I said he should go for it. The fact was, he was going nowhere with the paper. He was only a so-so writer, and

more than that, he didn't have the killer instinct you need to make it in this cut-throat business.'

'So you weren't surprised when he left.'

'No, not at all.'

'But it was all rather abrupt, wasn't it?' Maggie said. 'There wasn't a leaving do or anything like that?'

She heard Tremblay snort. '*I don't know. I doubt if I would have been invited even if there had been one.*'

Suddenly a thought came to Maggie. 'But still, was it all done officially? I mean, did he send in a resignation e-mail or letter or whatever the procedure is?'

The Canadian paused before replying. *'Good question. It wouldn't have come to me because I wasn't his boss, so I can't say for certain. But yes, I guess it would have been done properly. I know a couple of the folks in the HR department, and they definitely would have mentioned it to me if he'd just walked out without saying anything.'*

'Yes, I suppose that's true,' Maggie said uncertainly. So it all seemed very neat and tidy, but it wasn't actually getting her anywhere, she thought. And there was no getting away from the fact that this conversation was bloody awkward, given that Bainbridge Associates was working for her partner. Of course she had known that the conflict of interest would make things difficult, so she could hardly complain when it turned out to be true. But then it struck her that Dominique herself must be facing a similar conflict every day of her life. All these awards she had won for investigating and exposing the failings of the incumbent government, whilst at the same time her partner was vying for its leadership. Obviously he was inside the tent so to speak, and was bound to hear things, potentially embarrassing or damaging things, that would be like gold-dust to her as a journalist. And she, with her powerful media voice in the Globe, would have every opportunity to present her partner in a positive light. And yet, as far as Maggie could recall, Dominique hadn't done that. She wondered why.

'Okay, well thanks for sharing what you knew about Rory,' Maggie said. 'It's been a great help,' then added casually, 'By the way, I saw in your paper this morning that there's the big TV leadership debate coming up in the next couple of days. I guess you'll be rooting for Jack.'

'What makes you think that?' Dominique said sharply. *'Do you think I'm some sort of dutiful little political wife, standing by his side and smiling sweetly for the photographers?'*

Oops, Maggie thought, *struck a raw nerve there*, and then suddenly it all came into focus. The Urquharts were *jealous* of each other, and what a powerful emotion *that* was. It helped to explain why Dominique had been tracking her partner's phone use, and why Jack had hired a private investigator to follow her. Maggie already knew that he resented his partner's journalistic success, and now it seemed *she* felt the same way about *his* career. So rather than rooting for him she probably wanted him to lose the leadership contest. Whatever the truth of that, with all that undercurrent of mistrust, it was no wonder the relationship was in trouble. As indeed was the current conversation, and now she was anxious to end it as swiftly as possible.

'No no, not at all,' she replied, her words tumbling out. 'It was a daft thing to say, I'm sorry. Look, I guess you're really busy so I'll get off the line and let you get on. And thanks again for your help. Bye.'

After she hung up, Maggie gave a deep sigh of relief. It hadn't gone *well* exactly, but it could easily have been a lot worse. At least Dominique seemed to have forgotten the ludicrous suggestion that she was having an affair with her partner Jack Urquhart. But there was something else too, something that definitely didn't add up. She claimed she had very little to do with Rory Morrison on a day-to-day basis, and yet on the presumably few times she did interact with him, she was able to judge that he was totally consumed with the idea of quitting his job and moving to Ibiza. No, there was definitely something wrong there, something she would need to give some serious thought to. And then she sighed again. If only Jimmy was still around, because it was the kind of problem she used to love to chew over with him. Still, tomorrow she had a definite treat in store, because over breakfast that morning, Frank had mentioned that Yash Patel and his big fat *Chronicle* expense account had offered to buy them all lunch, *them all* being Lori, Frank, and the DCs Ronnie French and Lexy McDonald. And now, as heralded by a WhatsApp from Frank that she'd just caught sight of, and in a late change to the advertised programme, it seemed that the feisty Forensic IT wizard Eleanor Campbell was also to be present, having been summoned urgently northwards on some unspecified mission.

Surely, with all that collective investigative brain-power in one room, someone was bound to work out what to make of it all?

Chapter 13

Charlie McCrae gave a cheerful whistle as he propelled his cleaning trolley along the pavement, heading up towards the old Tron Kirk in the direction of the Castle. He wasn't exactly sure what the random tune was, but he thought it might be one of the Proclaimers hits, or maybe even a mash-up of a couple of them, because they all sounded exactly the same to his untutored musical ear. Just past two in the morning, it was a clear night with a full moon, although that was just a bonus, because there was more than enough illumination provided by the dazzling street lights. They had been changed to low-cost and powerful LED bulbs a year or so back, and now the upper reach of the Royal Mile was bathed in as much light as you got from the floodlights at Murrayfield Stadium. Except of course they hadn't been working on that horrible night two or three months back. The papers had made a big thing of the fact, after some dumb senior cop had publicly suggested the CCTV-and-streetlight blackout might have been caused by a cyber attack. That was pure bollocks of course, maintenance of the systems being the sole responsibility of the Edinburgh City Council. *Enough said.*

Still, finding these two gay lads all trussed up and with knives sticking out of them in the Castle Wind toilets wasn't a sight he would have wished on anybody, and not one he cared to remember either. Mind you, the episode hadn't been all bad. In fact, if he was being honest, it had turned out to be quite a big moment in his life. First off, he'd enjoyed his five minutes of fame, when he was the man of the moment, with all these TV and newspaper reporters clamouring for his attention. Some of them were pretty hot too, and in particular that wee minx from the BBC had delivered very pleasant dreams for quite a few nights on the trot. And after all that had calmed down, his workmate Kenny had suggested he might have grounds for a PTSD claim, given the nature of what he had been exposed to in the course of his work. Taking Kenny's advice, he paid a quick visit to his doctor, who was happy to provide a sick note and to extend it on request without question. As a result, Charlie had enjoyed eight weeks sitting on his arse at home, with just daytime telly and a few beers to keep him company. But he was of the belief that a man needed his work to give him a sense of dignity, even if that work was only cleaning the disgusting public toilets dotted along Edinburgh's famous Royal Mile. Or, to be more accurate, if that work *had* been cleaning toilets. Because that murder thing was a situation that just kept on giving. Surely it was unreasonable, he had said to his twat of a boss on his return to work, to ask me to go back to bog-cleaning after what I've been through? Which is why he was now the proud pilot of this fancy bit of kit, a top-of-the-range, electrically-assisted street-cleaning cart. And which was why his mate Kenny was now on the bog-cleaning roster. Kenny, understandably, wasn't too happy about this development, but Charlie wasn't bothered. After what he'd been through, some collateral damage was only to be expected.

Not that his new job was any picnic, especially right now with the tourist season being in full swing. There were plenty of litter bins along the Mile, but they were generally full to overflowing by early evening. Then at eleven o'clock or so, revellers would spill onto the streets, many in search of fast-food sustenance before heading to their accommodation or catching their buses back to the suburbs. By one o' clock in the morning, at least on a week-day like this, it was quiet, although the pavements were a bloody disgusting mess with a ton of discarded food and packaging. The big boys with the refuse trucks would swing by like the cavalry at four in the morning, but they liked the rubbish to be swept up into nice big piles first. That was a big part of his job, and if you asked him he would tell you it was bloody hard work. Especially of course when it came to the drunks. Every night there was always a handful of them, the pathetic guys and girls who'd got too pissed to know where they were, let alone having any ability to find their way home. The problem was, and this was looking at it from a street-cleaners' professional point of view, they somehow always seemed to make a habit of spewing their guts out, which left a great big bloody mess for Charlie to deal with. And, as luck would have it, it looked like he was going to have another one to deal with tonight. The guy was sitting slumped on one of the benches in front of the church, and as Charlie approached, his nose caught a whiff of an unpleasant smell. *Here we go again,* he thought. *Why can't blokes nowadays learn to hold their drink?*

But then, as he got closer, he realised it wasn't puke he was smelling, and it wasn't puke either that had congealed in a semi-liquid pool at the guy's feet. Not puke, but blood, which, as he got close enough to recognise the guy's face, was still trickling down from the stab wound in his chest.

Chapter 14

It was hardly surprising that the newspapers had picked up on the story that the Reverend Dr Donnie Morrison was to be prosecuted under the Domestic Abuse (Scotland) Act 2019, given the guy's former prominence and the fact that he had committed the assault on his wife right under the noses of two police officers. What had surprised Frank though was the fact that his mate, national hot-shot journo Yash Patel, was so interested in the story. That was until Yash had dropped his bombshell, causing Frank to get straight on the phone to Eleanor Campbell and summon her northwards. She hadn't been too pleased about it, but then again Eleanor was seldom pleased about anything, especially if it was anything to do with Frank. But his gaffer DCI Jill Smart had called Eleanor's boss over at Maida Vale labs and smoothed the way, which is why Frank and Lexy were now waiting at Glasgow's Central Station for her arrival on the first train up from Euston. That train having departed London at 5.41am, they weren't expecting to find her in the sunniest of moods. Especially as, according to the information boards, the train was running about half an hour late.

'It'll be good to see her again,' Lexy said as they loitered at the exit barrier of the arrival platform. 'She's a nice girl. I really like her.'

Frank nodded. 'I know you two are big mates. And before you say it yourself, I confess that's why I asked you to come along to this reception committee. I'm shameless I know, but with the lovely Eleanor you're always walking on egg-shells. At least I am.'

'You gave her away at her wedding sir,' Lexy laughed. 'Or have you already forgotten?'

'Weddings are all I think about at the moment,' he said with a wry smile. 'And no, I haven't forgotten. I still feel bad about that, the poor guy.' But that was a joke of course, because Eleanor was a special girl, and her husband, a big drip who went by the name of Lloyd, had been bloody lucky to bag her. 'Anyway, I can see a big red-and-white choo-choo pulling into the platform. I'll let you do the meet-and-greet if you don't mind.'

Eleanor had evidently been seated towards the front of the train, since she was one of the first to emerge through the gate, looking bleary-eyed and trailing a small carry-on-sized suitcase behind her. She spotted Frank first and gave a theatrical scowl before breaking into a seldom-seen smile as Lexy ran over to welcome her with a hug.

'Good journey Eleanor?' he asked after she had extricated herself from Lexy's embrace.

She scowled again. 'Like *yeah*. I just love a four-thirty minicab blowing its horn outside my front door, don't you?'

He laughed. 'Aye well it would already be daylight up here at this time of the year, and the best time of the day in my opinion. But anyway, it's brilliant that you could come. We've got a big BMW with a blue light on the top waiting outside on the double-yellows, and a packed programme ahead of us. So welcome to Glasgow and let's get the show on the road.'

It took them just twenty-five minutes in all, Frank piloting the motor along the outside lane of the motorway and watching with amusement as motorists caught sight of the marked cop-car in their mirrors, moving aside guiltily even though the majority had been keeping to the seventy mile-an-hour speed limit.

'Looks like a nice pub sir,' Lexy said as they pulled up outside. 'Or at least it might have been back in the fifties. The eighteen-fifties that is.'

Frank nodded. 'Aye, that's when it last had a lick of paint by the looks of it.'

'Why is it called the Greenock Tavern?' Eleanor asked. 'Because this isn't Greenock, it's Paisley, isn't it?'

'What, so you think it should be called the *Paisley* Tavern?' he said, giving her a sardonic look. 'So what would you call the other ninety-four pubs in the town?'

She made a face but didn't say anything. Ignoring her, Frank said,

'Right, let's get in there, see what we make of the place.'

It being just half-eleven in the morning, he didn't expect there to be much custom, but he had rung them up the previous evening to discover that they had recently started serving breakfast and so would be open. *Aye right*, he thought to himself, *breakfast*? Around here, that would be a bag of dry-roast peanuts and three pints of strong lager.

As he expected, the place was short of customers, the sole patrons being three old-age pensioners occupying a single table over in the back corner, playing dominoes and with a full pint in front of each of them. Behind them, a wide-screen telly was showing Sky Sports News, replaying the same highlights clips for the twentieth time that morning. Behind the bar, a man stood with his back to them, engaged in emptying glasses from a dishwasher.

'Are you Paddy, the manager?' Frank asked. 'I spoke to you yesterday about paying you a visit, remember? DCI Frank Stewart, Metropolitan Police. Department 12B for what it's worth.'

'Oh aye, right,' the man said, swinging round, his expression radiating indifference. Mind you, Frank thought, if you were running a place like this, visits from the police would be an almost every-day occurrence. 'What was it you wanted again?'

'We're having another look into the Donnie Morrison affair. You'll remember it I suppose, considering your place was swarming with TV cameras for more than a week after it happened.'

'Oh aye, I remember it alright. It was good for business actually. In fact, the brewery is thinking of setting up an article on our website, so our customers can get to know all about it.'

Frank laughed. 'Good idea to try and capture the tourist trade in this idyllic hotspot. Anyway Paddy, were you working that night can I ask?'

'Aye,' Paddy said. 'I'm always here. I live above the place. It's a perk of the job.'

'And this woman, Jade Niven. According to Dr Morrison, she was on shift until about half-nine, and that was why they'd arranged to meet at that time. Is that right Paddy?'

He shrugged. 'Far as I can remember. She did six to half-past-nine for me a few times a week. Her sister baby-sat for her. She's got a boy you see.'

'And the other woman Paddy?' Lexy said.

For a moment, he seemed confused. 'Eh...what?'

'The other woman sir,' Lexy repeated. 'The woman who took the videos.'

He smiled. 'Och aye I'd forgotten. Kylie Gilmour, aye, she was here right enough.'

'Good stuff,' Frank said. 'So to cut to the chase, did you yourself see Mr Morrison carry out the alleged sexual assault on the young woman? Or was it just this Kylie lassie?'

The man shook his head. 'Nah, I never saw nothing. Too busy working behind the bar here. But Kylie took a couple of videos, so she did.'

Lexy nodded. 'Yes, we've seen them. And where were they sitting, Mr Morrison and Miss Niven?'

He gestured with his head. 'Just over there. On them soft seats against the wall.'

'Thank you sir.' She walked over to the location he'd indicated and sat down on a red velour-cushioned bench.

'Okay then,' Frank said. 'Time for a reconstruction of the crime. So Eleanor, nip over and sit down nice and close to Lexy, and prepare to pretend you're the old pervert Donnie Morrison.'

She gave him a horrified look. 'Like *no way*. That's *disgusting*.'

He grinned. 'Well, obviously *I* can't do it. That would be *really* disgusting, don't you think, an old guy like me?' He reached into his pocket and removed a folded sheet of A4 paper. 'Right, so I've got a print-out of a couple of stills from those incriminating videos and what I want to try and do is see if we can re-create the scene.' He looked down at them, scratching his head. 'So the first one is where he's leaning over and sliding his hand up her leg.'

Eleanor looked as if she was about to protest again. He smiled sweetly at her and said, 'But perhaps if you just do the leaning over bit, and we'll forget about the hand up the skirt. Look, this is what it looks like.' He held up the photograph so she could see it.

She gave a loud sigh, her face like thunder. But to his amusement he saw that Lexy had started to laugh. 'Don't you fancy me then Eleanor?' she said. 'I'm hurt, really I am.' *Oops*, he thought, *that might cause a meltdown*, but to his surprise and to her credit, Eleanor just gave another grimace.

'That's *very* good,' he said, taking in the posed scene. Scratching his head again, he looked behind him to try and get the line of sight. 'Just hold it for a minute more please. Aye, that's where it must have been. The only place that works.' He gave them a thumbs-up. 'Okay, let's take a look at photo two now.' He held up his sheet of paper and studied the still. And then, when he realised what it was telling him, gave a sharp intake of breath. 'Actually you two, don't bother, I think we've got all we need.' Which was just as well, because that was one that showed Morrison trying to get his tongue down the throat of Jade Niven, and he hadn't fancied the conversation with Eleanor trying to get *that* one re-enacted.

He sauntered over to the opening at the end of the bar and pushed in. 'Excuse me,' he said to Paddy the manager as he squeezed passed him. The man shrugged then said in sarcastic tone, 'Sure, be my guest. And why not pull yourself a pint whilst you're at it?'

Ignoring him, Frank took out his phone and pointed it to where Lexy and Eleanor were sitting. In his other hand he held the printed still, switching his gaze from one to the other to try and work out the exact spot where the video had been shot. Satisfied, he called over to Lexy and Eleanor. 'Quick, nip round here if you will. I've got something really interesting to show you.' They did as requested, joining him behind the cramped bar.

'See? See what I'm saying?' he said, pointing to the screen of his phone. And of course, they saw it right away. That the only way Miss Kylie Gilmour could have taken that video was if she was five feet behind where they were standing now. Which would have put her five feet behind a solid brick wall.

Smiling, he leant over the bar and shouted to the manager, who was now out amongst the tables collecting glasses. 'Hey Paddy, just one more question before we leave you in peace. Just exactly how long was Jade Niven working for you?'

***

Yash Patel had booked a table at a popular Italian restaurant just off George Square in the centre of the city, chosen after Frank had made it clear that he and his team would be paying their own way and didn't want to go anywhere fancy. The place was part of a national chain, with a standardised menu and the kitchen a slick production-line from freezer to oven to table, but the dishes were tasty and filling, and Maggie's rumbling stomach had been looking forward to it all morning. Frank was already there when she arrived, chatting with Patel, Eleanor and Lexy at a little bar that evidently doubled as the reception desk. Spotting her arrival, he slipped over and gave her a squeeze.

'No Lori today?' he asked.

She shook her head. 'She's still on the Dominique Tremblay surveillance job I'm afraid. Me, I'd would be bored rigid by now, but she actually finds it exciting. She went on a car chase yesterday, which was quite interesting. Well it wasn't exactly a chase, but she had to follow Urquhart for more than twenty-five miles from the city. Down to the coast in fact, to some place called Gourock.'

He smiled. 'Oh aye, a lovely spot with great views right across to Helensburgh. And you can see Ben Lomond on a clear day. That's a Munro by the way. It's what they call any Scottish mountain above three thousand feet.'

'I know, you've told me that quite a few hundred times before,' she said, making a face. 'But have you heard, there's been another murder on the Royal Mile?'

Lexy jumped in. 'Yeah, the victim's that guy who did the MC job at the Taggarts' stupid Freedom Rally. Johnny Pallas he's called, the guy that was on that gay Love Island show. And according to my Edinburgh mates, it was the same cleaner that found him, the same poor guy that found these other two in the Castle Wind toilets.'

'That WhatsApp group of yours been in action again?' Frank said, with a hint of disapproval. 'I told you to watch your step with these.'

'Yes I know sir, but it's actually quite innocuous. It's just a bunch of mates from the detectives' training course.'

'Aye, you said that.'

'Honestly sir, I'm careful sir, ' she said. 'But it's the same M-O too. Tasered first before he was stabbed.'

'Tasered?' Frank said. 'I didn't know that. But that explains how the murderers were able to overcome these first two poor guys.' He shook his head. 'This will be tabloid gold, won't it? *Another murder makes the Mile a no-go area for gay community.*' He gave Patel a friendly dig in the ribs. 'What do you think Yash mate? Want me to write your headlines for you? I charge very competitive rates.'

Patel laughed. 'I wouldn't give up the day job just yet.'

A waitress had arrived carrying a stack of menus. She said, 'So if you guys are all ready, I'll pop you through to your table.' Her tone, delivered through a fixed smile, suggested this was a command, not a question.

'We're one short,' Frank said apologetically. 'A lady. You'll know who she is when she turns up because she's American. Goes by the name of Fisher.'

'We'll show her through when she arrives,' the waitress said, still wearing the corporate smile. 'This way please.'

'You didn't tell me your Carrie-Anne woman was coming,' Maggie said, giving him a playful punch on the arm. Although she wasn't exactly sure how playful she felt about it, given the number of times Frank had slipped the bloody woman's name into the conversation over the last few weeks. Still, at least she would now be able to get a good look at her.

He shrugged. 'Last minute decision, after what us three discovered this morning down in a seedy Seedhill pub. As soon as she I told her, she jumped straight on a train.'

'From Edinburgh?'

'Aye, it's only an hour door-to-door,' he said, sounding surprised by the question.

The table was compact but perfectly adequate, the seating arrangements comprising an upholstered bench along one wall and three individual chairs opposite. Maggie hesitated for a moment, guessing that Eleanor and Lexy would sit together. She watched as they squeezed into the wall seats, then quickly slipped in beside them before either of the men could make a move.

'And you two can sit opposite,' she said, nodding at Yash and Frank. 'And Yash, leave the one in the middle free please, so Carrie-Anne isn't stuck out on a limb when she arrives.'

She allowed herself a smile. *Two birds with one stone.* Firstly, she'd be able to get a properly good look at this Carrie-Anne Fisher creature without making it too obvious, and secondly, she would be able to observe first-hand the woman's body language when she was in proximity to her Frank. And if there was any body-language going on, then this bloody woman had better look out.

When the creature did arrive, a few minutes later, she was everything Maggie expected her to be and everything she hoped she wouldn't be. Forty perhaps, but only just, slim, naturally, quite tall, maybe five-seven or five-eight, looking cool and sophisticated in a simple black short-sleeved pinafore. Her hair, a rich glossy chestnut without a hint of grey, was the product of either great genes or an expensive colourist, tied up with a French plait which she had draped elegantly over one shoulder. And she was attractive of course - but probably not beautiful, Maggie decided, with rather shameful satisfaction.

'Here she is,' she said, gesturing at Frank, who at that moment was deep in conversation with Patel and hadn't noticed the woman's arrival. Alerted, he stood up and motioned towards the vacant chair.

'Oh hi Carrie-Anne, glad you could make it at such short notice. We've kept a seat warm for you.' He offered a hand in greeting, which she took, the duration commensurate with a professional greeting and no more. Maggie watched her closely as the woman took her seat. As well as the handshake, she had smiled at him, definitely, but it wasn't *that* kind of smile, and there had been no lingering eye-contact either. So far so good.

'I haven't met you guys,' the American said pleasantly. She had placed her hands on the table, allowing Maggie to hone in on the third finger of her left hand. Where, the old Motown classic immediately popping into her head, was where she wore a wedding band. *More good news*.

'Aye, sorry,' Frank said. 'Yash Patel, leading hack from the Chronicle newspaper, Detective Constable Lexy McDonald, my colleague from Police Scotland, Eleanor Campbell, genius Forensics wizard with the Metropolitan Police - and she's the woman I'm very keen for you to work with as far as all this Deep Fake stuff goes...'

'Like cool,' Eleanor interrupted, beaming a huge and uncharacteristic smile.

He paused for a moment, then pointed across the table.

'...and this is Maggie Bainbridge. She's a lawyer and a private investigator.'

And just so you know, she's also the woman I'll be marrying in a few months. That's what he didn't go on to say, and even although Maggie knew she was being stupid because this was one-hundred-percent a business meeting, she found herself wondering why not.

'Awesome,' Carrie-Anne said. 'Great to meet you all.' The waitress, who had lingered after escorting the American to the table, was now almost forcing menus into their hands, the smile still fixed but the air of impatience unmistakable and growing.

'Today's special is four-cheese lasagne and there's a two-for-one on our hand-kneaded sourdough garlic bread,' she rattled off.

Frank laughed. 'Nice though all of that sounds, I'd better not. I've got to squeeze into a fancy kilt in a few months.' He turned and smiled at Carrie-Anne. 'Everybody else here knows this and they're probably sick of me going on about it, but Maggie and I are getting married. Can you believe it? I mean, look at her and look at me. A mis-match made in heaven.'

'Actually sir, you hardly ever mention it,' Lexy said, deadpan. 'Only about ten times a day.'

'What? Nah, nothing like it,' he said, in mock protest.

'That's awesome,' Carrie-Anne said. 'Congratulations to both of you. So when's the big day?'

Frank jumped in before Maggie could answer. 'It's in ninety-eight days and...' He paused to glance at his watch. '...two hours and twenty-seven minutes. There or thereabouts. In a lovely place called Grassington. That's in Yorkshire, just so you know. Which is in England.'

Maggie gave a guilty smile, cursing herself for her sheer silliness. How could she have ever doubted her lovely Frank? And it turned out the American woman herself was married, no doubt with a handsome chisel-jawed hunk and a couple of perfect kids waiting for her at home. The thought made her smile, and immediately she began to feel better.

'Yes, we're really looking forward to it of course,' she said, pulling a face at the waitress, whose back was momentarily turned. 'But we'd better get on and order, otherwise we'll get chucked out I think.'

After ordering, it only took a few minutes for their meals to arrive, and at last Maggie hoped she would begin to understand why Fisher was here, Frank having been uncharacteristically evasive about the precise reason for her invitation.

'So to business,' he said, picking up a slice of garlic bread and taking a bite. 'This is really Yash's show, but I've asked Miss Fisher to come along as representative of the Security Services, and you'll understand why in a minute.' He gave the journalist a sympathetic smile. 'Thing is young Yash, we need to get wind of what you're planning to write in that esteemed rag of yours, given the seriousness of what's going on. Correction, what we *think* might be going on.'

'And if you don't like it?' Yash said, slightly sourly.

Frank shrugged. 'You know very well how this works mate. If we don't like it, we'll invoke the Official Secrets Act and there'll be a High Court injunction to shut you up. I know you won't like *that*, but at least you can storm off in a huff, then go and write a bitter and twisted piece about how the government's cracking down on the freedom of the press. But from what you've told me so far, it does seem reasonably likely it won't come to that.'

So there's something important going on, Maggie thought, something that might be big enough to involve the security services and big enough for them to see the need to import specialist expertise from the US. And it seemed to be something to do with the allegations of impropriety that had ruined the career of the husband of her new client Rose Morrison. Maybe that was why Frank had asked her to come to this lunch.

'Anyway,' Frank said, 'let's hear what you've got, and what you're planning to say about it.'

Yash nodded. 'Sure. So as I said before, I've come to realise that Frank's little pet theory - I mean the one about two dodgy occurrences *maybe* being a co-incidence but three of them *definitely* pointing to a conspiracy - well that's pretty much a law of nature. And so when the Nationalists up here started to get battered with scandal after scandal, I thought, hang on, all of this fits perfectly with the DCI Frank Stewart Law of Coincidence and Conspiracy. So I dug deeper, and I've uncovered enough iffy stuff to write what I think will be a sensational story.' He paused for a moment. 'You know how I work. I like to see the scene of the action for myself before I start writing a story. So first I went along to that Greenock Tavern place and then I popped over to the flat where Jade Niven used to live. And I realised right away that something didn't quite stack up with those videos in the pub and with that one outside her flat too. I mean that one was particularly crazy. The video had been stored on the building's CCTV computer system alright, but there was no way the camera could have caught Morrison leaving her flat because of the way it was pointing. Which is how I was able to tip you off.'

Frank gave a thumbs-up. 'Nice work mate. But just so you know, I won't be giving you the credit when I update my boss with progress.'

Patel laughed. 'Understood. Anyway, the title of my piece is going to be *The Curious Rise and Rise of Jack Urquhart*, and it's going to be bloody sensational. You'll all have heard of him I guess?'

'Urquhart?' Maggie said, unable to hide her surprise. '*He's* the subject of your story? Because he's my client at the moment.'

'I know,' Yash said unashamedly. 'Frank told me.'

Now she began to understand why she had been invited. Patel needed something for his big story, perhaps something to corroborate some fanciful supposition he'd made when piecing together the narrative. Whatever it was, it was evidently connected to Jack Urquhart in some way. He had found out from Frank that she was working for the politician, and figured that it might offer a way in.

Frank gave Maggie an apologetic smile. 'I hope you don't mind. I just thought Yash here might bring a bit of business your way. So long as it's nothing dodgy of course.'

'I'm not sure that it wouldn't be a conflict of interest, dodgy or not,' she said, furrowing her brow. 'At the very least, I imagine Jack Urquhart wouldn't be too pleased if he found out I was *investigating* him as well as working for him.'

'Don't worry, I wasn't planning to ask you to actually *do* anything,' Patel said. 'I'd just be grateful if you could maybe pass on anything that he might let slip in conversation, you know, something that might be relevant to my investigation. Nothing more than that. But I'll pay you of course, or at least the paper will.'

Maggie gave him a searching look. 'And how would I recognise what's relevant and what isn't, since I don't have the faintest idea what your investigation is all about?'

Patel nodded. 'I'm coming to that right now. So, in a nutshell, I think there's been some very fishy business going on to get Jack Urquhart into the pretty much unassailable position he now finds himself in. I'm talking about his bid to become the new First Minister, that's what I mean.'

Frank laughed. 'But you always were the king of the conspiracy theories, and when I say that, I mean it as a compliment.'

'You can laugh,' Patel said, 'but remember what you found out this morning? About Donnie Morrison? After my tip-off?'

'Aye, I remember. Seems like he was framed, just like he'd been claiming all along. But are you saying that Jack Urquhart is somehow behind all this? I mean, what's your evidence?'

Patel shrugged. 'It's all circumstantial at the moment I'll admit. But our man Donnie was very popular amongst many of the Nationalist membership and quite a few bookies had him as favourite to succeed Sheila McClelland. He was a major obstacle in Urquhart's way, and now he's not.'

'But what we found out this morning points to something very sophisticated,' Frank said. He turned and looked at Carrie-Anne Fisher. 'Some very clever image and video manipulation, if that's the right way to describe it.'

Eleanor jumped in. 'I've looked at it. It's like mega high-end video processing. AI-assisted I think. Next-generation defo.'

Fisher nodded. 'So Eleanor, it would qualify as Deep Fake do you think? In your professional opinion?'

'Hang on, hang on,' Frank said, interrupting. 'I thought it was all bad actors and foreign governments that were involved in this kind of thing? So are we now saying some tin-pot dictator has decided to employ the full power of their state apparatus to get a second-rate politician called Jack Urquhart elected in a tiny northern outpost of Europe? Nah, no way. That's ridiculous.'

'There is another explanation,' Patel said. He spoke slowly, then paused. 'Because you need to remember where Jack Urquhart went to University.'

'Where?' Frank said, shrugging.

Maggie nodded. 'Dundee I think. He studied at Abertay University I seem to remember, although I must confess that until I did some background research on him, I'd never actually heard of the place before.'

'Well you're right Maggie,' Patel said. 'But do you know what it's famous for?'

Frank shot him a look. 'What, is this bloody Mastermind or something? *I've* never heard of the place either.'

'*I* have, and I know what it's famous for too,' Lexy said. 'It's one of the leading places in the world for video game development. Loads of the global games publishers have software centres there, and students come from all over the world to study at Abertay Uni. They do lots of specialist degrees in the subject. It's basically geeks-ville Scotland.'

Patel gave a smug smile. 'Exactly Lexy. So knocking out these fancy fake videos of Donnie Morrison would have been a piece of cake for any number of the aforementioned dweebs who call the place home. And Jack Urquhart would have met plenty of them in his time at the Uni.'

'But that seems a lot of complication and conspiracy when Urquhart already has a lot going for him,' Maggie said, thinking out loud. 'I mean, he's no mastermind but he's very *presentable*, isn't he? And image is very important for politicians. Style over substance, that's what they often say.'

'But he's only been a junior minister for a year or two,' Patel argued, 'and that was in a role that wasn't exactly demanding. And he didn't exactly make a huge success of it either, by all accounts. Whereas Livvy Foden is equally young and arguably as good-looking as he is, and *she* was bloody Finance Minister.'

'Until she was accused of swindling that development fund,' Frank pointed out.

'Which she denies,' Patel said. *'Which she denies.'*

Frank gave him a scornful look. 'So you're suggesting that was Urquhart's doing too was it? Hacked into her bank account and sent her half-a-million quid?'

'Why not? If you've got the tech skills to write a video game you can hack into a web-site. Any of Urquhart's old Uni mates could have done that, no sweat.'

'And evidence?' Frank asked again. 'Like maybe a name of one of these mates of his?'

Patel laughed. 'That's the difference between my job and your job Frank. I'm allowed to spin a web of supposition and theory, whereas you need all that tiresome evidence stuff before you can do anything. But *obviously* I'm not going to be stupid enough to accuse Urquhart outright. It'll all be grade-one journalistic what-iffery. *What if there are secret forces behind the curious rise of this mediocre politician?* We just ask the questions and let our readers' imaginations do the rest.'

Frank shook his head, and Maggie was pretty sure what he was going to say. She was right.

'It all seems like a load of shameful bollocks to me, total bollocks. But if you want to write the story, then that's up to you. Go ahead.'

'Except it's not *all* bollocks, is it?' Patel said, with more than a hint of smugness. 'Not in the case of Donnie Morrison for a start. You've seen that with your own eyes this morning, and you had two of your own colleagues as witnesses too. He was definitely framed, so why couldn't it be the case with Foden too?' Once again, he paused theatrically. 'And now I've dug up another one. The one that absolutely proves this whole shebang can't be just dismissed as coincidence.'

'What's that then?' Frank said, still sounding unconvinced.

'Turns out the party chairman Willie Paterson's been a very naughty boy. Or should I say, it's *alleged* he's been a naughty boy. Another sex scandal, and this time the woman in question is saying she was the victim of a serious sexual assault. At last year's party conference.'

Frank gave him a doubtful look. 'And she's saying this to who exactly?'

'Well, to me for a start. As I said, I've been doing some digging. That's what us journos do. Let's just say there had been rumours and I simply followed the trail.'

'But this woman hasn't reported the matter to the police?'

Patel shrugged. 'She was trying to get on their party's candidates' list for the next election. She was worried if she brought the matter up it would end her political career before it had even started. And not just that. She confessed to me that she might just have led him on a bit, you know, gave him the wrong impression. Because she says she had invited him to have a drink with her, to get him to support her application to become a candidate.'

'But agreeing to a drink isn't agreeing to sex,' Maggie said sharply. 'There's a bloody important distinction.'

'I know that, I know that,' Patel protested, holding out his hands in front of him. 'But you see the thing is, this woman is a big supporter of Jack Urquhart's leadership bid. And not only that, there's been rumours, if you know what I mean. About her and Urquhart and the exact nature of their relationship.'

'What, are you suggesting this anonymous woman is a honey-trapper too?' Frank said, his tone cynical. 'And that she was put up to it by Urquhart?'

Patel shrugged again. 'Why not, it happens. People will do anything when they get the sniff of power, you know that.'

'Aye, but this sounds like *complete* bollocks, even by your standards,' Frank shot back.

But much as Frank might protest, Maggie thought, why *couldn't* Yash be on to something? There was just so many strands of this whole tangled affair that invited questions. Never mind the curious rise of her client Jack Urquhart, what about the equally sensational ascent of the appalling Tommy Taggart and his barbie-doll wife Sienna? With the election to the Scottish Parliament a mere eighteen months away, it was Taggart who stood to benefit most from the chaos and scandal that had lately enveloped the ruling Nationalist party. Could it be true that a conspiracy was afoot, but one that was designed to ease Taggart's Scottish Freedom Party's bid for power, rather than to promote the candidacy of Jack Urquhart as First Minister, which was what Yash clearly believed?

But all of that wasn't what had *really* sent Maggie's head spinning. It had been that murder yesterday on the Royal

Mile of the unfortunate minor celebratory Johnny Pallas, the guy who had been a vocal supporter of the Taggarts and their Scottish Freedom Party. That news had seriously pulled her up short, because for a moment, when she had first read about it, she'd had a sinking feeling that the victim was going to be identified as Rory Morrison, son of the disgraced politician Donnie. Except, it now seemed to have turned out, the father had been the victim of a sophisticated frame-up, allegedly orchestrated by a shadowy cohort of Dundee-based video-game nerds, and may have been innocent all along as he had always claimed. The thing was though, Yash's casting of her client Jack Urquhart as the brains behind some crazy scheme somehow just didn't ring true. Urquhart was charismatic on telly it was true, but in the flesh, his whole was a lot less than the sum of his parts. Good looking, yes, but she had found him weak and a bit vain, and if Maggie was being honest, a little bit dim too.

But one way or the other, he seemed to be pretty central to this whole affair. Could it be that in the background there was some mysterious Svengali figure, someone who was pulling Urquhart's strings behind the scenes, making him the puppet figurehead of some dark conspiracy? The thought of which caused her to laugh out loud, drawing puzzled looks from her fellow diners. Because of course, the whole thing was complete and utter tosh, a construct so improbable as to invite nothing but derision. But what the hell, she had to meet with Urquhart again anyway, to bring him up to speed on Lori's curious discovery down in Gourock. So yes, she would accept Patel's commission, and at some point during that meeting she would simply ask

Urquhart outright as to the veracity of the journalist's wildly implausible premise.

Although she herself, just like Frank, had already made up her mind. It just *had* to be complete bollocks. *Surely?*

Chapter 15

The sensational discovery that the Reverend Doctor Donnie Morrison, sanctimonious politician and part-time minister of the Free Church of Scotland, had indeed been the victim of an outrageous frame-up, had sent Frank's investigation into a bit of a tail-spin. Prior to the discovery, he had been pretty much just going through the motions, making sure he did a competent and thorough-enough job without really expecting anything much to come of either strand of the case. But now of course it was a whole different story, and doubly complicated by the fact that his annoying hotshot reporter mate Yash Patel knew all about it too, having put Frank and his colleagues onto the trail in the first place, and in a day or two the story was going to be splashed all over his paper's Sunday edition. *Chronicle Proves Morrison Victim of Deep Fake Attack.* That would be the gist of Patel's story, and once it was out there it couldn't be ignored. Not only that, but in an hour's time he had a phone-call scheduled with his gaffer, a call in which ACC Natalie Young would doubtless ask awkward questions and might even become slightly tetchy when it emerged that the breakthrough, if you could call it that, was down to a two-bit newspaper scribbler.

So now it was a time for the gathering of thoughts, to make an attempt to work out where the hell they were with the case and, more critically, where the hell they should go next. And that was why he'd set up his own mid-morning gathering of his crack team, at this precise moment assembled in the canteen of New Gorbals nick. In deference to the expected importance of the session, he'd pinched an easel-mounted whiteboard from one of the upstairs incident rooms and was presently standing in front of it, a marker pen in one hand and a half-eaten bacon roll in the other. Present, and also equipped with breakfast essentials, were his DCs Lexy McDonald and Ronnie French, together with Principal Forensic Officer Eleanor Campbell of Maida Vale Labs, London, W9.

'Right then boys and girls,' he said through a mouthful of roll, 'I'd be most grateful if we could all engage our massive brains and see if we can figure out a plan of action for this goddamned holy mess of an investigation. But before that, I need to refresh myself on what I was asked to look at in the first place. Everybody okay with that?'

'Sure guv,' French said. Frank quite reasonably assumed he was speaking for everyone, so gave a thumbs-up and continued.

'Right then. So you will recall that my first mission was to look into Donnie Morrison's ludicrous assertion that he was set up by the Jade Niven woman in order to force a by-election and thus open the door for the nut-job Tommy Taggart to win his seat. The second mission was to look into allegations of funny business surrounding the aforementioned by-election, said funny business designed to smooth Taggart's passage to our Mickey-Mouse Holyrood parliament. And ratcheting the nonsense level up to eleven was the suggestion by an imported CIA spook that there might be shady foreign agents involved in the whole bloody ridiculous shebang.'

'You thought it was all rubbish sir,' Lexy said, smiling. 'And I can see why.'

He nodded. 'Precisely. But now what we've discovered in regard to these videos taken at the Greenock Tavern and at the nearby rented flat of Jade Niven has tossed a bloody great spanner into the works. To put it bluntly, it's all gone somewhat tits-up.' He paused for a moment then smiled. 'But no matter, there's always a Plan B. I'm just not quite sure what it is yet.'

'And what about this Jack Urquhart geezer?' French interjected. 'Is it all his doing like Patel seems to think, or is that all bollocks too?'

Frank shrugged. 'Well at first I thought it was a pile of grade-A tosh, that was until our boy Yash reminded us that Dundee is the video-game capital of Scotland, if not the whole UK. So now I'm not so sure. But there's a quiet wee lassie here that might be able to help us answer that question.' He shot Eleanor a wry smile. 'Miss Campbell, you've not said much this morning. Actually, you've not said anything at all. Have you fallen out with us?'

She gave him a dismissive look. 'I've been like *thinking*. I'm allowed to do that, aren't I?'

'That's what we pay you for,' he said, laughing. 'So anyway, these videos. Is there anything we can do with them? I mean, to see if they can tell us anything?'

'That's what I've been thinking about.' She paused for a moment. 'I've worked out that we need a memory-resident algorithmic decompilation engine with multi-threading de-encryption.'

'Aye, I could have told you that,' Frank said, making a face.

She ignored him. 'But we haven't got one, the UK I mean. Well actually GCHQ have *got* one, but it doesn't like *work*.' It was said in the smugly dismissive tone he'd heard her use before when revelling in the failures of rival techie geeks. 'And they've been trying for like *years*,' she added, her pleasure self-evident.

'The Germans have got a word for what you've just been saying. But what about that MI6 lad Zak you're so pally with? I thought he was the maestro of all that sort of stuff?'

She shrugged. 'He's like left the service, remember? He's gone totally private now with his ethical hacking business.'

Frank sighed. 'Aye *right*, I remember now, and he's making a bloody fortune too. So anyway, what exactly does one of these de-what's-it engines do exactly?'

'You wouldn't understand even if I told you.'

'I wouldn't. But I still want to know, just so I can bore my pals down the pub. They're all big fans of that de-compiling stuff down at the Horseshoe Bar. After a couple of beers that's all they want to talk about.'

She gave him a sour look. 'I'll need to make it like *really* simple.'

He laughed. 'I know. But just get on with it, we haven't got all morning.'

She gave him another look, this one even more sour, if that was possible. 'So software is built from *code*. That's instructions written in like a *language*.' She spoke slowly, as if she was an infant teacher going at a pace to suit a class of particularly dim five-year-olds.

'Understand,' Frank nodded, although he didn't.

'I tried to learn Basic on an old Spectrum once,' French said guilessly. 'Wrote a program to play bleeding knots and crosses, and the bleeding computer beat me every time.'

Eleanor ignored him. 'Then to enable the program to run on the target hardware environment...'

'What's that?' Frank asked.

French jumped in, evidently enjoying his self-appointed role as IT guru to the group. 'She just means a computer or a smartphone. Geeks use them fancy words to make them sound smarter than they are, that's all.'

She glowered at both of them before continuing. '.. to enable the program to run on the *target hardware environment* it goes through a *compiler,* which converts it into an industry-standard format, which in our case is an MP4 video file. Once the code is compiled, it can be run but it can't be like *read*. It's then encrypted for double security. To make doubly sure no-one can copy or steal the code.'

'Okay *right*,' Frank said, and this time he thought he nearly understood. 'So that's why you need one of these de-compiler gizmos. So that you can get back to the original language?' It was half-question, half-statement. 'And is a computer language like well... like a *language*? So is there English computer-speak and French computer-speak and Russian computer-speak and so on?'

'No,' Eleanor said flatly.

'What do you mean, *no*?' he said, recognising he was fast reaching the point that inevitably arrived in any technical conversation with Eleanor Campbell, or in fact in any sort of conversation with her at all. The point where irritation began to trump amused indulgence.

'They're *all* English-like,' she said. 'All programming languages are. Since like the beginning of time.'

He assumed she meant since the start of the computer age, but decided this wasn't the best time to indulge in pedantry, no matter how pleasing that would be.

'So I ask again. How will having one of these mystical de-compiler thingies help us?'

'Coders write comments in their code. To remind themselves how and why they've added a particular bit of logic to the program. And it's like *obvious* they would write these comments in their own language.'

And finally he *did* understand. 'Right, *right,* I get it now. So if the code for our dodgy videos is full of *och-aye-the-noos* and stuff like that, we can assume it's one of our Dundee geniuses who have done the fancy Deep Fake programming...'

Lexy laughed. 'The city's a magnet for games developers from all round the world sir. They're probably not *all* Scottish.'

'Sure sure, I know that,' he said, grinning. 'But if it turns out to be the Chinese or one of the other baddies who are responsible, then the language of their comments is going to give them away, I think that's what I'm understanding.' He gave Eleanor a thumbs-up. 'And thanks for explaining it so clearly Eleanor,' he said, winking at Lexy. 'So I guess you'll be wanting me to speak to my new best friend Carrie-Anne Fisher of the CIA and see if we can get you working with their Langley super-geeks? Because they're bound to have de-compliers coming out of their ears over there. Ten-a-penny probably.'

'Like *awesome*,' she beamed, not bothering to disguise her joy at the prospect. Which was unusual to say the least, because in Frank's experience Eleanor didn't normally do joy.

'Consider it done.' He glanced at his watch. 'Right then, just forty-one minutes before my grilling with the ACC. So, what's next on the agenda folks?'

'I think we need to speak to the two women, don't we sir?' Lexy said. 'Jade Niven and the girl who took the videos. What was her name again, I keep forgetting?' She whipped out her notebook from a back pocket. 'Yes, Kylie Gilmour, that was it.'

Frank nodded. 'Except we now know this Kylie couldn't have taken them, don't we? Not unless she can walk through walls.'

'And I'll tell you something else guv,' French said. 'That manager geezer at the pub must be in on the scam too. Because he confirmed that the Kylie bird had taken them videos, didn't he? And yet she didn't.'

'Aye, good point Frenchie,' Frank said, not for the first time reflecting that you underestimated his slovenly DC at your peril. Because inside the uninspiring exterior lurked a surprisingly smart and perceptive detective. When he could be arsed, that was, which wasn't very often. 'So Lexy, can you make these lassies your priority. Chase them up and see what they have to say for themselves. And Ronnie, maybe you can pay our manager man Paddy a visit when you're in the area. Which brings me to your ongoing enquiries. How are you getting on with your door-to-doors? Found anyone who can understand a word you're saying?'

French laughed. 'That's cruel guv. All us East-Enders speak proper, not like you bloody Jocks. But yeah, it's been quite interesting. I can tell you something, there's a lot of support on the ground for Tommy Taggart and his party. I'm not much of a student of Jock-land politics, but I'd say people are seriously pissed off about the mess the Nationalists have made of running the place, so plenty of people gave him their vote without any persuasion.'

'So no evidence of intimidation or anything like that?'

'Well I wouldn't say that guv, not entirely. What I *did* hear from a load of folks was that Taggart's goons were out in force at the polling stations right enough. But mostly they weren't doing the heavy intimidation stuff. Mostly they were handing out goody-bags.'

'What?'

'Goody-bags guv,' French repeated. 'You know, like you do after a kid's birthday party. They made up goody-bags with the party's logo printed on it and lots of stuff in it. *Scottish* stuff. Shortbread, whisky miniatures, caramel wavers and the like. All the healthy stuff you Jocks love.'

'You're kidding,' Frank said. 'What, Tommy's party has been *bribing* the voters with bloody caramel wavers and cans of Irn Bru?'

French shrugged. 'Yeah, but I don't think they were breaking any law.'

'But doesn't it depend on how much they spent on the stuff?' Lexy said, evidently thinking out loud. 'Because I'm pretty sure there are laws limiting campaign budgets and that sort of thing.'

'Aye, probably,' Frank said, 'and that's something we'll have to take a look at, unfortunately. But before we get too dejected, I think I heard you use the words *not entirely* Frenchie. Am I right or am I right?'

'Spot on guv. From what I can make out, there *was* a bit of argy-bargy going on outside some of the polling stations, but that seems to have been squarely targeted at the opposition's leafleting squads, not the punters. Basically Taggart's thugs were suggesting to the Nationalist supporters that they should f**k off if they didn't want their f**king heads kicked in.'

Frank nodded. 'No surprise that. I recall their defeated candidate made complaints along these lines at the time, but it seems our esteemed Police Scotland boys couldn't raise the energy to investigate.'

'Yeah, but they were probably getting their goody-bags too guv,' French said, laughing. 'Only theirs would be big fat wads of cash in a plain envelope.'

'That's no bloody joking matter Frenchie,' Frank said, giving him a stiff look. 'Because the last thing I need is a police corruption allegation heaped on top of all this other crap.'

'But maybe Ronnie's right sir,' Lexy intervened. 'Because there were rumours going round the rank and file at the time it was all kicking off. The boys and girls on the beat saw what was happening on the street, and we were all asking the same question. Why's the brass not doing anything about this?'

Frank sighed. 'Bloody brilliant, that's all I can say. But just for a laugh, I'll risk my pension and what I laughably call my career by bringing it up with the ACC. I'm sure she'll be thrilled to hear all about it.'

'Yeah, ask her how much she trousered herself,' French said, grinning.

'*That's* not going to happen, I can assure you,' Frank said, adopting an expression of mock horror. But that raised the question of what exactly he *would* be saying to ACC Young when they spoke in less than half an hour's time. Fortunately, there was one tangible development to report, even though he and his team couldn't take much credit for the discovery of the bizarre Donnie Morrison honey-trap affair. But he was going to have to say something about what the motive behind the hi-tech crime was - if it indeed *was* a crime, and he wasn't even sure about that- and who might be the perpetrator. *A group linked to First Minister candidate Jack Urquhart,* that's what the Chronicle would be speculating in a couple of days' time, so he would need to be ahead of the game and have some opinion on whether there could possibly be any truth to the allegations. It was rubbish, of course it was, surely, but he couldn't say that outright to the ACC, just in case it turned out not to be. No, he would have to hedge his bets on that one, much as he found the idea distasteful. But looking on the bright side, he at least had got Eleanor Campbell working on the case, and if anyone was going to be able to discover the provenance of these fake videos, then it would be her. And that was bound to take time, given he had to set the thing up with Carrie-Anne Fisher, and she would doubtless have to do the same with her spook friends Stateside, and then there would be security hoops for Eleanor to jump through before she would be allowed to get her hands on the fancy technology. It would be two or three weeks minimum before she even got started, Frank reckoned, which was actually quite good, because it would stop the impatient ACC badgering him for updates every five minutes. As for the Taggarts and the allegations of electoral malpractice, the suggestion that they may have been chasing their opponents away from the polling stations with threats of violence meant there was something worthy of further investigation. Mind you, it was a moot point if stopping some soppy Nationalists handing out their stupid leaflets was a crime or merely doing the public a service. But he would definitely mention it to Young, and on balance, he probably had *just* enough to get through the call without looking a total eejit.

'Right then guys,' he said, feeling relieved. 'We're probably done here, and thanks for your help. You all know what's next on your agendas so get on to it, quick as you can.'

'Before we finish, can I just raise another thing too sir?' Lexy said. 'It's just something about these Royal Mile murders. Random thoughts that popped into my head last night when I was watching some rubbish on the telly.'

He laughed. 'What, working out of hours Lexy? If you think I'm paying you overtime, then you can forget it. But aye, let's hear what you've got.'

'Okay sir. So the latest victim you'll remember turned out to be Johnny Pallas, you know, the reality TV guy. My mates on the investigation tell me he was a regular at that Harley-Dee's place. And you'll also remember that was where the two last victims worked as well, *and* it turns out they knew Pallas pretty well apparently. So the guys on the investigation team are working on the supposition that the murderer might be someone who frequented that club.'

'Good to see we've got some geniuses working the case through there,' Frank said. 'And Pallas was a supporter of the Taggarts and their Freedom party of course.'

'Not just a supporter, he was a member too. And that got me thinking about something else.'

'See Ronnie?' Frank said, directing a wry grin at his Cockney colleague. ' Lexy's been expending brain power in her spare time. You could learn something from that.'

'I already have guv,' he said, deadpan. 'Leave it to her.'

'Anyway Lexy,' Frank continued, suppressing a laugh. 'What more is it that you've been contemplating?'

She smiled. 'I thought I would take a look at the other two victims to see if maybe they were members of the SFP too. Andy and Rab McVie, that's their names by the way.'

'What, brothers?' Frank said, surprised.

'No, they were married,' Lexy answered. 'Just last year.'

He shook his head. 'Just adds to the tragedy. But did you find out if they were members of Taggart's rabble?'

'No. What I mean, is no I haven't found out, because the SFP won't let us have access to their membership list, and so unless people come out publicly like Pallas did, then you won't know. But I did find *this* on their social media.' She thrust her phone towards him so that he could see the picture on the screen. It was evidently the McVies, striking a lewd pose, their hands grabbing each other's crotch.

Frank laughed. 'Very tasteful, and these boys really did love their leather shorts, didn't they? But just because they're wearing Scotland football shirts doesn't mean they're members of the SFP.'

'I know sir', Lexy conceded, 'but it makes you think, doesn't it? Coincidences and conspiracies and all that.'

He laughed. 'I've done quite enough head-scratching for now, but aye, there might be something in it I suppose. Add it to your list.'

'Right-oh sir. I'll chase it up.'

'Good stuff. So wish me luck with my call. I just hope the ACC's in a good mood. Mind you, even when she's cheery it's hard to tell the difference.'

He checked his watch again, then tried to remember if he was to call the ACC or she was going to ring him. Shrugging to himself, he decided he would let her have the honour, and he would take the call right here in the canteen, giving him just enough time to wander up to the counter and grab another coffee and a chocolate biscuit. Although maybe he should pass on the latter, given the impending need to be able to squeeze into that kilt for his wedding. It gave him a warm feeling just thinking about it, him and Maggie getting married, with Jimmy as best man and little Ollie as head usher. Aye, that day was going to be the red-letter day to end all red-letter days, as opposed to today, which was looking like it would probably be best forgotten.

Unlike tomorrow, which although he didn't know it yet, was going to be one of the worst days of his life. And then it was going to get a whole lot worse.

Chapter 16

It was going to be an especially busy day, with Maggie needing to have a detailed catch-up with Lori before grabbing a train to Edinburgh for her lunch-time meeting with her client Jack Urquhart. Then she had to whizz back to Glasgow for a tea-time meeting with Rose Morrison, a meeting she wasn't much looking forward to on account of the slow progress they were making on the search for the truth about what happened to her son. But at least on the Urquhart front, the news that his partner Dominique had arranged a seemingly shady meeting with an unknown person at a location twenty-five miles away from her Glasgow city-centre office was something positive to report to him, even if the details were as yet sketchy. Although, as Frank had pointed out rather uncharitably over breakfast that morning, having shady meetings was surely the basic job description of a journalist. Talking of that breakfast, she wondered now whether he'd noticed the she'd made a special effort with her appearance that day, slapping on a bit more make-up than normal, and choosing a sleek emerald-green dress from her wardrobe that wouldn't have been out of place on a night out, the outfit a complete contrast to the sober grey or navy dresses she generally favoured as work-wear. She had justified it to herself on the basis that the lunch venue was the up-market Royal Mile Grampian hotel on the capital city's famous thoroughfare, a venue much favoured by the Edinburgh political classes due to its relative proximity to the Holyrood parliament buildings. And, she reflected, less than a hundred metres from the spot where Johnny Pallas had been found murdered, the pictures on the local TV news bulletins confirming that the location was still cordoned off by striped crime-scene tape. If Frank had noticed her attire, he hadn't said anything, but then again he had been preoccupied with his own upcoming workday, which was to centre around a public announcement that the police were to open an investigation into the circumstances surrounding the Donnie Morrison scandal, timed to pre-empt the unveiling of the story by Yash Patel in the Sunday edition of the *Chronicle*.

Lori was still on surveillance duties outside the offices of Dominique Tremblay's newspaper, so they had arranged to meet at the tiny coffee-shop across the street which she had made her base for the duration of the mission. She was already there when Maggie arrived, but she wasn't alone as expected, sharing a table with a floppy-haired youth in a black hoodie. Puzzled at first as to his identity, she suddenly remembered. It was Nathan Duke, one of the paper's IT team and the guy they had informally co-opted to feed them any internal gossip about Miss Tremblay that might be relevant to their case. Now she knew who he was, but she still hadn't expected him to be here this morning.

'Hi,' Maggie said, giving Lori a look that said *what's he doing here*?

'Oh hi Maggie,' she said brightly. 'You remember Nathan, don't you?'

'Of course. Hi Nathan, good to see you again. Have we sorted you out with a coffee?'

'Yeah ta,' he mumbled, holding up his cup in acknowledgment. 'Sweet.'

'Nathan knew Rory Morrison,' Lori said. 'It just came out when I was chatting to him the other day. That's right, isn't it Nathan?'

'Yeah', he mumbled again. 'We were kinda mates I suppose. He was a funny guy.'

Now Maggie understood why he was here, and she wondered why she hadn't thought of quizzing the lad before on the subject of what he knew of Donnie and Rose Morrison's boy. Rory and Nathan weren't much different in age, and it was quite usual for work colleagues to form a friendship when they had things in common, age being one of them. Although of course Rory had been based in Edinburgh, whereas Nathan worked here in Glasgow, but that was hardly a barrier these days, where much if not all social interaction was conducted online.

'So he would have talked to you a lot about his grand plans then?' Maggie asked. 'He must have been really excited about it all.'

He shook his head slowly without speaking. Then just as it seemed he was about to elaborate, Lori intervened. 'That's the thing Maggie. He never mentioned it, did he Nathan? Not once.'

'Nope,' he confirmed. 'Kept it a complete secret. Absolutely schtum.' The way he said it suggested the omission had caused some offence. Now she wondered if there had perhaps been something more to the friendship. Was she mistaken, or was she detecting the faintest scent of unrequited love from this shy youth?

'Why was that, do you think?' Maggie asked, as gently as possible.

He shrugged. 'Don't know. But I followed his Instagram for a while. He seems very happy. I'm glad.'

She nodded sympathetically. 'And has he kept in touch with you? I mean, through WhatsApp or whatever? With you personally?'

He shrugged again. 'I guess he's too busy with his wonderful new life.' Maggie took that as a *no,* the hurt now fully on display. But that was what sometimes happened in life wasn't it? People move on, that was the cliché, but the trouble was, so often they forgot about the people they left behind.

'Yes, perhaps,' she said. 'But do you try to keep in touch with him?'

He gave a sigh. 'Yeah, at least I did for a while. I know he was reading all my messages but he never replied. Well, except just once and that was just two words. *Doing fine*. That's all I got. After that, he didn't even bother to read them.'

'And when was this?' Maggie asked, furrowing her brow. 'I mean, when you got that short reply?'

'I don't know. Four, maybe five months ago.' Which was the same time his parents lost touch with him, Maggie thought with some dismay.

She smiled. 'Okay Nathan, I really appreciate you telling us this. Lori will have told you we're working for his parents to try and track him down I suppose? Because they're very worried about him.'

He nodded. 'Yeah, she told me.'

'And of course we'll let you know as soon as we know anything. And perhaps you'll let us know if he suddenly gets in touch again.'

'I will,' he said, getting up from his seat. 'See you.'

'Gosh, that was a turn up for the books, wasn't it?' Maggie said after he'd gone. 'Well done to you Miss Logan.'

Lori grinned. 'Yeah, well it just came out when I was getting an update from him yesterday. I slipped him twenty quid for his trouble by the way, I hope that was alright.'

'Absolutely fine. So what about Miss Tremblay, did he have anything to say about her?'

'Not much. She's not popular, but I guess we knew that already. Full of herself and doesn't suffer fools, that's what everyone seems to think. But obviously I did ask Nathan if there were any rumours about her and any of the men who worked there, and he said there wasn't as far as he knew. Although he reckoned there's plenty who might like to try it on with her, based on the water-cooler chat.'

Maggie smiled. 'Well, she's annoyingly attractive and not short of what they used to call sex appeal either, so I'm not surprised about that. But I suppose that's one bit of good news I can report back to her partner.'

'If you ignore her dodgy meeting the other day,' Lori said.

'Yes, exactly, that's what I want to hear all about next. Tell me what happened.'

'Aye, nae bother. So I followed her westwards out of the city, down the M8 and A8 all the way down to Greenock. She was tanking along in that fancy Porsche of hers but fair play to your plucky wee Golf, it had no trouble keeping up. Mind you, I had my foot through the floor most of the way.'

Maggie gave her a look of mock horror. 'I told you it's my pride and joy, that car. It's been with me through thick and thin.'

Lori laughed. 'I was very nice to it, honest. So anyway, Dominique headed through the town then out along the coast for a few miles until she reached Gourock. She parked up by the seafront in one of these spaces where the car's facing the esplanade, if that's what you call it. Then about ten minutes later another car drew up alongside, this one a big fancy SUV. The driver got out and got into Dominique's car, but it all happened too quickly for me to get much of a photo. And the other person was wearing a hoodie so I had no chance of recognising anyone of course, and her sports car's got a tiny back window so you can't really see through it from outside. And obviously I couldn't brazenly stick my phone in front of their windscreen to get a better shot.'

'Obviously not,' Maggie said, giving an involuntary giggle as she imagined the brazen Miss Lori Logan doing just that.

'But I did get out of my car...' She smiled, seeing Maggie's look. '... I mean, *your* car and took a casual walk past them, giving them a swift glance out of the corner of my eye, you know, kind of sneakily. But that didn't really help because they other person was wearing sunglasses. Ray-Bans I thought, expensive designer ones.'

Maggie laughed. 'I'll need to defer to your expertise. Although you say you didn't get a look at the guy's face at all?'

She shook her head. 'Nah, nae chance of that, not with the hoodie pulled up, plus only seeing the other person mainly from the back.' She paused for a moment. 'But see, the thing is, even a shapeless hoodie can't hide a nice pair of tits. Boob-job I would say, the way they were standing up for themselves. Made me jealous they did.'

'What?' Maggie said incredulously. 'Are you saying it was a *woman*?'

She nodded. 'Aye, I would say so. Not one hundred percent defo, but *fairly* certain. And if it was a man, and they were meeting up for a shag, they would have been snogging, and they weren't.'

'So what were they doing?' Maggie asked. 'If you could tell.'

Lori shrugged. 'No, I couldn't, not for sure. But they weren't laughing, but they weren't arguing or anything either. Anyway, I got the make and registration number of the other car of course, so I expect your Frank will be able to tell us whose it is.'

Maggie gave her a wry look. 'If only it was that easy. Accessing the Vehicle Licensing database without an official reason is gross misconduct for policemen, even senior DCIs like Frank. He'd be booted out the door and it would be bye-bye to his pension too. But it's good that we know about the car of course. Because there's maybe a chance our client will know whose it is.'

Thinking about what Lori had just told her, she allowed herself a smile of satisfaction. Suddenly and unexpectedly, and with lunch with her client just two hours ahead, there was real progress on the case to report. It seemed Jack Urquhart's suspicions of infidelity had proved to be inaccurate, but maybe, just maybe his partner had something to hide.

The only thing was, they hadn't a clue what that something was.

***

Maggie didn't know Edinburgh at all, but Google Maps had seamlessly guided her on foot from Waverley Station to her destination on the Royal Mile. Which, she had been surprised to discover, wasn't an actual street name, but a term apparently dreamed up for the benefit of the tourists by the now-forgotten author of a guide book published as recently as the nineteen-twenties. It seemed to encompass three or four streets that stretched from Holyrood House up to the Castle, and got its *Royal* moniker, she had read, from it being the ancient processional route of Scottish monarchs on their succession to the throne. Also, and this was perhaps taking her geeky anorak tendencies too far, it was actually nearly two of today's miles in extent, the Scots having operated with a different-length mile before they joined up with the English back in the sixteenth century. All of this was moderately interesting undoubtedly, and it served to explain why her lunch venue, the Royal Mile Grampian hotel, actually sported a Canongate address.

Disappointingly though, rather than the grand Victorian palace she had been expecting, it turned out to be both modern and blandly undistinguished in appearance. But it was evidently still grand enough to employ a fully-uniformed doorman, who greeted her with a discreet salute and a warm *good day madam* as she ascended the three or four wide steps that led to the entrance.

As arranged, she selected one of the sumptuous leather armchairs that were dotted around the expansive reception area and awaited his arrival. Sinking back in her seat, her eye was drawn to a group of four or five women sitting at a table a few feet away, whom she assumed, like her, had gathered before making their way through to the restaurant. Mostly young and self-evidently prosperous, if their exquisite dress and coiffure could be taken as a measure, and radiating entitled self-confidence, she speculated they might be fast-track civil servants from the nearby parliament, or perhaps some of those special advisors without which no politician seemed to be able to operate these days. And then, looking again, she realised she recognised one of them. It was Livvy Foden, the embattled Finance Minister, and Jack Urquhart's main rival for the vacant leadership of the Nationalist party and thus, by default, for the post of First Minister. In recent days, it had emerged that Foden was planning legal action against the *Globe*, Dominique Tremblay's paper and the one that had broken the story of her alleged embezzlement of a vast sum from a development fund destined for the Western Isles. And about to be introduced to the plot-line of this already crazy soap-opera was the fact that the veteran Nationalist politician Donnie Morrison had been the victim of an outrageous miscarriage of justice, the perpetrator or perpetrators as yet unknown. Later today, that fact was going to be made public by her darling Frank, and she wondered if Morrison might now sensationally decide to re-enter the leadership race himself. All in all, it was turning out to be an interesting period in Scottish politics, to say the least.

Jack Urquhart arrived pretty much on schedule, sweeping purposefully in through the revolving doors, causing five pairs of female eyes at the adjacent table to do an involuntary double-take as he bounded into the reception area. He really was a *very* good-looking guy, Maggie reflected, and she was glad, if a little guilty, that she had made the effort to dress up for the occasion. She stood up to greet him, and to her surprise he swept her into a deep embrace before kissing her - quite lingeringly she thought, if there was such a word - on the cheek. Shamefully she thought of the five pair of eyes on her, five pairs of *jealous* eyes, as once again she imagined herself the willowy heroine in one of her mum's trashy romantic novels. And then, out of the corner of an eye, she caught a glimpse of Livvy Foden, on her feet and with camera-phone pointed in their direction. *Damn*. But what the hell, she thought, it was all perfectly innocent, and anyway, if she and Urquhart were having an affair, would they conduct it so openly, in the reception area of one of Edinburgh's busiest hotels? And more to the point, she reflected wryly, would he be having an affair with a slightly care-worn forty-four-year-old mum?

Evidently catching sight of Foden himself, he extricated himself from their embrace and shouted across to the photographer. 'Afternoon Livvy,' he said, shooting her a smile. 'Another one of me to frame and put on your desk, eh? I hope you got my good side.'

'You haven't got a good side Jack,' she said, smiling back. 'But when this makes the papers tomorrow, everyone will be wondering why you need a private detective.'

He laughed. 'You see Maggie, you're famous all over Scotland. It must have been all that good work on the Lomond Tower case. Anyway, time to eat.'

As they made their way through to the restaurant, Maggie said, slightly alarmed, 'Do you think she *will* send it to a newspaper?'

He shrugged. 'She might. But so what? It won't do me any harm, and it might even be good publicity for your agency.'

'I'm getting married in a couple of months,' she said, annoyed by how easily he had dismissed the threat. 'I don't want my lovely fiancé seeing me on the front page of some dodgy Scottish tabloid.'

'Yes, I know, I'm sorry. But I guess I'm just a touchy-feely sort of guy. And you're pretty irresistible, if you don't mind me saying so.'

And now, probably for the first time, she began to see what sort of a man Jack Urquhart really was. Self-centred of course, but wasn't that true of most politicians? No, there was something else too, something just a tiny bit creepy about the guy. She'd met the type plenty of times when she was a barrister at Drake Chambers, those entitled men with their money and their gilded careers who thought they could just help themselves to any woman who took their fancy, as if it was sport.

'Actually Jack, I *do* mind you saying so,' she said, quite sharply. 'Maybe it would be best if we kept to business, don't you think?' His face took on an apologetic expression. Smiling, he said, 'Yes, you're right Maggie, I'm sorry. Business. Of course. But let's just enjoy a lovely lunch. The food's amazing here, I'm sure you'll love it.' She doubted if he really was sorry, but he sounded maddeningly convincing. But then again, she guessed he'd probably had a lot of practice.

Whatever the truth of that, he hadn't been lying about the food, the menu a delectable pot-pouri of her favourite dishes, and she had no trouble in coming to a decision, eventually plumping for a simple if extortionately-priced steak. Somewhat stressed by the earlier events, she had also succumbed to his insistence that they should have wine with their lunch. She'd let him choose, and given her menu selection, he had not unreasonably gone for a rich Shiraz, which as she moved onto her second generously-sized glass, she wondered if he had picked it because of its especially strong alcohol content. She could feel her mood rapidly mellowing, causing her to make a mental note to cover her glass with her hand the next time the attentive waiter tried to top her up. But now it was time to talk business.

'So Jack, as I told you, we've been conducting a surveillance operation at your wife's place of work over the last twelve days, and as you know, we have an informant who works for the paper and is feeding us whatever information he can. And finally two days ago, as I mentioned on the phone, something occurred which we think is important.'

He nodded. 'She met someone. In Gourock you say. Bloody Gourock.' For some reason, mention of the seaside town seemed to amuse him. 'I should explain. That's where Dominique and I used to meet... well you know, before I left my first wife. Quiet little place.'

'That's interesting,' Maggie said, although it really wasn't. 'We're working on the basis that this might be a regular arrangement and so they might meet again same time next week.'

'Makes sense.'

'Right,' she said. 'If we're properly prepared this time, we're hoping we can get a clear photograph of the person's face. So that you might be able to identify...' She paused for a moment '... to identify *her*.'

'What, it's a bloody *woman*?' he said, not able to hide his shock at the revelation. 'I suppose it might just be one of her pals, or a work contact maybe?'

Maggie shrugged. 'Possibly Jack. We don't know, but we have details of the car of course. So we'd hope to find out who it is.'

'Bloody *great*,' he spat out. 'So Dominique prefers some dyke stuffing a big rubber dildo up her to her own husband? That's bloody something, isn't it?'

'I don't think we can say that,' Maggie said, trying not to show her distaste for his crudeness. 'There was a considerable amount of subterfuge about the meeting, which does arouse suspicion I admit, but there was no evidence that it was a romantic assignation. It could very well be a work contact, and considering your wife's profession, that isn't a far-fetched assumption.'

'Show me the car,' he said, evidently still angry. 'I might know it.'

She fumbled in her bag for her phone. 'It's a Range-Rover, a big expensive SUV. No private plate or anything, but it's nearly new, with a last year registration prefix. FB22 something-or-other I think it is.' She swiped through her photo album until she came to it. 'Yeah, here it is,' she said, pointing the screen towards him. He looked at it carefully then shrugged. 'Don't recognise it off the top of my head. But I want to know who it is, so carry on with your investigation.'

'Fine,' Maggie said, 'but just so you know, we'll be closing down our surveillance op at the end of this week. I think we've taken it as far as we can for now. We'll try to identify who Dominique has been seeing and then we'll be wrapping up the case. I expect we'll be finished by the end of next week, one way or the other. Is that okay?'

He smiled, seemingly already over the surprise of her revelation. 'Yes, that's perfect, of course. And you've done a fabulous job, thank you for that.'

'It's just what we do,' she said, finding herself returning the smile without wanting to.

The waiter had returned to their table and was reaching across for the wine bottle. 'Not for me thanks,' she said, catching his eye. 'It's lovely, but I've had enough.'

'Aw come on,' Urquhart said. 'Just a little sip to celebrate a successful outcome. Because it's a huge weight off my mind, now that I know. Go ahead, fill her up George.'

She sighed. 'Okay, but just half a glass please.' *And then I'm out of here*, she thought. But before then, there was just one more item of business to be dealt with.

'I don't expect you'll have heard,' she said casually, 'but it turns out Donnie Morrison's claims that he was the victim of some sort of honey-trap have been proven to be true. The police are going to announce today that they're opening an investigation to find out who was responsible. I only know this because it's my fiancé Frank who's running with the case.'

She saw him shrug. 'That's nice, but really, who cares?' he said. 'Morrison's an old has-been, in fact more like a never-was. It's well known around Holyrood that he was a right old creep with the women.' Maggie smiled to herself, the phrase *takes one to know one* instantly springing to mind. Except of course Jack Urquhart wasn't old, and she could imagine plenty of women welcoming *his* attentions.

'So you don't know anything about it then?' she asked.

He looked at her, clearly puzzled. 'Know anything? Why should I? I hardly know the guy, and let's face it, he's not exactly a rival is he? As I said, he never amounted to much in the first place, and he's definitely past it now.' The answer was convincing, and she looked forward to reporting back to Frank that his assessment of Yash Patel's crazy Urquhart-and-Dundee-geek conspiracy theory - that it was nuts -was almost certainly true.

But now it was time to go. She leaned down to pick up her handbag, slipping it over her shoulder as she began to get up. 'Thank you for a lovely lunch Jack,' she said, 'but I need to rush off to Waverley now to catch my train back to Glasgow. I've got a meeting with another client and I don't want to be late.'

'Are you sure?' he said, his eyes piercing hers. Reaching into the pocket of his jacket, he removed what turned out to be a key-card and placed it on the table. Then, he reached across the table and took her hand in hers, squeezing enough for it to hurt. 'Because I hope you don't mind, but I took the liberty of booking us a very nice room on the top floor with a wonderful view right along the Mile. After all, is there anything nicer than a little afternoon delight?'

***

She was still absolutely seething when she reached the entrance to the station. The bloody *gall* of the man, believing all he had to do was to smile that bloody smile at her and she would then jump into bed with him! What sort of a woman did he think she was? Somehow she had managed to restrain herself from slapping him across the face, but she had made it bloody clear that their business arrangement was now over, and he could bloody well find out for himself the identity of the woman - yes, the *woman* - who might be shagging his partner. Now she just wanted to get home to Frank and her little boy, to wrap herself in the warmth of her lovely little family. Never again would she succumb to the stupid burst of schoolgirl vanity she had so shamefully experienced as a result of Urquhart's insincere flattery.

As she walked onto the concourse, she began to realise that something was going on. There were hundreds of people milling around and glancing up, and when she looked, she saw that the electronic arrival and departure information boards were completely blank.

'What's happening?' she asked a girl standing next to her.

'Everything's down,' the girl said. 'All the information systems and the signalling too apparently. Nothing's running right now. It's a total nightmare.'

'Have they said what the problem is and when it will be fixed?'

The girl shrugged. 'Not sure exactly, but some people are tweeting there's been another cyber attack. That's about the fifth one this year. But the station staff told us ten minutes ago they're hoping to switch to back-up systems and get some trains running in a couple of hours. That's what they're saying anyway, but who knows? We're all waiting for another update.'

'Okay thanks.' Frustrated but realising there wasn't much she could do about it, Maggie wandered over to a kiosk on the concourse that sold coffee, and although she didn't really need anything after her lunch, ordered an americano just to pass the time. Looking around, she saw there was no chance of grabbing one of the few seats, all of which were occupied, but she did manage to find a protruding ledge next to one of the platform gates which provided some relief for her aching feet, unaccustomed as they were to wearing such high heels. And then she heard her phone emitting an odd but rhythmic beeping, like an extended notification, but not one she ever recalled having heard before. Puzzled, she took it out of her bag and swiped down to her notifications. As far as she could see, there was nothing, and she began to wonder if she had imagined it or if it had emanated from someone else's device. With a mental shrug, she decided that yes, she must have been mistaken. *No worries.* But now she had got her phone out, she might as well give Rose Morrison a ring now. It was a shame, but with the day she was having, she would have to put their meeting off, a great pity since she had been anxious to report what Nathan Duke had told her earlier about the woman's son. She swiped down and selected Rose's number, pressing the phone tight against her ear as she waited for it to ring. Hearing nothing after nearly a minute, she gave a puzzled glance at the screen. *Network unavailable.* She supposed that was hardly surprising with hundreds of folks trying to phone home or make other travel arrangements, but it was bloody inconvenient nonetheless. Not being exactly technically savvy, she wondered if WhatsApp would still be working. She tapped on the icon to open up her chats, selecting first Frank so that she could drop him a quick line to let him know what was happening. Mystified, she stared again at her phone. *This was odd.* All her messages to and from Frank seemed to have disappeared. Confused, she next looked at her recent chats with Lori. *Same thing, all gone, every one of them.* Trying to make sense of it, she reasoned that maybe all her message data was held on that thing they called the cloud, and so when the network was down you couldn't access anything. Sighing, she realised that whatever the reason, there was absolutely nothing she could do about it. Hopefully Frank would have heard about the situation on the news and would have headed home early to relieve their after-school child-minder. Hopefully too, the train company would kick in with their contingency plans and get her travelling westward as soon as they could, even if only on a bus. In the meantime, the best she could do was to find a seat, try and calm down a bit, and wait for the unfortunate situation to resolve itself. At least it would give her time to compose herself, and she could use the waiting period to figure out if there was anything more she should be doing to expedite the Rory Morrison investigation.

In the event, it was nearly two hours before the train operators managed to get anything running again, but at least they hadn't resorted to the dreaded replacement bus service, an outcome that would have tripled the journey time between Scotland's two largest cities. But even still, it was nearly eight o' clock before she was finally walking the last few hundred yards along the road on which lay their smart little rented bungalow.

Where three police cars stood waiting, their blue lights flashing ostentatiously.

Chapter 17

It had been almost nine o'clock in the evening when Jimmy had received the frantic call from his brother, and given he was nearly two thousand feet up on the Lairig Ghru pass, it was a bloody miracle he'd been able to get any kind of signal at all. Even still, he'd only caught about every third word as the call crackled and broke up, but it was enough to send his heart crashing crazily in his chest. *Maggie's been arrested for murder. She needs a solicitor urgently. You need to get your arse down here right away.* Which was not exactly going to be easy. He was half-way through one of his outward-bound courses, up in the mountains with his partner Stew Edwards and a bunch of overweight middle-managers from a Perth insurance company. An hour earlier they'd set up camp for the night, and a late dinner of unappetising tinned stew was bubbling away on the portable gas stoves. The next day was going to be the toughest part of the mission, with a climb up to the summit at nearly two thousand seven hundred feet before the long and tricky descent down the pass to Braemar. Given the fitness and experience of their charges, it wouldn't be safe for Stew to chaperone them on his own, and the last thing their embryonic but growing business needed was to leave a bunch of dead bodies littered all over the mountain. But after some head-scratching, Edwards had come up with a solution. He was pals with a woman from the Coylumbridge Mountain Rescue Team, a school-teacher called Philly Scott, and he would ask her to trek up to them at first light and take over from Jimmy. She'd get to the camp around mid-morning, Stew reckoned, which would afford the insurance guys a welcome lie-in and still give them plenty of time to get off the mountain before it started to get dark.

So at quarter to five in the morning, just as the sun was rising, Jimmy had slung his heavy rucksack on his back and headed at speed back down the pass towards the tiny settlement of Coylumbridge, a mile or so distant from Aviemore, where he could catch the train to Glasgow. It was about a ten-mile trek in all, and as expected he'd met Philly Scott when he'd completed about two-thirds of the journey. He'd exchanged a few words with her, getting out his Ordinance Survey map to show her the exact location of the camp. She was a super-fit-looking woman whom Jimmy estimated to be in her mid to late forties, and very attractive too. With some amusement, he guessed her willingness to drop everything and come to their rescue was because she was one of Stew's many female conquests. Generally-speaking he didn't approve of his business partner's promiscuity, but he had to admit that on this occasion it had come in very handy.

He'd got to Aviemore station just before eight o'clock to find a timetable in chaos. *Everything's been cancelled because of yesterday's cyber attack*, an apologetic uniformed official from the train company had told him. *All the trains are in the wrong place and so are the drivers.* But the good news had been that there was a replacement bus service, and the vehicle had been outside waiting to depart and scheduled to stop only at Perth and Dunblane. The journey south had been completed without major incident, the coach delivering them to the entrance of Queens Street station, from where he'd grabbed a taxi to take him to New Gorbals police station. Now he stood in the tiny entrance area, awaiting Frank's arrival. A few minutes later, he heard the click of the electronic lock as a door swung open and his brother stepped through.

'Thank God you got here so quick,' Frank said as he shook Jimmy's hand. 'The last twelve hours have been a bloody nightmare.'

'So what the hell happened?' Jimmy said. 'What are they saying she's done?'

'Murder, I told you that,' Frank said brusquely. 'The victim's that guy Urquhart, the MSP. He was found dead in a hotel room yesterday afternoon. He thought his partner was cheating on him so he had engaged Maggie to look into it. To be honest, they're being a bit cagey with me as far as the M-O goes, but I'm hearing around the station that he was stabbed. And the really bad news is they're saying that *they* were lovers, Maggie and him.'

Jimmy looked at him in disbelief. 'No no, that's complete crap, you know that. You don't believe that for one minute do you?'

Frank shrugged. 'Of course I don't. But they *did* meet at that fancy hotel for lunch yesterday. And she was all dolled up too, you know, make-up and a nice dress. I noticed that when she left home yesterday morning but I didn't want to say anything. And they're saying they've got evidence. I don't know exactly what, but that's what they're saying.'

'Okay,' Jimmy said, nodding. 'So who's the investigation officer then? Do you know him?'

'It's a *her*,' Frank said. 'DI Steph McNeil. I don't know her other than a brief nod across the canteen. Lexy says she's alright, but that she's mega-ambitious.'

'Is that a problem?'

Frank sighed. 'It might be, if the brass start pressurising her for a result. That's when even the most honest cop thinks about cutting corners if it's going to help advance their careers.'

'And how long have they still got with Maggie? She got arrested, when, fifteen, sixteen hours ago, something like that?'

'Aye, they dragged out the formalities to nearly eleven o'clock last night. They took her fingerprints and a DNA swab when she arrived, and then left her in a cell whilst they filled in all the paperwork. So by my reckoning they've got about another nine or ten hours to decide whether to charge her or not. Obviously they're not keeping me in the loop as far as that goes.'

'Aye, understandable,' Jimmy said. 'So I guess I'd better get in there then. Wish me luck.'

***

The interview room was stark and windowless, with a metal table and four chairs, and the recording machine mounted on a stand to one side. A desk sergeant escorted him along the corridor to the room, swiping an access card on arrival to temporarily unlock the door. 'In you go pal,' he said, ushering Jimmy through, then closing the door behind him.

Two police officers, both female, sat at the table opposite Maggie. As he entered, one spoke. 'So you're the solicitor I presume? I'm DI McNeil and this is DS Curran. Just so you know, your client has been arrested on the suspicion of the murder of Mr Jack Urquhart, and she has been held in custody for...' the detective glanced at her watch then paused as she did the calculation. '... for fourteen hours and twelve minutes approximately. She's been made aware of her rights but we understand that the suspect is herself a lawyer so she's probably well aware of them already.'

'Aye she is,' Jimmy said. 'And I'm Jimmy Stewart by the way.' He pulled out the chair next to Maggie and sat down, then leant over to her. 'How've you been?' he whispered, smiling.

'Pretty shit as you can imagine. I just want this mess cleared up so I can get out of here. How's Ollie, is he okay?' she added anxiously.

Jimmy nodded. 'He's fine, don't worry. Frank got back home at five last night and he'll be back to relieve the babysitter tonight in good time. The boy's being well taken care of.'

'Okay,' McNeil said, already showing some signs of irritation, 'we haven't got much time so we'll make a start.' She gave instructions to her detective-sergeant to switch on the recorder then said, 'So Magdalene Bainbridge, you're here on suspicion of the murder of Mr Jack Kingsley Urquhart, a man we are led to believe was your lover.' She paused, then leant forward to peer at Maggie, evidently awaiting a response.

'Don't need to say anything Maggie,' Jimmy said, swinging back on his metal chair, 'because I don't think that was actually a question. Carry on Detective Inspector, please.'

McNeil shrugged and directed a smile towards her DS. 'Okay, so what we're going to do is try to reconstruct the events of the afternoon in question. We'll go through it, and all you need to do is tell us if we're right or wrong, okay? So Magdalene, you had arranged to meet Mr Urquhart for lunch at the Royal Mile Grampian hotel, meeting him in the reception area at approximately twelve-forty, where it was reported you greeted each other with a warm embrace. A more-than-friends embrace, in fact, as it was described to us by an eye-witness.'

'No,' Maggie said, shaking her head vigorously. *'He* embraced *me*. I wasn't expecting it, and I didn't want it either. It took me completely by surprise.'

McNeil smiled. 'You say that, but we have a photograph of that aforementioned embrace from a reliable witness, a Government Minister no less, that perhaps suggests otherwise. For the tape, we're showing the suspect Exhibit One.' She nodded to the DS, who slid a print-out across the table.

Jimmy looked at it briefly and shrugged. 'Proves nothing. And it's obvious he's taking the initiative.'

'Miss Bainbridge has her arms around him too you will observe,' McNeil said, poking at the image with her forefinger before sliding it away again. 'As the witness observed, this looks a bit more than a just-friends thing.'

'But that was just a reflex action,' Maggie protested. 'Actually, I think he's a bit of a creep. Sorry, *was* a bit of a creep. I didn't want him touching me at all, no way.'

'So you say,' McNeil said. 'Anyway, the pair of you then sat down for your romantic lunch at twelve minutes to one, which continued, according to your waiter, to approximately five minutes past two, when we have evidence you both went up to a pre-booked room on the fifth floor for what we can assume was an encounter of a sexual nature.'

'No, absolutely *not,*' Maggie said, her voice rising to a shout. 'It *wasn't* a bloody romantic lunch as you put it. He's my client, nothing else, and he engaged my investigations agency because he thinks his partner Dominique Tremblay is having an affair. It was a business meeting pure and simple, and we only met at that hotel because it was convenient for his workplace. He chose it and I went along with it simply because he's the client. That's what you do in business. You do what the client wants.'

McNeil smiled. 'And does that include having intimate relations I wonder? Because your waiter told us you were holding hands at the table. Forgive me, but that doesn't suggest a business meeting to me.'

'That's ridiculous,' Maggie shouted again. 'He reached out and grabbed my hand. And yes, he told me had booked a room for us, but I told him to sling his hook in no uncertain terms. In fact, I said there and then that our business was over, and then I left no more than two minutes after that.'

The detective raised an eyebrow. 'That's your story I know. But there is a problem with it, isn't there?'

Jimmy looked at her sharply. 'What do you mean?'

'We have a witness. A chambermaid from the hotel who saw you both walking along the fifth-floor corridor that leads to room 507. According to the maid, you were holding hands with Mr Urquhart and smiling. Well, more than that to be honest. She described you as all loved-up and giggling like a schoolgirl.'

Maggie shook her head again. 'No, absolutely *not*. She's either mistaken or lying, can't you see that? Because after I told Urquhart what I thought about his vile proposition, I walked straight out of the door of the restaurant, and I was bloody seething I can tell you, all the way to the railway station.'

'And yet you didn't arrive home until nearly eight o'clock that evening. I don't think that timetable quite stacks up, do you? Our reconstruction suggests let's see... just over an hour for lunch, then maybe two hours or so having sex, during which there was an argument which resulted in the murder of the victim. At four to four-thirty you left the crime scene, made the twenty-minute walk to Waverley station and caught the next train to Glasgow.'

Jimmy gave her a dismissive look. 'Inspector, you must be the only person in Scotland who doesn't know about the cyber attack yesterday afternoon. No trains, no CCTV, no mobile networks, no nothing. Or maybe you're just choosing to ignore that inconvenient fact. Really, I'm not quite sure what you're trying to prove here.'

McNeil smiled. 'We're trying to show that Magdalene had ample time and opportunity to carry out the killing. And I think, as my thumb-nail reconstruction shows, my hypothesis is amply supported by the facts.'

Jimmy snorted. 'Facts, what facts? As far as I can see, all you have is that fairy-story you just told us, which I don't think somehow counts. And tell me, how exactly was Miss Bainbridge meant to have carried out this crime? Because you haven't even told us yet what was supposed to have happened.'

'He was found stabbed to death,' McNeil said blandly. 'What more do you need to know? And of course, Magdalene here knows already, doesn't she? She was there after all.'

Jimmy jumped in again before Maggie could protest. 'So you say. Me, I'm not hearing any evidence. So who found the body?' he asked, changing tack. 'The same chambermaid who supposedly saw them all loved up in the corridor, as you put it?'

'As it happens, yes,' McNeil said, sounding as if she was parting with the information with great reluctance.

'Aye, very convenient that,' Jimmy said. He was silent for a moment then said, 'So the problem I see - and one of many you've got actually - is that *Magdalene* here has got absolutely no motive and no prior evidence of intent to kill the victim. So good luck when you meet with the Procurator Fiscal guys in what, an hour or so? Because you'll need it.

This time McNeil laughed. 'Mr Stewart, right now I think we'll be happy just to put your client at the scene of the crime. Because we all know that nine times out of ten it's the other party in a relationship who is responsible. In fact, it's true ninety-nine times out of a hundred.'

'I keep telling you,' Maggie protested again. 'There *was* no bloody relationship. He was a client, that was all, pure and simple. Why can't you understand that? And I was *never* in that damn room, no matter what your supposed witness tells you.'

This time McNeil's face took on a smug expression, which suddenly made Jimmy's heart sink. *They must have something, something that's not going to be good for us*. And now he needed to flush it out, no matter how bad it turned out to be.

'Look, I'm enjoying this fairy story,' he said, speaking slowly, 'but if you're going to be charging my client, you're going to be needing some proper evidence, and right now you've got two-thirds of nothing at all. So unless you've got something else to tell us, I'm afraid this chat will be coming to an end, and pronto.'

McNeil smirked. 'Right now, our experts are examining the mobile telephone records of the victim. I suspect Miss Bainbridge, you will have some idea of what they will reveal.'

Maggie gave her a puzzled look. 'No I don't, why should I? I doubt if I exchanged more than half a dozen messages with him, if that.'

The DS looked at her boss and gave a smirk. 'Do you want to show them what we've found so far ma'am? Because I think it paints a different picture from the one she's been telling us. Pretty X-rated stuff if you ask me.'

McNeil laughed. 'Nah, let's wait until our guys have got the full story, shall we? The SOCO guys are still sweeping the room and they *never* come away empty-handed.'

Jimmy looked at Maggie who was sitting in absolute stunned silence, shaking her head.

'I never sent any messages like *that*,' she said, her voice reduced to a whisper. But then she was silent for a moment. 'Well, not about *sex*.'

***

At that point, DI McNeil had brought the interview to an abrupt close, dismissing Jimmy's attempts to find out what they intended to do next. A uniformed constable had arrived to take Maggie down to the detention cells, leaving Jimmy sitting alone to ponder whilst he waited for his escort back to the entrance area. Time was running out for the questioning detectives under the twenty-four hour custody rule, so he knew that the Procurator Fiscal's lawyer would already be running a fine-toothed comb over the evidence to see if the police had enough to charge Maggie at this early stage in the investigation. His assessment was that they didn't, because if they'd already had something really concrete - like for example her DNA or fingerprints on the murder weapon - that would have come up in the interview. But given this was only the day after the crime had been committed, there would still be a ton of forensic work going on at the scene and back at the labs. No, the chances were they would have to release her, but it would be with conditions, which would be in force for twenty-eight days, with the hundred-percent likelihood that she would be pulled back in for questioning multiple times during that period. And the undeniable fact was that the public show of intimacy with the victim, even if his attentions had been unwelcome, when added to the eye-witness statement of the chambermaid, was going to be hugely damaging. Of course Maggie had vehemently denied their veracity, and he had wanted so much to believe her, but then, when the police had brought up the subject of some unseen but apparently damning WhatsApp messages, she had seemed a little uncomfortable. The reason for that he intended to find out, but whatever way you looked at it, she was in deep trouble.

And now, in about thirty second's time, he was going to have to update Frank on how the interview had went, an assignment he was now approaching with a sinking heart. As it turned out, he didn't have to wait even that long, as he heard once again the click of the door unlocking, followed by Frank's head peering round the gap. 'Let's wander down to the canteen and we'll get ourselves a coffee,' his brother said as he led them along a corridor, 'and you can tell me everything that happened.' Jimmy sighed. *Aye, this was going to be awkward.*

Being late afternoon, the place was quiet, Frank directing him to a vacant table before going up to the counter to fetch their drinks. He returned with them a minute or so later, when Jimmy quickly updated him on everything he knew. As expected, it didn't go down well.

'Look, it's all mainly circumstantial,' he said, 'but they've got a witness who says she saw them in a corridor together. So one day into the investigation and she's already their prime suspect. And you know how it works Frank. They won't be looking too hard at anyone else. All their efforts will be going in to making the case against Maggie stick.' He paused for a moment. 'But you know it's all rubbish bruv, you know it is. Because she wouldn't do this.' He paused again. 'Maggie wouldn't cheat on you. She just wouldn't. Any more than you would cheat on her.'

'No, I know she wouldn't,' Frank said, but there was a doubtful look on his face, as if he was trying to convince himself.

'Come on,' Jimmy said, concerned. 'What's bugging you mate?'

'Ah, nothing. It's just me being an arse, that's all.'

'Come on. Tell me.'

Frank shrugged. 'Yesterday, when she went to that lunch with Urquhart. The dress she wore. She looked really... well, sexy in it. And she put on lots of make-up, and perfume too. I noticed, but I didn't say anything.'

'Maggie's a bloody nice-looking woman,' Jimmy said. 'I mean, it's a bit embarrassing for a future brother-in-law to say it, but she is. Or are you just too blind or stupid to see it? Oh and by the way, she was going out to lunch at a fancy hotel in Edinburgh, wasn't she, so *of course* she's going to dress up.' He shook his head and gave a wry smile. 'It's what women *do*, you eejit. Believe me, it's got absolutely nothing to do with us men, and I'm surprised you don't know that. It's so they look their best for all the other *women* who'll be there. It's *them* they want looking at them, not the men. One hundred percent.'

Frank smiled wanly. 'Aye, I suppose you're right.'

Jimmy nodded. 'You know I am. But the big question is, what the hell are we going to do now? Because we need to do something, and bloody quickly too. She's in serious trouble.'

And of course that didn't need explaining to his brother, because Frank knew only too well how the police worked in these circumstances. The truth was, the brass in general didn't give a stuff about justice. They just wanted results and they wanted them fast, and even if DI McNeil had her doubts about Maggie's guilt, she'd soon be under pressure to set them aside. A high-profile politician had been murdered and naturally it was the biggest story in town. From the brass's viewpoint, they'd already identified a perfect prime suspect, and with a bit more to-and-froing with the prosecutors to knock the evidence into shape, they would be able to charge her, leaving the courts to do the rest. *Result*. It wasn't difficult to see either how damning the case could be in the hand of a skilled and persuasive prosecuting advocate. Jimmy could easily imagine a damaging tale being woven, the story of the pretty private investigator who had fallen for the handsome and charismatic politician, she knowing that his relationship was falling apart and seeing the opportunity to replace his partner. Except that hadn't been part of Jack Urquhart's plan. He had just been looking for easy, no-strings-attached sex, and when the accused had realised that, she had murdered him in a fit of rage.

Sure, none of it was true, but it didn't have to be. It only needed to be convincing enough for a jury to say *guilty*.

Chapter 18

They'd kept her locked up to the very last possible moment allowed by the law, literally releasing her twenty-four hours to the second from when they had first taken her into custody. As a result, it was past eleven before they finally got away from the police station, and on the drive home, Frank had been uncharacteristically taciturn. She hadn't said much either, her head swirling with a million confusing thoughts, none of which made any sense. Added to all of that was of course concern for the well-being of her darling Ollie, presently safely tucked up in bed and under the supervision of the hastily-organised teenage babysitter, a reliable girl who was the daughter of one of their neighbours. With the prospect of her being arrested again without warning, Maggie would have to make more permanent arrangements for him to be looked after, and she couldn't ask her mum to come up to her, not with her father's condition continuing to deteriorate. So Ollie would have to go to Yorkshire, and that would mean there would be complications about his schooling, which she didn't want to even think about right now. Frank had continued to be uncommunicative over breakfast the next morning, and now as she walked the last few steps to her Byers Road office, she began to wonder if he might be doubting her version of what had happened. The thought of that made her sad and angry at the same time. How could he possibly believe she could be unfaithful to him? It was simply unthinkable. But with a pang of guilt she remembered her extended preparations for the lunch that day. That *bloody* dress and the make-up and the perfume too. Deep down, she knew she had done it all for Urquhart, driven by a stupid *stupid* schoolgirl vanity, and now she was paying the price. And then of course, there was that dumb bloody WhatsApp, definitely not her finest moment.

Lori was already there when she arrived of course, Maggie having come to learn that ridiculously early starts were just one of her brilliant new assistant's many excellent attributes, but, glory upon glory, Jimmy was there too. And goodness, how his presence was welcome right now.

'Morning morning,' he said brightly as she closed the door behind her. 'Me and young Lori here have just been getting reacquainted. She's been telling me all about her big surveillance job and the exciting car chase.'

'Well that particular investigation's well and truly over now,' Maggie said with an ironic smile, tossing her shoulder-bag on the floor as she plonked herself behind her desk, 'and that was even before I decided to murder the client. That is, if you believe the police and their spurned-lover motive.'

Lori gave her a serious look. 'I'm sorry Maggie, but you're just not the sort of woman who does sex, are you? I mean, no offence but you're more Women's Guild than sultry temptress.'

Maggie laughed. 'Well thanks very much for your support Lori. I suppose I should take it as a compliment. Or is it an insult?'

'No, honestly,' the girl said hurriedly, evidently worried she might have caused upset. 'But the thing is, *anyone* can see that just looking at you. And that would include a jury, *obviously*. Because they're just ordinary people I think.'

Jimmy grinned. 'Aye, twelve good men and true, although they use fifteen up here for some cases and they let women on as well of course. But you're right, they're just ordinary folks. And yes, they'll definitely be on Maggie's side.'

'You say that Jimmy, but I'm not so sure,' Maggie said ruefully, 'and I'm not certain Frank sees it that way at the moment either.'

Jimmy shook his head. 'No no, he's a hundred percent on your side, of course he is. He'll be fine. But let's not worry about him right now, it's you we need to be concerned about.' He paused for a moment before continuing, sounding as if he was reading from a list. 'So, they didn't charge you, which was good, because it means the Fiscal's office wasn't happy with the evidence at this point. You were released with conditions, which stay in force for twenty-eight days. We could go to court and contest them of course, but I don't think there's any point because I don't think we'd win. Do you agree Maggie?'

She nodded. 'Yeah, there would be no point. I need to hand in my passport and my mobile phone by five o'clock this evening, and I need to inform the police if I intend to travel more than thirty miles from my place of work. That's about it, isn't it? Yes...'

Suddenly, she remembered what had happened as she sat at Waverley Station waiting for her train back to Glasgow. 'My phone... so when I tried to WhatsApp Frank that day, I found all my messages had gone. Same thing with Lori's too. At the time I thought it was something to do with the cyber attack, but now I'm not so sure.'

'Aye, well I read there was stuff like that going on,' Lori said, evidently unconcerned. 'But you've got to hand it in haven't you? But there's nothing to worry about there I assume. No dodgy messages or suchlike.' It was posed more as a question than a statement, and it caused Maggie to shuffle uncomfortably.

'Look, I *did* send him a message. Just once. It was really stupid.'

Jimmy gave her a sharp look. 'What did it say?'

She shrugged. 'Not much. He was being a bit forward, something along the lines of *can we have dinner, and then we'll see what happens afterwards*. And I replied saying *what kind of woman do you think I am*, or something like that. But I added a smiley emoji...' She hesitated. 'And a kiss. I don't know why I did that. I think I was just trying to gently de-escalate the situation, but it wasn't my smartest move in retrospect.'

'What, is *that* all?' Lori said, laughing. 'All my pals add kisses to every message. Everybody does. It doesn't mean they want to shag you.'

Jimmy grinned. 'Well I wouldn't have put it that way Lori, but aye, lots of people do it automatically. It can be bloody annoying actually. But it doesn't mean anything.'

'But they'll think it's suspicious,' Maggie said suddenly. 'I mean, that all my messages have been suddenly deleted. They'll think I cleared my phone because I've got something to hide.'

'So it still there?' Lori said. 'That daft message. Is it still there?'

Maggie reached down for her bag and took out her phone, opened up WhatsApp and navigated to Urquhart's chat. And as she started to read the first of the messages, a wave of horror swept through her.

'Oh my God!' she blurted out. 'Oh my God!' Shocked and stunned, she thrust the phone in Lori's direction. 'Read that. And tell me I'm imagining it. *Please* tell me I'm imagining it.'

With a look of surprise, the girl took the phone and began to read. 'Bloody hell. God, Maggie, you didn't write any of this did you?'

'No!' Maggie said, her hands shooting up to cover her mouth. 'No way. Oh God, how the *hell* could this have happened?'

'What is it?' Jimmy said anxiously.

'Deep shit, that's what it is,' Lori said. 'Here, take a look.'

He took the phone from her and started to read the first message in the chat. 'Good God, this is bad, really bad.'

'But I *didn't* send these messages, you know I didn't,' Maggie said, her voice betraying desperation. 'Here, give me the phone, I need to delete them. Right now.'

'No,' Jimmy said firmly, stretching his arm out to move the device out of her reach. 'You didn't write them and you didn't send them. So we need them as evidence.' He took out his own phone from his pocket. 'I'm going to photograph them and then I'm going to email them to

Frank, as insurance, in case down the line there's any funny business with my phone too.'

She was silent for several seconds as she desperately tried to process what was happening. Jimmy was right of course, because if she *was* the murderer, and she *had* composed these highly-explicit messages to Jack Urquhart, surely the first thing she would have done following her arrest was to delete them before she had to hand over her phone to the police? But how had they got there, that was the question? Something strange had happened to her phone on the day of the murder, and it must be the case that somehow this devastating development had to be connected to that, even if she had no idea how. But there was one thing she was now certain of, even if she hadn't been before.

Someone was trying to frame her for the murder of Jack Urquhart.

***

Earlier, Frank's head had been spinning as he'd hung about outside the office of ACC Natalie Young, waiting to be summoned for what he had known would be a stern talking-to. The news about the incriminating WhatsApp messages that had been found on Maggie's phone, conveyed to him in an urgent call from his brother Jimmy ten minutes earlier, had added to the bizarre confusion surrounding the last twenty-four hours, and for all his head-scratching, he'd been unable to make any sense of it at all. But now, despite the meeting with ACC Young having gone exactly as he had expected it to - that is, badly - the fog was beginning to lift and for the first time he could see a way forward, albeit along a path that was still rather dimly-lit. A path that led, once again, to the canteen at New Gorbals police station.

Having grabbed a coffee and a chocolate bar, he selected a quiet table along the far wall, sat down and took out his phone, selecting an entry from his *frequent* list. He paused for a moment before he tapped the number, stealing a wry glance at his watch then letting out a restrained laugh. Aye, it was no more than five minutes since he'd exited the ACC's office, where she had warned him in no uncertain terms that getting involved in his fiancé's murder investigation would be treated as both gross misconduct and an attempt to pervert the course of justice, which, she had explained as if he didn't know, was an *extremely* serious offence. So no more than five minutes since he was listening to her sanctimonious sermon, here he was, about to ignore it. *What the hell.* He clicked the number and waited for the recipient to pick up, which she eventually did after about a dozen rings.

'Hello Miss Campbell,' he said brightly. 'Long time no speak with the queen of IT Forensics. Glad you could find the time to press that green button on your phone.'

'You called me the day before yesterday, when I got back to London,' she answered. *'What do you want now? I'm busy.'*

'Naturally,' he said, grinning to himself as he pictured her irritated expression. 'So, just a couple of quick things. Firstly, Carrie-Anne Fisher tells me that she's got four of the six signatures she needs to get you access to that big Langley Virginia toy-box you're so excited about, and she's hopeful that she'll get the last two by the end of the week.

Then I suppose you'll be given a user-code and a password and Robert will be your uncle.'

'They use twin-retina biometric recognition, not user codes,' she said dismissively, *'and three-factor authentication too. It's like mega secure. Next level.'*

He laughed. 'Good to know. Anyway, I've told Carrie-Anne how urgent it is, and so you should be getting your eyeballs scanned no later than twelve hundred hours Eastern Standard Time this Friday. That's five o'clock over here, just so you know.'

'*Cool.*'

'Aye, it is. That'll be good won't it?' He didn't wait for her to reply. 'So my next question is a daft one. I know it is, so please don't take the piss after I've asked it, because I'm just a simple man and I don't understand all of that next-level techie stuff that you love so much.'

He heard her chuckle, which was not exactly a common event. Taking advantage, he pressed on. 'So the question is Eleanor, is it possible to deep fake text messages? Or to be more exact, WhatsApp messages, although I'm not sure what the difference is. And I don't know if deep fake is the right term by the way.'

'They're like encrypted,' she said, then fell silent. He waited patiently, but evidently she wasn't proposing to offer further elaboration.

'Right, I think I know what that means,' he said. 'It's like some sort of code or cipher, isn't it? But I'm not sure it answers my question. And I'm really scratching my head to work out what it all means.'

She gave a short-tempered *harrumph. 'Tell me what's happened.'*

He smiled to himself, as he recognised Eleanor's natural curiosity about any technical poser starting to overcome her natural obstructiveness.

'It's my Maggie,' he said quickly. 'She's found some messages on her mobile that she definitely didn't write or send.' And then, as he said it, he suddenly had a thought. 'Eleanor, this is exactly like that case we had a couple of years back, that Salisbury Plain one, isn't it? You know, that phone cloning thing and these IM-something-or-other numbers you told me about.'

'No it isn't. Nothing like it,' she replied, her tone scathing. This was good, Frank thought. Now there was every chance he would be at the end of a long and complex technical explanation, mainly designed to demonstrate how dumb he was. And he wasn't the least bit bothered about this, because he knew it wasn't personal. Eleanor was like this with everyone, and if he could manage to listen without interrupting - because Eleanor *hated* to be interrupted during her monologues - there was every chance he would find out what he needed to know.

'So, tell me more,' he said, suppressing a grin, 'and please, in words of one syllable or less.'

'You can't clone WhatsApp messages,' she said. *'The technology is hyper-secure and it uses like a secret two-fifty-*

six-bit algorithm to tie the physical device to the messaging account. They designed it specifically for privacy. Even law enforcement agencies aren't allowed access. And that obviously can also prevent cloning hacks by bad actors.'

He didn't begin to understand the technicalities, but with a sinking heart, he thought he might know the consequences. 'So you're saying it's not possible? I mean to plant WhatsApps on somebody's phone, if that's the right terminology?'

'Someone could steal the phone and then give it back. Like, obviously.'

He nodded. 'Aye, I know, but I don't think that was what happened.' He paused for a moment as something came back to him. 'Listen, Maggie said that on the day of the crime she thought she heard a sort of weird *beep-beep-beep* on her phone, but of a kind she'd never heard before. And then when she looked, she saw she'd lost a ton of her messages. It was that day when the railways suffered that big cyber attack and some of the phone networks were down too I think.'

There was silence at the end of the phone, and for a moment he wondered if she had hung up on him, an occurrence that wouldn't have been unique in his dealings with the tricky forensic guru. But no, it appeared she had simply been thinking, because she suddenly said, *'Handshake.'*

'What?' he said, mystified.

'I said handshake,' she repeated. *'Handshake.'*

'Aye, I know what you said, but what does it mean?'

'It's what you do when you're trying to establish a network connection to a remote device. That's what Maggie would have heard. The handshake sequence.'

'Sorry, not with you,' he said truthfully.

'The hackers speed-cycle through a megabase of automated high-resolution cipher combinations to crack the connection credentials,' she said, her tone authoritative. He assumed he was meant to find this helpful, and although it wasn't, he didn't want her detecting the fact and then throwing a paddy and storming off in a huff, if that wasn't an over-mixing of the metaphors.

'Aye, I kinda get that,' he lied, but quite convincingly he thought. 'And that means they can then do stuff on the phone, like deleting or writing WhatsApp messages?'

'Deletion, defo,' Eleanor said. *'It's what hackers like to do most because they're bad guys and vandals at heart. But writing and sending WhatsApps is a lot more difficult. In fact, I don't know how it can be done. You'd need like mega technical capability. Off the scale.'*

'Because of that hyper-secure algorithm thing you just told me about?'

'Like yeah.'

'But do you think Maggie's phone could have been the victim of one of these handshake things?' he persisted.

'Yeah. Possibly. If that was the notification she thought she heard.'

'But how could you find out for definite?' he pressed. 'Would you need to get your hands on the phone itself?' And then he stopped himself, because there was no way he could get Eleanor involved in this, given what the ACC had said to him ten minutes earlier. Backpedalling, he said, 'Look, I'm not asking for your help, just to be absolutely clear, I'm just looking for information. But *someone* would have to get their hands on it physically, am I right?'

'No', she answered instantly. *'The actual phone tells you nothing. Someone would need access to the phone company data logs, but then it's definite the hackers would have covered their tracks. I would,'* she added. *'Defo.'*

'That doesn't sound too good,' Frank said, his heart sinking. 'Does that mean that there's nothing anybody can do then?'

'I could take a look,' Eleanor said unexpectedly. *'It's like super-interesting. I just need her number.'*

'Absolutely no way,' he shot back, alarmed. 'You can't go within a million miles of this and that's a bloody order.'

'You're not my boss,' she said, matter-of-factly. *'Patrick is my boss. I only take orders from Patrick. I can ask him.'*

'Don't bloody touch this,' he said, now seriously worried about what he had unleashed. 'I mean it Eleanor, this is a murder enquiry.'

There was more silence at the end of the line, which he took as a good sign, signalling that she recognised the seriousness of the situation.

'I won't', she said finally. *'Promise. But I'm gonna check something out that I saw in a GCHQ technical bulletin the other day.'*

'Well, what's that?' he said, concerned.

'There's credible evidence that Chinese hackers might have cracked the WhatsApp security algorithm.'

***

If his head had been spinning before, then it was going round about a thousand times quicker after his conversation with Eleanor. Somehow, someone had achieved the impossible by faking WhatsApp messages on Maggie's phone. The objective was to frame her for Urquhart's murder, that seemed clear, but *why* and *who*? The whole thing was just totally bizarre and unfathomable, making no sense whatsoever. And the crazy thing was, whoever was behind this had access to state-of the-art technology, a technology that, if Eleanor was to be believed, originally emanated from the Chinese state. Eleanor and her former MI6 mate Zak had told him all about the Dark Web of course, where criminals could buy and sell that sort of stuff like it was on Amazon. Maybe that's where they had got it, and now they -whoever *they* were - were using it against his Maggie. But no, that stretched the bounds of credibility too far. But then again, so did the situation with Donnie Morrison. Someone very clever had gone to enormous trouble to fake these videos of him with Jade Niven, and as Frank drained the last dregs from his coffee cup, the similarities between the two cases came into stark focus. On the face of it, there was absolutely no way they could be connected, and yet they were, if only by their common use of high-tech capability to frame an innocent person.

He was abruptly jerked out of his contemplations by the ringing of his phone. Glancing down, he saw it was DC Lexy McDonald. 'Hi Lexy,' he said. 'How's tricks?'

She didn't answer immediately. *'Sir, there's been a development. In Maggie's case.'* Her voice was quiet and she spoke slowly, as if she wished to put off the reason for her call for as long as she could. *'I heard it on the station grapevine and I thought you needed to know. It's not good sir.'*

'What is it?' he said, feeling his mouth start to dry.

He heard her draw breath. *'The forensic guys have found something sir.'* She paused again. *'In the hotel room. It was some hair on the pillow. And there's been a positive DNA match. I'm sorry sir. Look, have to go.'* Abruptly, she hung up, evidently not wishing to extend the difficult conversation a second longer than necessary. Trying desperately to process this new and devastating information, Frank began to properly realise the mess that Maggie was now in. The incriminating phone messages, the public displays of intimacy during that lunch, the eye-witness statement from the chamber-maid, and now this bombshell. Anytime soon, she was going to be arrested and charged with the murder of Jack Urquhart. It was certain she would be remanded in prison awaiting trial, a process that could take nine months or more given the current backlog in the courts. Instantly, he came to a decision, one that had every prospect of going seriously pear-shaped, a decision that could destroy the lives of everyone and everything it came into contact with. *But he had no choice.*

Grabbing his phone, he stabbed a thick finger on his brother's number. Jimmy answered within a couple of rings.

'Hey Frank,' he said in a breezy tone, unaware of what was coming. *'I'm just here in the office with Maggie and Lori. How's it going pal?'*

'Totally rubbish, since you ask,' Frank said. 'Listen, you need to get Maggie out of Glasgow, and fast. I don't care where you take her, but just get her as far away from here as possible. And it's bloody important you don't tell me where she's going, okay? Just get it done, and get it done quick.'

Chapter 19

It had been one hell of a twenty-four hours, that was for sure. One moment she had been sitting in the office with her colleagues, desperately trying to figure out what to do about the calamity that had befallen her, the next, Jimmy was pushing her out through the door and into Byers Road with barely a word of explanation. His car had been parked a few streets away, and he had driven the few miles back to Milngavie at what she considered a dangerous speed. They'd gone straight to the school, where Maggie had made up a story of a surprise phone call from the doctor's surgery offering an immediate appointment for Ollie due to a cancellation. Two minutes later, she had been stuffing some clothes and their tooth-brushes into a sports bag and throwing it into the boot. They had driven north without stopping until they reached the outskirts of Perth, where, unexpectedly but evidently pre-arranged, Jimmy had pulled into a service area. Just a few minutes later, she and her little son were being bundled into an old Land Rover driven by Jimmy's business partner Stew Edwards. She didn't know the roads up in that part of the world, but she'd seen signposts first for Blairgowrie and then Braemar, so had had a pretty good idea where they were heading. Ollie, of course, had been buzzing with excitement at this great adventure; she was quite a bit less excited as it began to dawn on her that she was now a fugitive from the law. She guessed her face would soon be all over the media, like an outlaw on one of these old Wild West posters. *Danger! Have You Seen This Woman?* Wryly she wondered if they might offer a reward, dead or alive.

Stew had been his normal chatty self on the journey north, evidently unconcerned that he was now an accessory to a serious crime. 'I've got a nice little hidey-hole up there,' he'd explained, then lowered his voice to a whisper, presumably so that Ollie couldn't hear. 'It's a *bit* embarrassing, but I sometimes take the occasional woman or two there for.. well, you know what for.' He'd grinned at that, showing no hint of embarrassment at all as far as Maggie could detect. 'I've got it done up lovely, you and Ollie will be really comfortable. And it's in the middle of nowhere. In fact, you head for the middle of nowhere and keep going. But it's got broadband, so you can be holed up there for weeks, no bother at all. Although Tesco won't deliver. That's the only problem.' She wasn't sure if he'd been joking or not.

His description had proved accurate in regard to both remoteness and comfort, the small stone-built structure surrounded by pine trees and located at the end of a rough bridleway nearly three miles distant from the main road. She guessed it had perhaps been a shepherd's hut at one time in its history, but now it had been extended and refurbished to form a cosy holiday bolt-hole, comprising a combined living area and kitchen with an open fireplace and a separate bedroom, dominated by a king-size bed warmly dressed in linen duvet and pillows. In the corner, Stew had erected a camp-bed for Ollie, which her son had seized upon with great joy. Their host was right, they *would* be very comfortable here. Until the police helicopters and their searchlights started circling overhead, she thought with wry amusement. Although the fact was, tucked in amongst thick trees as the place was, you could easily miss it even if you were just a few metres away. Stew had only waited with them for ten minutes or so, just long enough to show them where everything was and how the small bottled gas stove worked. Before he left, he'd handed Maggie a phone. 'Burner,' he'd said, this time with a slight hint of shame. 'Always got a few kicking around. I've given Jimmy one too. Very handy, if you know what I mean. It's already set up with the Wi-Fi password, but there isn't a phone signal for about ten miles so don't go wandering in the woods.'

Now it was half-past-eight the next morning, and an earlier email from Jimmy had invited her to a video call with himself, Frank and Lori. She settled herself on the comfortable sofa and punched in the number of his just-acquired burner phone, courtesy of Stew. Her assumption was that Jimmy and Lori would be in the office, but as for Frank, she had no idea, wondering with huge trepidation whether he was going to tell her that he had gone on the run too. But as it happened, they were all together, she instantly recognising the venue as the Bikini Barista cafe, and each of them was already equipped with steaming coffees.

Frank spoke first, his sagging features suggesting he hadn't slept much last night, his voice rough, the tone anxious. 'How are you Maggie? And how's Ollie? Both okay? And remember, I don't know where you are and I don't want you to tell me. Because obviously I'm going to be hauled in and questioned about this, as soon as they realise you've gone AWOL.'

Maggie gave a half-smile. 'Actually, I've no idea where we are. I remember we passed a sign saying eleven miles to

Braemar but other than that, I haven't a clue. But yeah, we're both fine. Ollie's still asleep.'

'That's great,' Frank said, taking a sip of his drink. 'Now obviously, what I asked you to do was a bloody drastic step, and I can't give any promises that it won't seriously unravel and slap us all in the face big-time. But what we have to remember through all of this is that you, Maggie, are totally innocent, and when we prove this - and believe me, we bloody well will, no matter what it takes - then we'll all be in the clear. That's how I'm justifying my actions, and I'll tell you all now, just so you know, that I take full responsibility for any consequences that come out of this. Me, and me alone.'

'I wasn't exactly kidnapped, was I?' Maggie said. 'I've got massive reservations about this, I can't deny that, but I'm here, aren't I? My own decision.'

'Aye, I know,' Frank said, 'and it's bloody serious for you, I appreciate that, and I'm worried sick about it too. But the evidence they've got, well it's frightening. The thing is, if I was in charge of a case like this, I'd probably be pressing for charges myself, that's what's so scary. And there's every chance a jury would convict you, and then it might take years and years for an appeal to be heard, and even then it might not be successful.' He paused for a moment, then shook his head. 'And there was *no way* I was subjecting you to that Maggie. No way.'

'So what we gonnae do then?' Lori asked anxiously. 'Because we've got to do something dead quick, because they *will* find her, won't they? Eventually. It might take them a week, but they will.'

Frank nodded. 'Aye, you're correct Lori. But the clock's not *quite* started ticking yet. Right now DI McNeil and her pals will be sitting down with the Fiscal's lawyers over at New Gorbals nick, just making sure that they've got enough to press the *charge* button. Assuming they get the nod, which they will, then they'll send out the blue lights to bring her in. At which point, they'll discover that Maggie has legged it.'

'And then they'll start asking *you* questions,' Maggie said, concerned. 'And they'll soon find out too that I disappeared yesterday around midday if they talk to Ollie's school. So what are you going to say about that, when they ask you *did you know*?'

He gave a wry smile. 'I hate to admit it, but I'll be shamelessly lying, although only in the interests of justice, mind. I'll tell them we had a big row at breakfast about the wedding, and that you said you were minded to call it off, and you threatened to go back to London that very day. I thought it would all blow over, but when I got back home last night I was devastated to find you weren't there. I tried to call you, but you'd left your phone behind on the kitchen table, presumably because you knew it had to be handed into the police. I tried your parents and phoned your place in London and got no answer, and since then I've been worried sick, because I've no idea where you might have gone.'

'Some story,' Jimmy said. 'Almost believable in fact.'

Frank smiled. 'Thanks. They'll suspect it's bollocks of course, but there's no way they'll be able to prove otherwise for a while. But anyway, we can worry about that later. As Lori says, we have to do something, and that's why we're here, to work out what that something should be.' He paused again to take another swig of his coffee. 'So, I'll give you my take on things first and if any of you have anything to add, don't hold back. We need all our brains firing on all cylinders if we're going to crack this. All agreed?'

'Agreed,' Jimmy and Lori said, simultaneously.

'Agreed,' Maggie said, although she was unsure if her brain was capable of firing on any cylinders at all, given the turmoil of the preceding few hours.

'Right,' Frank said briskly. 'We're going to have to have two lines of attack here. The first, and the most important, is to prove that the so-called evidence they've got against Maggie is a huge pile of poo. *We* know that it is, and we know too that it's all part of a conspiracy to frame her, orchestrated by person or persons unknown, for reasons that are also unknown.'

'But what have they got, really?' Jimmy said. 'A few dodgy WhatsApps, a suspect eye-witness statement, a strand of Maggie's hair. It's not much, is it?'

'Aye, it's not much but it's enough,' Frank said. 'That's my worry. But okay then, where do we start? Suggestions anyone?'

Lori jumped in before anyone else could answer. 'But they're all lies, right? Every one of them. Which is good.'

Maggie wasn't quite sure she had heard properly. 'Did you say it's *good*?' she asked.

'Yeah, I did,' Lori said, her expression animated. 'You see, if we prove *one* of them is a lie, then they all like *collapse*, don't they? All of them. If one's a lie, they must all be.'

Frank nodded, although his frown suggested that he didn't agree one hundred percent with her contention. 'Aye, well there is something in that Lori, but the trouble is, if the SIO is determined enough, they might still try to push through the conviction, lies or no lies.'

'But you were telling me it was going to be impossible to prove how these WhatsApps got there, weren't you?' Jimmy said to Frank. 'So no point in wasting time on *them* right now, is there?'

'It's got to be the chambermaid first,' Maggie interjected. 'She lied, she *must* have, or at least she was badly mistaken. If we get her to admit that, then they can't put me at the scene of the crime. Then it gets very difficult for them.'

'But what about the hair on the pillow?' Lori asked.

'A defence barrister would have no trouble shooting that down in flames,' Jimmy said confidently. 'Okay, it's Maggie's hair, but remember how Urquhart kissed her when he arrived for lunch? Their heads came together, so a strand could easily have got transferred during that encounter. And remember, the police have a photograph of the embrace so there's no denying it happened. No, I don't think there's much of a chance they could build a case around *that*. Not on its own. It's flimsy to say the least.'

'Aye, well maybe,' Frank said, his tone dubious. 'But regardless, I agree it makes sense to start with the chambermaid. That's going to be a job for Jimmy or Lori, or both. Obviously it would be a lot easier if I waltzed in flashing my warrant card and started asking questions, but if I did that, I suspect it would be my last act as a policeman.'

'No bother,' Jimmy said. 'Me and Lori will get our heads together with Maggie and work out a plan.' He looked straight at his phone and smiled at her. 'Is that okay boss?'

She laughed. 'Have you forgotten, I'm not your boss any more. But yes, we can chat it through.'

'Great stuff,' Frank said. 'So the other big thing we need to do is *one*, see if we can work out who actually *did* kill Urquhart, or at least work out what the motive was, and *two*, try and figure out *how* it was done. This will be a lot more difficult, obviously. And before you ask, this will be purely brain-work, because with this being a live murder case, there's a limit to how much tramping all over a police enquiry we can do. It'll be the exercising of the little grey cells, as some fat fictional detective once said.' Lori gave him a blank look, and Maggie wondered if she'd ever heard of either Poirot or indeed Agatha Christie.

'But to help you with this,' Frank continued, 'we need to consider the absolutely crazy stuff that's going down in our country right now, and all of it, I should say, is centred around bloody politics. We've got Jack Urquhart being murdered at the start of a leadership contest. We've got that old goat Donnie Morrison being discredited by way of a very sophisticated honey-trap sting or scam, call it what you will. We've got the emergence of numerous scandals linked to senior figures in the ruling Nationalist government, as joyfully reported by Dominique Tremblay and the Globe. And last, but definitely not least, we've got the meteoric rise of Tommy and Sienna Taggart and their ghastly Scottish Freedom Party.' He paused for a moment to take another sip from his coffee, giving it a look of mild disappointment when he realised it was empty. 'You see, that's just way too much *stuff* for a sleepy nation like ours, so I'm telling you something. It's all linked together, every last bit of it. I don't know *how*, and I don't know *why*, but if and when we figure it all out, we'll have the key to this whole bloody blancmange.'

He paused again, this time evidently for effect. 'So that's your mission folks, simple and straightforward. Figure it all out. And quick as you like.' He picked up his cardboard cup, and threw it expertly into the nearby waste-bin. 'Oh and just one more thing,' he said, his comment aimed at Jimmy and Lori. 'I wouldn't be going back to the office this morning, because I think it might be getting a visit from the police sometime soon. So, if you don't mind, I'll love you and leave you.'

And he was right of course, Maggie thought after the call had ended, about everything being linked together. There was just too much that had happened in such a short space of time for it to be mere coincidence, she totally agreed with that. But Frank had forgotten something else, something so equally extraordinary that it surely had to be added to the mix. That was of course the Royal Mile Murders. Three gay men had been killed during the exact-same period that all of these political shenanigans had been in full flight, their bodies being discovered barely a mile away from the Parliament building itself. And what of Rory

Morrison, another gay man and the estranged son of the politician caught in a honey-trap conspiracy? A gay man who had disappeared about the same time as everything else that was happening, after giving up his job for a life of hedonism on a Mediterranean island? Was that just a coincidence too? *No way.*

Her own situation might be a mess, Maggie reflected, there was no denying that, but she had promised Rose Morrison she would find out what had happened to her son, and it was a promise she fully intended to keep. But where to start, that was the question, with their enquiries on Ibiza having so far produced nothing, and precious few other leads to go on. There was *one* thing that had been preying on her mind, and that was the conflicting reports that she had got from Dominique Tremblay and the IT geek Nathan Duke about Rory's mood prior to him taking off to Ibiza. According to Tremblay, Rory couldn't stop talking about it in the days and weeks before, whereas according to Duke, a young man who was close enough to Rory to be considered a friend, he hadn't mentioned it at all. Kicking herself, she realised that with an earlier and more methodical review of what she knew about the case, she might have noticed the variation before. But whether she had or whether she hadn't, she couldn't help but recognise it for what it was.

Clutching at straws.

Chapter 20

Frank had expected it all to kick off big-time as soon as Maggie's disappearance was discovered, and he hadn't been disappointed. After the video call with the Bainbridge team, he'd sped back to New Gorbals nick, where he had been accosted on arrival by his mate DC Lexy McDonald, keen to share some sensational breaking news with him. An hour earlier, two squad cars had simultaneously been dispatched to arrest murder suspect Magdalene Bainbridge, one to her rented Milngavie bungalow and one to her Byers Road office, where in both locations they had found her not present. On hearing of this disturbing setback, the ACC had dragged DI McNeil into her lair, where presumably the detective was on the end of a severe bollocking for not having arrested the prime suspect when she'd had the chance.

Having conveyed all of this to Frank with barely-hidden amusement, Lexy had suggested they slink off down to the canteen for a late breakfast roll and a quick update on the Morrison investigation, where apparently there had been developments. The comestibles ordered and taken delivery of, they were now occupying a quiet table tucked away in the corner, he anxious to keep as low a profile as possible. Not that this was going to be able to be maintained for long, especially after Lexy said, 'And by the way sir, ACC Young's after you next, once she's done with the Inspector. Is there anything you want to tell me?'

'Maggie's left me I think,' he said, cursing inwardly at having to spout this necessary deception. 'We've not been getting on, and it's all just come to a head, with everything that's happening to her. She's just not been herself, and I'm worried sick of course.'

Lexy gave him a questioning look. 'I don't mean to be disrespectful sir, but was that a rehearsal of what you're going to say to the ACC?'

'Was I that terrible?' he asked ruefully.

'I've seen worst acting sir,' she replied, grinning, 'but only at my four-year-old niece's Nativity play.'

He smiled. 'Aye it's a fair cop. But look, just to make it absolutely clear, I don't want you going within a million miles of the Urquhart investigation. It would be bad for you and, much more importantly, it would be bad for me too. And that's all I'm saying on the subject.'

She laughed. 'I understand how bad it would be for you sir. And seriously, I won't go anywhere near it either. My career's too important to me, you know that.'

He nodded. 'As it bloody well should be too. But we'll see what the ACC's got to say for herself in a bit. Anyway, you told me you had some updates on the Morrison deep-fake investigation. So come on, spill the beans.'

'Right sir. So as you'll remember, I've been looking into Jade Niven to see what we can find out about her, and I'll tell you something sir, there something really dodgy going on there. We knew that before of course,' she added, anticipating his interjection, 'but this is *really* dodgy. Off the scale.'

'How so?' he asked, interested.

'Well, as far as her Seedhill flat and the landlord chucking her out and all that are concerned, that was definitely a lie. I talked to the guy on the phone, and he said straight off he had no problems with her at all. She'd only been there three months for a start, but the rent had come in every month on the dot, and far from wanting to chuck her out, he wished that all his tenants were as reliable. And the second thing was, he said he didn't think she actually lived there, or at least she was taking her time moving in. Because anytime he called round she wasn't there, and he says none of the neighbours ever remembered seeing her either.'

'I thought she had a kid too,' Frank said. 'Or did I get that wrong?'

'No you're right sir. Jade told Donnie Morrison that she was the single mother of an eleven-year old boy. But I'm thinking that might have been a lie too, to garner more sympathy from Morrison. Because no-one had ever seen the kid either.'

'Interesting,' Frank said. 'And she doesn't live there now, I think I remember hearing. Have you managed to track her down? Mind you, I know it was a couple of years ago now since it all happened.'

She shook her head. 'Well that's the weird thing, I haven't. I know it's mental sir, but the fact is, I'm beginning to think that Jade Niven doesn't actually exist at all. Because I checked with HMRC, and there's no record of a National Insurance number for anyone with that name and that approximate date of birth. And no tax records either, obviously.'

'She was mid or maybe late thirties wasn't she?'

'That's what the videos suggests sir, yes. But there's no-one on their database that fits that age profile.'

Frank nodded. 'But she *did* meet with Morrison, whoever she was. So does that mean that Paddy, our slippery host at the Greenock Tavern, was paying Miss Whoever cash in hand?'

She gave him a wry smile. 'Frenchie got to the bottom of all that sir. He had a chat with Paddy like you asked him to.'

He laughed. 'Aye, I know all about Ronnie's chats. Is the guy still walking?'

'Just about, I think,' she said, smiling. 'Apparently, Jade approached Paddy with a story that she was trying to build up her CV and she needed some bar-work experience, so she would work for below minimum wage, cash in hand. And of course Paddy, being a slimy git, agreed right away. And guess what else sir?' she continued.

Frank had already worked it out. 'Let me think.' He stroked his chin in an exaggerated manner then said, 'There's no such person as Kylie Gilmour, our mystery video director and fellow part-time barmaid. Am I right?'

'Got it in one sir,' Lexy said, impressed. 'Paddy said Jade slipped him a hundred quid to say it was this Kylie woman, if anybody asked who took the videos.'

'But the thing is,' Frank said, thinking out loud, 'the Jade lassie did media interviews at the time didn't she? Telly and everything. So she was definitely real.'

'Yes she did sir', Lexy agreed, 'but they wouldn't have dug very deep into her background. And in fact, most of her media work was with Dominique Tremblay of the Globe. Now *there's* a coincidence for you.'

'Aye, interesting that,' he said. 'But what about us cops? Because we do an identity check as a matter of course when we bring someone in for questioning. Matter of routine.'

'She was never questioned,' Lexy said. 'Because no-one believed a word of what Morrison was saying at the time. It all sounded totally ridiculous when he claimed these videos must have been faked, so the police up here didn't want to know. Understandably I think, looking back.'

'Of course,' Frank said, nodding. 'Well I tell you what, this is bloody good work from both of you. It absolutely proves that Donnie Morrison was set up, even if we kinda knew that already. All we need now is for wee Eleanor to unravel the provenance of these videos and we might even get to know who was behind it all.' He paused for a moment. 'Although what I don't understand is, if they were so desperate to get rid of him, why they didn't just wrap him up in a concrete suit and chuck him into the Clyde.'

'I do, at least I *think* I do sir,' Lexy said. 'This way, they discredited him, and by default they discredited the Nationalist party too. That's what it was really all about sir. Yes, whoever was behind this wanted him to stand down from his seat, but they wanted to throw mud at the Nationalists at the same time. Whereas if they'd killed him, there would be a wave of sympathy for the ruling party. That's what I think anyway.'

'Aye, that makes sense,' he conceded. 'Anyway, a good job well done, and maybe that'll win me some credit with the ACC, even although I didn't do anything myself.' He paused for a moment, and as he did so, reality suddenly struck. 'Although I wouldn't be surprised if she decides to arrest me on the spot instead. So let's enjoy this breakfast, because if they bang me up, we won't be seeing one another for a while.'

***

Suspended from duty. It wasn't his worst-case scenario, but it was bloody not far off. The ACC had started by asking him if he knew where Maggie was, which he could answer truthfully. But after that, the meeting had gone rapidly downhill. The next question was the bloody obvious one, asking whether he'd had any involvement in her disappearance, which of course forced him to respond with a lie. Squirming inside, he'd reprised the Maggie's-left-me tale, his spirits plunging as he realised the depth of the hole he was digging for himself. Unamused, the ACC had informed him that his behaviour would be the subject of a formal disciplinary enquiry, but until then he was to be suspended from all duties on full pay, pending its outcome. A DCI would be appointed to take over the Taggart and Morrison enquiries, and after effecting a handover of all relevant information, he should stay away from all Police Scotland premises until further notice. Less than five minutes after entering her office, he was back out in the corridor, his world crashing around him. What an *idiot* he had been, to ever think he could get away with this farrago. His own predicament was bad, sure it was, but it was Maggie who was his only concern. She'd had plans to launch a legal practice alongside her detective agency. Well that was never going to happen now, not now and not ever. The regulators barred anyone with a criminal record from practicing, and that's what Maggie was going to end up with, one way or another. What *madness* had persuaded him to take this course of action, to make his Maggie a fugitive from the law, when he should have entrusted her fate to the Scottish Criminal Justice system? Maybe it still wasn't too late, maybe she should hand herself in and he would take the blame for persuading her to run away against her better judgement. But now, to coin a cliché, he was up the creek without a paddle, cut off from the vast investigative resources of his employer, and cut off too from the irreplaceable talents of Eleanor, Lexy and Ronnie. *Aye, you're a real genius Frank Stewart*, he thought with growing self-disgust, *definitely your finest hour and make no mistake*. Dejected, he thrust his hands in his pockets and shuffled off towards the canteen. He was just pushing through the double doors when his phone rang. He removed it from his pocket, gave it a quick glance, then prodded the answer button.

'Well hello Ronnie, how's tricks? I've lost track, are you still in Glasgow?'

'Yeah guv, last day before I head back to the Smoke for a while,' French said. *'Catching the twelve o'clock train south. But I'm having an interesting chat at the moment with a guy.'*

'Oh really? Where are you?'

'Paisley Sorting Depot guv. It's a bloody massive place. Anyway, I've found a geezer who's willing to talk to me

about that postal vote stuff. It was a couple of years back mind, but he remembers it fine. Answar's the guy's name. He's an Asian guy obviously. And I get the feeling that they're not exactly champions of diversity on this shop floor.'

'Aye, I can imagine,' Frank said disapprovingly. 'And I bet the boy Answar's no fan of Tommy Taggart either.'

'No, he ain't. But anyway, Answar says he remembers some of them postal vote envelopes being opened by a couple of the shop floor lads, a pair of racist bastards he calls them. At the time he wanted to say something to management, he says, but he was worried about his job so he kept schtum. It doesn't prove anything guv, but I would say they were probably chucking away any that voted for the Nationalists. Not all of them, 'cos that would invite suspicion, but maybe enough to make a difference to the vote.'

'And did your boy have any idea why they were doing this? What I mean was, were they Taggart activists or what?'

'They might have been guv, but Answar reckons they were slipped quite a few quid, because he remembers them laughing and joking at the time about having a giant piss-up.'

'And do these guys still work there?'

'Yeah they do guv. Hang on a minute.' Ronnie was silent for a moment, Frank assuming he was scanning the sorting office to see if he could locate them. *'Yup, I can see them now. What do you want me to do? Shall I bring them in for a chat with you before I go?'*

'Eh, right...,' Frank said, then paused. 'So Ronnie, there's a bit of an issue with that...' Hesitantly, he explained the outcome of his meeting with ACC Young.

'They'll bring in a new DCI to take over my cases, and it wouldn't surprise me if they stand you down and use one of the local DC's instead. Sorry about that Ronnie, because I know how much you like your holidays up here.'

His reply surprised and touched Frank in equal measure. *'That's a bloody travesty guv, I'm really sorry to hear that. And as for me, I've only got a few more months before I retire and I don't want to be working with some other plonker. You're my guv, always will be.'*

'And I love you too Ronnie,' Frank replied, laughing. 'But listen, this will all sort itself out in time, so I'll say the same to you as I've said to Lexy and I'll be saying to Eleanor as well. I don't want you going anywhere near any of this, and especially not the Jack Urquhart murder case. Because I don't want to be responsible for you losing your pension. Understand?'

'Sorry guv, you're breaking up. Didn't hear that. Hello? Hello?' And then he hung up.

Frank grinned involuntarily and shook his head. It was Ronnie's inability or unwillingness to follow orders that had landed him in Department 12B's Atlee House in the first place, the Metropolitan Police's warehouse for mavericks, has-beens and never-had-it-in-the-first-place losers. Thirty-five years into his non-glittering career, Ronnie wasn't going to be changing any time soon. He just hoped that the corpulent DC wouldn't do anything really stupid. But then again, Ronnie was so lazy it took a lot to get him to do anything at all, stupid or otherwise. Now, to his great relief, Frank recognised his gloomy mood beginning to disperse, in no small measure because of his uplifting conversation with the incorrigible French.

Aye, they might have suspended him, but that didn't mean the fight for justice was over. *Au contraire.* His resources might be severely depleted, amounting to just three very amateur sleuths, but one was the woman he loved, the second was the brother he loved nearly as much, and the third was some mad ex-waitress lassie, new to the game but whom he suspected was easy to underestimate. The stakes were high, and failure would mean the end of his career and probably Maggie's too.

But failure wasn't an option he was contemplating.

Chapter 21

It had been six days, Jimmy reckoned, doing the calculation in his head, six long days of being able to do nothing useful to fix Maggie's awful situation, and six days where the four of them - himself, Maggie, Frank and Lori - had been by necessity *incommunicado*. The police had hauled him and Lori in of course, immediately they had discovered that Maggie was missing, to 'help with their enquiries', as the over-used euphemism put it. These sessions, stretching over the full twenty-four hours allowed by the law and incorporating a overnight stay in the luxurious detention cells of New Gorbals police station, had certainly been no pleasure cruise. He knew that his business partner Stew had taken her to his secret love-nest somewhere up in the Grampian Mountains, although luckily he didn't know its exact location, which allowed him to reply half-truthfully to their insistent questioning. But it would only have taken one call to Stew to find out where it was, a fact that luckily he managed to keep to himself. As for Lori, she genuinely knew nothing, but that didn't stop them putting her under the metaphorical cosh for the full period.

Meanwhile Frank was stuck on what they were calling gardening leave up at the Milngavie bungalow, although Jimmy doubted if his brother had much of an appetite for any horticulture. A patrol car was parked across the street, manned twenty-four-by-seven on a rotating shift basis, presumably in case Maggie should return, or more likely just to piss his brother off, which it had succeeded in doing. Frank was pretty sure too that all their regular phones would have been tapped, so he had ordered that they go easy on calling or texting each other for the time being, even when using the two burner phones which he knew Maggie and Jimmy had, courtesy of Stew Edwards. *Just try and behave normally* was his message. But what was normal in these far-from-normal circumstances, that was the question? If your fiancé or business partner had disappeared into thin air, normal would be worrying yourself sick and doing everything in your power to find her, so that's what they had to pretend to do. There were enquiring phone calls to her elderly parents in Yorkshire, who of course could not be let in on what was happening and so were suffering indescribable agonies, and to her best friend Asvina Rani, a senior partner of the famous London law firm Addison Redburn, who also knew nothing but suspected the truth. Additionally, Frank had been offered the opportunity to make a straight-to-camera appeal for information on the evening news, but had turned it down because of how bad it would look once the truth emerged.

And then of course, there was Yash Patel. With some amusement, Jimmy imagined the crack reporter's state of mind after Maggie's sensational disappearance had became the only story anyone in Scotland was talking about, two days after he had debuted *his* story about Jack Urquhart, the geeks of Abertay University and the conspiracy to discredit Donnie Morrison and a bunch of other leading Nationalist politicians. Since then, he'd been calling or messaging Jimmy about a hundred times a day, and it could be assumed that he was doing the same to Maggie and Frank, probably unaware that her phone was currently in the possession of the police. He would be completely livid, no doubt about it, since he quite reasonably regarded Maggie, Frank and Jimmy as good friends, and so would be gutted that he wasn't in on the secret. Now, he was reduced to writing speculative opinion pieces with headlines like *'What Has Happened to my Best Friend Maggie?'*, which Jimmy knew would be sticking in his throat. But friend or no friend, Yash was a journalist first and foremost, and the consensus was he would have been unable to resist the lure of a big scoop. Jimmy could just imagine the headline. *Chronicle Exclusive: We Reveal Fugitive Maggie's Secret Hideaway.* No, that wouldn't have been a good idea at all.

For Jimmy, normal also meant his embryonic but growing business up in Braemar, so with nothing constructive to be accomplished in Glasgow or Edinburgh, he'd headed back up north, where he and Stew were booked to lead another party of unfit business executives up the Lairig Ghru. They overnighted as normal at the remote mountaineers' bothy, three thousand feet up at the top of the pass, then led the group back down to Coylumbridge the next day without incident. Totally normal, except that on the trek he'd had a word with his partner on the subject of the stock of burner phones he knew Stew kept tucked away in his sock drawer, the outcome of which was two more devices promised for Frank and Miss Lorilynn Logan, to be couriered southwards as soon as they got back to Braemar.

So finally, a full seven days after Frank had been suspended from duty, they were able at last to contemplate actually *doing* something. On their last telephone conference, his brother had set out the task in simple terms. *One*, track down the chambermaid who had lied about seeing Maggie and Jack Urquhart heading hand-in-hand to that hotel bedroom. *Two* - this one infinitely more difficult - find out who actually *had* murdered the man-of-the-moment politician. Now a follow-up video call had been scheduled, where everyone would be expected to throw their ideas into the ring and together, they would try to agree on a concrete plan of action. Whatever the outcome, he'd assumed he would soon be heading south again, so he'd arranged for Stew's school-teacher-cum-lover Philly Scott to stand in for him for a week. Now he sat at his desk in their tiny office in the Highland village, ready for the call. He pulled the burner phone from his pocket, propped it up against a book so he could easily see the screen, then clicked on the meeting link. *Frank joining, Maggie joining, Lorilynn joining...* One by one, their heads popped into view.

'Well hello guys,' he said. 'Great to see you all again, literally.' He directed an enquiring look at Maggie's image. 'And how's the fugitive surviving? Stew's keeping you well-supplied I hear.'

She smiled back, but he thought it looked a bit forced. *'He's lovely Jimmy, and yes I'm getting by. But, if you want to know the truth, I'm gradually going stir-crazy up here, and Ollie's really missing his friends. Honestly, I don't know if I can put up with this much longer. But on the bright side, I've had plenty of time to think.'*

'I've been thinking too,' Lori interjected, with what looked like a self-satisfied smile. *'But I've been doing stuff too, not just thinking.'*

'Oh my goodness,' Maggie said, laughing. *'That sounds ominous. But then again, that's why I took you on Lori. I knew you had mountains of initiative.'*

'And looks like you're getting mountains of value for money too,' Jimmy said to Maggie, giving her a wink. 'If Miss Logan here is thinking *and* doing too. So Lori, are you going to tell us now what you've been up to, or are we going to look at the big picture first?' The question was directed at the group in general, although he was expecting Frank to jump in and lead the discussions as per usual. But weirdly, his brother just continued to stare out silently from the phone, with an expression that definitely radiated a degree of smugness. Something was going on here, Jimmy thought with puzzlement, because staying quiet in any discussion was as far from Frank's *modus operandi* as it was possible to get. Jimmy paused for another moment to allow his brother a bit longer to respond, but no, he evidently wasn't going to say anything. Giving a mental shrug he said, 'So Maggie, what do you think? Big picture or....?'

'I'm absolutely desperate to hear what Lori's been up to,' she said, jumping in. *'Definitely. So Miss Logan, tell us all, please.'*

'Sure Maggie, sure. So with Jack Urquhart dead, then obviously that was the end of our investigation, especially since we wouldn't be getting paid and carrying on for free would be really dumb, wouldn't it?' Lori blasted the words out at a hundred miles per hour, her expression earnest and radiating passion at the same time. *'But you see, I just couldn't give it up. I needed to find out who Dominique Tremblay was seeing and why she was keeping it so secret, because that didn't make any sense to me since it wasn't as if she was shagging some man on the side and keeping it from her partner, it was just a woman she was seeing, so why did she have to keep it so hush-hush? That's what I*

couldn't understand, and I wanted to understand it, I really did. And especially after her partner Jack Urquhart was killed. I mean, why should she care if she was seen after that, why did she still have to keep it such a secret? And there was something else too. She hasn't been showing any signs of like mourning or anything like that, and you would be mourning if your dearest love had been brutally murdered, wouldn't you? I thought that was really suspicious too.'

Maggie laughed. *'Phew, I think I caught most of that Lori. But maybe you could slow down just a little bit for us old folk?'*

'I'm sorry, I'll try, honest I will,' the girl said, with no discernible decrease in pace. *'So anyway, I followed her again down to the same place in Gourock. That was last Thursday and I don't know if you remember, but it was a bloody hot day.'* If anybody did remember, she evidently wasn't intending to give them a chance to say so. *'Too hot to keep a hoodie on for any length of time, that was what I was thinking. And I was right too. You see, as soon as Dominique parked up, I got out of Maggie's Golf and positioned myself in one of these wooden shelters they have dotted along the seafront. You know, where the old-age pensioners sit with their flasks and tupperware boxes with their ham sandwiches. So I squeezed in between two old dears, as if I was their grand-daughter or something, and slipped my phone out to be ready to take a picture or a vid. I thought that was quite a smart move actually.'*

Jimmy looked at Frank again, expecting him to make some smart-arsed crack in response to Lori's last remark, but no, he was still just sitting there with a seraphic half-grin on his face. *Bloody strange*.

'So I just like waited,' Lori continued, *'and sure enough, the other woman turned up again in the same fancy car, big sunglasses and wearing her hoodie same as before. And same as before, she parked beside Dominique and got into the passenger seat.'* Unexpectedly, she paused, not for breath, Jimmy surmised, but for dramatic effect. *'And of course, being so bloody hot, she had to put her hood down, and that's when I got her.'* Once more she fell into silence, like a stand-up comedian waiting for applause at the end of a long humorous routine.

'So who was it?' Jimmy asked impatiently. 'Did you recognise her?'

Lori gave a triumphant smile. *'Red hair, big tits. Aye, I recognised her, nae bother. It was Jade Niven. I've seen her photos in the Globe. She's a right tart so she is.'*

'What?' Maggie exclaimed. *'The woman who set up the Rev Morrison? But wait a minute. Frank, I thought you told me that she had disappeared into thin air? Or was I mistaken?'*

Jimmy gave his brother a quizzical look. Surely this time he had to say *something*, especially since it was Maggie who had directed the question at him?

'That's what DC McDonald tells me, aye,' Frank said, nodding. *'We've been trying to track her down but it looks as if you've beat us to it. Nice work.'*

Lori gave a proud smile, which quickly changed to a frown. *'Aye, well I saw her alright, but I didn't actually track her down. You see, afterwards I tried to follow her back to Glasgow, but I lost her. The M8 was dead busy so I was able to keep up for a while, but then she cut on to that M77 and really put her foot down. And well, Maggie's wee Golf was no match for her big motor. Soz Maggie, but it isn't,'* she added apologetically.

'I won't tell him if you won't,' Maggie said, smiling. *'He's a very sensitive little car. But you've done brilliantly Lori. Great work.'*

'Aye, brilliant work Lori,' Jimmy said, and he meant it too. The problem was though, did it actually get them any closer to resolving Maggie's terrible situation? On the face of it, it didn't, especially since there were question marks as to whether this Jade Niven was a real person or not. It had to mean something, granted, but right now it seemed beyond his brain-power to figure out exactly what. He looked at Maggie, and hoped to see that expression he loved and revered in equal measure. Lips pursed, brow furrowed, deep in thought, her mind racing through scenarios and theories and possibilities, like lines of code in a complicated computer program. But no, she looked rather deflated, he guessing that whilst like him she was pleased with Lori's initiative, she too was disappointed by the outcome.

'So what do you think Frank?' Jimmy said, determined to finally get his brother involved in the conversation. *'You've sat there hardly saying a word. Come on, what should we do next?'*

Frank jabbed at his phone with his index finger, and then drew back before it landed on the screen. And then he gave a perplexed look. *'There's been developments, courtesy of*

Lexy McDonald. She sent me a WhatsApp thingy earlier - at great risk to herself I hasten to add - and I'd like to read it to you, but I don't know if I can do that and stay on this damn video call at the same time.'

Jimmy laughed. '*We* could, *you* couldn't, Mr Techno-Useless. So why don't you just give us the gist, whilst you still remember some of it.' Frank returned a look which Jimmy took to be the equivalent of a one-finger salute, then said. *'Aye, well alright then.'* He was silent for a moment. *'But listen, and this goes especially for you Miss Maggie Bainbridge, when I've told you what I'm about to tell you, I don't want you all going bloody nuts and doing stupid things, because it doesn't mean we've cracked the situation by any means. Promise?*'

'We don't know what it is yet, so how can we promise?' Jimmy said warily.

'*We promise,*' Maggie interjected. *'Just bloody get on with it.'*

Frank shrugged. *'Lexy had a quiet word with one of her mates on the murder squad. They're in a WhatsApp group and apparently this guy fancies her like mad. So she took full and shameless advantage of that situation, without compromising her honour I hasten to add. But as a result, she found out something DI McNeil and co have been very anxious to keep to themselves.'*

'Bloody hell, not the M-O of the Urquhart murder?' Jimmy said.

'Exactly that. Exactly that.' Frank was silent for a moment. *'You see, Jack Urquhart was tasered before he was stabbed. The same M-O that was used for these two pole-dancers and for that Johnny Pallas guy too. Interesting, don't you think?'*

'Bloody hell,' Jimmy said again, unable to think of anything that better voiced his astonishment.

'*Bloody too right*,' Frank said with a wry grin. *'And in a couple of minutes I'm going to be on the phone to our pal Yash Patel, and I'll be giving him a proper scoop for him to get his teeth into. And just so you know, I'll be writing the headline for him. Word for word. '*

***

The piece had made the *Chronicle Online's* early-evening update, the sensational story broken by its star investigative reporter Yash Patel. *Leak of Urquhart murder method throws Bainbridge investigation into disarray.* Patel had gone to town, putting the boot into Police Scotland for the obvious ineptitude of the Urquhart investigation, so much so that just an hour after the story had gone public, the Chief Constable was forced to issue a written statement. And as Frank had correctly predicted, it was clear that in the eyes of the brass, nothing was going to change. According to the statement, they had a witness who had seen the fugitive en-route to the murder scene with the victim, they had concrete forensic evidence placing the accused at the scene, they had motive and opportunity. As for means, tasers were regrettably but easily available on the black market, and as a private investigator and former criminal barrister, the fugitive Magdalene Bainbridge was doubtless in contact with shady individuals who could supply the said device with no questions asked. At some point of course the whole ridiculous edifice was going to crumble, everyone knew that, but the problem was, that might not happen until Maggie was serving a life sentence for murder, her fate in the hands of the Court of Appeal.

However, despite the ongoing difficulties of her current situation, this new and sensational development was, to Maggie's growing excitement, threatening to shine an illuminating spotlight on the tangled web of complexity that characterised these crazily-interlinked cases. *At last*. It was nine o'clock in the evening, and Ollie had not long gone to bed after an exhausting day of play in the secluded woodland garden that surrounded Stew Edward's cosy little love-nest. Now she lolled back on the sofa in the small but comfortable lounge with a large and nicely-chilled glass of Chardonnay in her hand, courtesy of Stew's efficient supply-chain, and began to *think.* Past experience had taught her that the solution to an investigation always came not from charging around like headless chickens, but from the creative side of the brain, although she couldn't quite remember whether that was the left side or the right side, not that it mattered. You used your imagination to come up with a theory, and then you gathered in facts that either supported that theory or quickly blew the whole thing to pieces. The problem was, this far into a case she usually had *something,* even it was ridiculously sketchy or far-fetched. But on this case, she had nothing. *Zilch.*

Undeterred, she took out her phone and fired up the *Notes* app to record both what she knew so far, and also the gaps in her knowledge that had to be filled in as quickly as possible. Hopefully she would then be able to formulate a plan of action for Jimmy, Lori and Frank. So fact one, and the new and critical one, was that the killings of Jack Urquhart, Johnny Pallas, and married gay couple Andy and Rab McVie were identical, and so almost certainly were carried out by the same person or persons. But what then was the link between the victims, since Urquhart was different in not being gay? Taking another sip of her wine, she tapped *link* into her phone and added a question mark. Yeah, easy to do that, but what *was* the bloody link? Was there a common motive perhaps, although on the face of it that seemed unlikely? Most murders were one-offs, frequently caused by anger or betrayal within family relationships, the cheating wife killed by the jealous husband or the abusive partner killed after years of silent suffering. But in the case of Johnny Pallas and the married McVies, this was a crime clearly targeted at gay men, or at least these gay men in particular. *Those* two murders were linked for sure, but the killing of Urquhart didn't fit in with it at all. So maybe it wasn't the *motive* that was linked, because of course it didn't have to be. No reason at all why it couldn't be the same killer but a completely *different* motive, a realisation that made her give a loud sigh of frustration. This thing seemed to be getting *more* bloody complicated, not less.

So come on, she thought, taking a generous gulp from her wine glass, let's try and brainstorm what else it could be, starting with possible motives for the killing of Jack Urquhart. He was a politician and when you looked around the world, you saw that it was far from unusual for politicians to be murdered by their political opponents. But this was Scotland for God's sake, not some tin-pot dictatorship, although she smiled to herself when she thought of what Frank might have to say about that. Nonetheless, it was just about plausible, wasn't it? Jack Urquhart had looked certain to win the upcoming Nationalist leadership contest and thus become First Minister. But whilst there were many who might vehemently oppose that outcome, were there any who would actually *kill* to prevent it? Instantly she thought of Tommy Taggart and his Scottish Freedom Party. But whilst they were unquestionably vile, and a demonstrable threat to public order in Scotland too, they also seemed amateurish and faintly ludicrous. They might talk the talk, to employ the common cliché, but she had serious doubts if they could also walk the walk. Couldn't be ruled out of course, but it seemed a bit unlikely.

So coming back to the motive, the police, ridiculously, had decided almost from the first minute that it was a *crime passionnel*, with her as the perpetrator. In support, they had a witness, a chambermaid at the hotel, who had seen her hand-in-hand with Urquhart heading for an afternoon of sex in a fifth-floor bedroom. Yes, that was fact two, she thought, typing it into her phone. *Lying chambermaid, but who set that up?* Tomorrow she would send Lori and Jimmy off to the Royal Mile Grampian hotel to investigate, and hopefully that would shed a bit more light on that aspect of the case. But what was even more ridiculous, she thought, was that the police had seemed to have given no consideration at all to the possibility of his partner Dominique Tremblay being the murderer, despite years of statistics backing up the fact that the other half was always the most likely prime suspect. Nor had they bothered to quiz the young civil servant with whom, it had been alleged, he had been having an affair a year or so back.

Now that she had time to think about it, it dawned on her that the relationship of Dominique Tremblay and Jack Urquhart was an odd thing indeed. She was smart, successful, beautiful and powerfully alluring, and so she could understand why Jack had evidently gone crazy for the woman, causing him to callously dump his wife and children without apparent regret. Likewise, he was pretty irresistible too, a fact that she had shamefully though innocently experienced for herself and now bitterly regretted. And yet the relationship had turned out to be an arid affair, so much so that Jack, without a trace of irony given his own track-record of infidelity, had suspected his partner of having an affair, and so had engaged Bainbridge Associates to investigate. But four weeks of surveillance by Lori had turned up nothing in that regard. Instead, though equally interesting in Maggie's opinion, Dominique Tremblay had engaged in a series of clandestine meetings with a woman who turned out, sensationally, to be Jade Niven, the same woman who had run the honey-trap operation to discredit the Reverend Donnie Morrison. That was bizarre and inexplicable in equal measure, but surely it had to be explained if they were to make any progress in the case. And to do that, she realised she needed to know *much* more about Miss Tremblay.

Bringing up Google, it wasn't hard to find a mountain of information online about the prominent journalist's Scottish career. But what Maggie was most interested in was the journalist's back-story, which currently was mostly a blank to her. From her Wikipedia profile, she had noted the woman had worked on a French-language paper in her native Quebec province, *Le Journal de Montréal,* before moving to Scotland and joining the *Globe*. But what of her life before then? She punched in *Dominique Tremblay Journalist Canada* and clicked *search*. There wasn't much, but perhaps Dominique's career had really only taken off once she had moved to Scotland. Most of the information was obviously in French, again no surprise. Maggie clicked on a link which opened what looked like a local version of Wikipedia, the text again all in French. Her schoolgirl knowledge of the language wasn't all that bad she considered, having obtained a decent A-Level in the subject, but nowadays you didn't have to struggle with all of that stuff. With a slight feeling of shame, she selected the *translate* option and read on, in English. Apparently, Dominique Tremblay had grown up in a small town called Saint Sauveur, about 80km north of Montreal, and then took a journalism degree at La Salle College, an institution that Maggie quite reasonably had never heard of. But as far as her career at the prestigious Montreal newspaper was concerned, there was nothing. *Puzzling*. She did a search for the website of the newspaper itself, clicking to alight on its homepage. It was in French of course, but a button helpfully allowed an instant translation into English. At the top, there was a search box. Maggie paused for a moment, pondering, then typed in *Dominique Tremblay articles*, expecting to find a slew of the journalist's work. But to her surprise, the search returned *nothing*. Or to be more exact, just one result. And then, to her utter astonishment, she read the text of that link.

Tragic death of La Salle graduate in skiing accident.

Clicking into the article, she saw it was a short three-paragraph piece in tribute to one Dominique Tremblay (23), a former student of La Salle College, who had died after a collision on her home slopes above Saint Sauveur. And then Maggie looked more closely at the photograph that accompanied the article, which at first glance looked like one of the annual class photographs from back in her Yorkshire school days, except this was evidently a University equivalent. *La Classe de Journalisme 2003* was superimposed in a title box at the top of the group picture, and along the bottom were the names of that year's graduating students, about forty in all. And in the front row, helpfully circled by the newspaper, sat one Dominique Tremblay. Except this woman didn't look *anything* like the woman she had met.

Excitedly, she picked up her notebook and leafed through to where she had scribbled down a dozen or so important numbers, when she knew she would have to hand her regular phone over to the police. Picking up the burner phone, she punched in Tremblay's number from the list. She knew of course that what she was about to do was crazy, and it was impossible to predict what the consequences would be. But equally, she knew too that it had to be done. She prodded the number, raised her phone to her ear and waited for Tremblay to answer, hoping that the woman would not ignore it on account of not recognising the number. But after half-a-dozen rings, it was answered with a tentative *Tremblay?* Adopting a heavily-caricatured accent which she hoped would disguise her own speaking voice, Maggie said brightly, *'Bon jour Mademoiselle Tremblay. Quel est votre vrai nom?'*

'Excuse me?' the woman answered, clearly perplexed. But Maggie had heard enough, immediately ending the call.

A Quebecor who didn't speak French? *No way.* Especially one who was already dead.

Chapter 22

For Frank, it had been another day of not much happening, stuck at home in the Milngavie bungalow save for a trip across the river at around three o'clock in the afternoon. But at least with the emergence of the Jack Urquhart *modus operandi*, the case had got one solid foundation stone they could build upon. In his opinion, it was going to be virtually impossible now for the Procurator Fiscal to make a credible case against Maggie, or at least to have any chance of making it stick. Consequently, he was certain that at this very moment at the Crown Office headquarters in Edinburgh, there would be senior-level huddles going on to decide what to do next, the only objective being to make sure that should they decide to press ahead, they wouldn't get the blame if it all went tits-up when it got to court. They would know that the evidence was thin, and would be thinking that maybe it would be best to just throw the towel in now before they incurred the great expense of a full-blown murder trial. But that would mean a very public contradiction of the Chief Constable's very public stance, a humiliation that some in the Fiscal's office might relish, but that would surely damage them too. Still, the risk was that there would be voices in Edinburgh arguing that they should let the courts sort it out, which might not be in Maggie's best interests. No, he thought, that wasn't going to happen. Sensible heads would eventually prevail. The only problem was, *eventually* was a time period of indeterminate length.

Nonetheless, the new development had the effect of freeing his personal shackles somewhat. He still wasn't going to go within a million miles of Lexy, Ronnie or Eleanor because he didn't want them getting into any trouble -

something he'd reminded Lexy of *fortissimo* after she had sent him that explosive WhatsApp - but given that the final outcome of Maggie's situation was no longer in doubt, he could take a few more risks himself. *Especially* after what he had found out just a few hours earlier on his drive over to the posh suburb of Newton Mearns. Now, having watched a bit of football on the telly, he'd just got up to fetch himself a beer from the kitchen when he heard the *buzz-buzz* of the burner phone. He scrambled back to the living-room, snatched it up from the coffee table, punched *speakerphone* and flopped down on the couch.

'*Darling, I'm bloody missing you like crazy,*' were her opening words, causing his heart to skip about a thousand beats.

'And I'm bloody missing you too,' he said. 'Aye, like crazy as well. Are you in bed?'

'Would you like me to be?' Maggie said mischievously.

He grinned. 'Too bloody right I would. So how are you doing? And how's Ollie?'

'I'm fine, he's knackered, which is good,' she said, and he heard her laugh. *'But listen, you'll never guess what. Something incredibly interesting.'*

'What's that?' he responded, as he assumed he was supposed to.

'Dominique Tremblay isn't who she says she is. I'm one hundred percent certain of that. In fact, I'm one thousand percent sure'.

'How come you're so sure?' he said, puzzled and intrigued at the same time.

'Because she died in a skiing accident about twenty years ago.'

'What?'

'She died. In a skiing accident.'

'Aye, you said that. But I don't understand what you're telling me.'

'I did some digging. There was a Dominique Tremblay, and she did grow up near Montreal and she went to Uni there and graduated with a degree in journalism. But then tragically, she died in a collision on the slopes near her home town.'

'Bloody hell,' Frank said, struggling to process this bombshell. 'So who the hell is the woman who works for the Globe then?'

'I don't know. But I did ask her. In French. At least, in my terrible schoolgirl French. And it flummoxed her. Don't you see Frank? A native French speaker would have answered back in French automatically, without even thinking. But she was taken by surprise, so she didn't. So she's not even French-Canadian, like she claims.'

'What?' he exploded. 'You *asked* her?'

She sounded taken aback by his obvious incredulity. *'Well yeah, but she wouldn't have known it was me. I used the burner phone and put on a French accent.'*

Despite himself, he couldn't help but laugh. 'Aye, she'll never know it was you because there's a million people speak French with a Yorkshire accent.' He paused for a moment and drew a breath. 'But I suppose it's bloody done now.' And now they would have to deal with the consequences, whatever they might be. On the positive side, the bad guys might now feel under some pressure, which in his experience often led to mistakes. But then again, they might feel threatened, which might unleash consequences that weren't so clever. Whatever the case, he decided it was best to make no further comment on what he considered to be a rash action on her part. Instead he said, 'But as I said, if she's not Dominique Tremblay, who the hell is she?'

'That's what we need to find out, don't we?' Maggie said. *'And bloody quickly too. Because although I'm hoping she didn't recognise my voice, she'll now know that someone's on to her, and God knows where that might lead.'*

'Aye, exactly,' Frank said, trying not to sound as if he was telling her off, but not being sure he'd succeeded. Sensing a change of focus was called for he said, 'Well, I've not been sitting on my backside either, I'll have you know. Because *I* found out today that Jade Niven isn't who she says she is either.'

'What?' Maggie blurted out, making them both laugh.

'Aye, it was your Lori that got me thinking when she said Jade had sped off down the M77 when she was chasing her back from Gourock that day. Because you see, that's the way you go to Newton Mearns, which is where the Taggarts live. So on a hunch, I tooled round there this afternoon and banged on their front door. Obviously I don't have my warrant card at the moment, so I gave a quick flash of my library card. '

'Bloody hell Frank,' she said, sounding annoyed. *'You're suspended.'* But then he heard her laugh again. *'You're a bloody nutcase, really you are. That's one of the many reasons why I love you.'*

'For me, it's your body mainly,' he said, grinning. 'But anyway, do you want to hear the rest of my story or don't you?'

'Have I any choice?'

'Nope. So as I said, I went round and knocked their knocker. I don't think either of the Taggarts were in, but the gay lad who looks after Tommy's diary answered the door.'

'Hang on, did you say a gay lad?' Maggie said, evidently surprised.

'Aye, a gay lad, and his name's Jimmy would you believe,' Frank said. 'Jimmy Petrie. He was the boy who was wearing the Harley-Dee's T-shirt last time me and Ronnie French called round. But let me finish my story, will you?'

'But it might be important,' she protested. *'But yes, of course I'll let you finish. Go ahead.'*

'Fine, I will. So I stuck my phone in his face and says to Jimmy-boy, do you recognise this registration number? I was showing him the number that Lori had clocked on the big SUV that had parked up alongside Dominique. And he looked at it for a few seconds, saying nothing, because it was obvious he *did* recognise it and he was wondering what he should do. And then eventually he says, *aye, it's Mrs Taggart's. It's her big Range Rover.*'

'What?' Maggie said again. *'So Jade had borrowed Sienna Taggart's big car for her meetings with Dominique?'*

'Well that's one explanation,' Frank said, enjoying her surprise. 'But I've got a better one.'

'No,' Maggie said, evidently cottoning on to where he was going with this. *'No way.'*

'Way,' he said. 'Same age, same tartyness if that's a word, same surgically-enhanced boobs - you'll remember that Lori pointed that out specifically first time she saw her. And the big mane of red hair, which is obviously a Dolly Parton-style wig, and the thick rings of mascara round her eyes. All of that makes you look totally different, doesn't it? So mental though it seems, I'm running up the flagpole the contention that Jade Niven and Sierra Taggart are one and the same person.'

'But why?' Maggie said plaintively. *'What the hell is this all about? Why should she be doing all of this?'*

'That's another thing for us to figure out I guess. But before we think about that, what's this gay lad thing you're worried about?'

'Well, it runs right through this case, doesn't it?' she said. *'Those Royal Mile murders, and my missing person Rory Morrison - who, may I remind you, is the son of the Reverend Donnie Morrison - and now Tommy and Sienna Taggart's house-boy or whatever you call him. After all, it's you that's always going about two things maybe being a coincidence, but three definitely being a conspiracy.'*

'Aye, you're right,' he conceded. 'But Jimmy the house-boy's not dead or missing, is he? That's the difference.'

There was silence at the end of the line, which he took to indicate that she was thinking about something that had just occurred to her. And then she spoke.

'No, he isn't. Not yet anyway. Not yet.' She paused again. *'No, forget I said that. A crazy idea popped into my head, but it can't be right.'*

He smiled. 'Well you often are, so I wouldn't beat yourself up. But anyway, this is a right turn up for the books, is it not? Two women who're central to our case, and who are obviously in cahoots, but who aren't who they say they are. And it's funny, because I remember thinking the first time me and Lexy McDonald talked to Sienna Taggart in that motor-home that there was something not quite right about her. Aye, I need to do a bit a digging, definitely. What was her maiden name again, can you remember?'

'Lomond. Nice and easy to remember. Agnes Lomond. And she grew up in some rough area not far from the loch itself I seem to recall.'

'Oh aye,' Frank said, his memory refreshed. 'Renton. Which believe me, is a bit different from Newton Mearns. So maybe I need to take a drive down there, call in at her primary school and see if anybody still remembers her.' He paused for a moment, thinking. 'Alright then,' he continued. 'What we need I think is a bit of divide-and-separate brainstorming tomorrow morning, after we've had the benefit of a good night's sleep. And then we can catch up maybe in the afternoon and see where we've got to. Jimmy's coming down tomorrow, isn't he, to meet up with your Lorilynn?'

'Yeah he is. They're going to the Royal Mile Grampian to investigate that chambermaid. She won't be able to sleep tonight thinking about her date with her beau.'

He laughed. 'Aye, she is a bit besotted by the lad. But she'll get over it once she gets to know him better.'

'You're horrible,' she said fondly. *'But yes, let's spend tomorrow morning trying to make sense of all this craziness and then we'll talk again.'* She paused for a moment. *'Goodnight. And I love you.'*

'I love you too,' he said, reflecting yet again that he had never been more sure of anything in his life.

So tomorrow there would be a run down to Renton in search of the truth about Sienna Taggart, the woman formally known as Agnes Lomond. Maybe on reflection he'd be better heading for the secondary school to take a look at their class photos. Because given what he'd just heard about Dominique Tremblay, he expected that Mrs Taggart might also have changed quite a bit in her transformation from being Agnes.

***

As far as Maggie was concerned, the morning couldn't really have got off to a worse start. First of all, there had been an early call from Lori, en-route to the Royal Mile Grampian hotel to begin her investigation into the lying chambermaid. The previous day, her assistant had apparently suffered a full-on berating from Rose Morrison. Their client had been bemoaning, with complete justification it had to be said, the complete shambles of the investigation into her son's disappearance. *I've already paid you eighteen hundred pounds*, she had complained, *for basically nothing, and now your boss Bainbridge has disappeared with my money. It's an absolute scandal and I'll be getting a proper lawyer to sue you*. Lori had tried her best to placate her, but the truth was, the investigation had been close to a total disaster.

The second setback, although possibly of much less consequence, was a headline that had caught her eye on her phone's news app, evidently sourced from one of the country's down-market tabloid newspapers. *Sultry Paige boasts of all-night bonk with Love Island stud*. A soap actress whom Maggie had never heard of, was claiming that her 'good friend 'Johnny Pallas hadn't been the least bit gay, but had only appeared on the show to become famous, and as proof, she had provided the tabloid with graphic descriptions of their regular and vigorous love-making. The actress had gone on to add that she was missing him terribly and that it was just vile and jealous people on social media who were spreading these terrible lies about him.

Whatever the truth of the matter, to Maggie it raised a definite question mark about the theory that somehow their case was centred around gay men. It was discouraging, that was for sure, but she felt she had little option but to ignore this late-breaking and inconvenient fact.

Still, there was plenty to focus on and plenty to do to take her mind of these undoubted difficulties. Jimmy was on his way to Edinburgh, where he would meet with Lori at the Royal Mile Grampian, and she hoped and expected that between them they would get to the bottom of the chambermaid situation. It would be mid-afternoon at the earliest before they reported back, leaving her plenty of time for a bit more thinking, which was no real burden, because in many ways it was the part of the job she liked the most. It was hardly an original allegory of course, but she regarded an investigation very much like a giant jigsaw puzzle, where you had some idea of what the big picture looked like but you needed every single piece to be slotted into place before the case could be reliably solved. And like a jigsaw, there was great satisfaction both in seeking out each piece and then seeing how they all fitted together. And on this one, although not yet perfectly in focus, she thought she was, at last, starting to see the big picture. Taking out the notebook she kept specifically for her brainstorming activities, she turned to a fresh page and began scribbling. She jotted down and underlined a heading before moving on to the facts as she saw them.

What We Know So Far.

- *Two women who are seemingly - no, definitely - not what (or even who) they say they are*

- Two women who are co-conspirators in some as yet-unknown plot or scheme
- Two women who are married to up-and-coming politicians

That last point got her thinking about her Urquhart case and she added:

- The relationship of Jack Urquhart and Dominique Tremblay was (according to him at least) a sexless affair

Chewing on her pen, she paused for a moment as she reminded herself of the first rule of brainstorming. *Get all the ideas on the table, no matter how seemingly bonkers they might be.* So she wrote:

- Two women who are of exceptional desirability - not simply attractive, but notably sexy too

Was that significant, she wondered? It certainly explained why Jack Urquhart had been driven to leave his wife and children, unable to resist the powerful allure of the beautiful Dominique. Yes, she nodded to herself, this *is* significant. So what more do we know? Furrowing her brow, she scribbled down a few more lines:

- Sierra Taggart - extraordinarily - is also Jade Niven
- Jade Niven/Sienna Taggart was the honey-trappist who tried to discredit Donnie Morrison
- Donnie Morrison's homosexual son has disappeared
- Rory Morrison had links to Harley-Dee's gay club

- Patrons of that club have been found murdered on the Royal Mile
- Sophisticated deep-fake technology was used in the Morrison conspiracy

She paused for a moment, contemplating. Yes, it was all rather disjointed, but it was easy to forget about that last point, that some very hi-tech wizardry had been deployed to pull off the Morrison honey-trap. That made her wonder how Eleanor Campbell was getting on with the investigation into the provenance of these videos. On the spur of the moment, she picked up her phone and swiped Frank's number. It took a while for him to answer, she smiling to himself as she pictured him thrusting a hand into each pocket in turn, having forgotten, as usual, which one he'd put it in.

'Morning darling,' she said, amused. 'It sounds as if you're outside, from the whistling gale in the background.'

'Aye,' he laughed, *'and it's pissing down too. Typical Scottish weather, with the school holidays a few days from starting. Actually, I'm outside the front gates of Renton Secondary School. You can't just stroll onto school grounds so the head's coming down to collect me. But the good news is she says she's got a class photograph with Agnes in it.'*

'That'll be interesting,' Maggie said.

'Aye it will be,' he said, laughing again. *'I said they must be very proud of what Agnes stroke Sienna had achieved and there was a deadly silence at the end of the line. Anyway, to what do I owe the honour of this call?'*

'I don't suppose you've heard from Eleanor?' she asked. 'But then I don't suppose you're allowed to speak to her, are you?'

'No, and I wouldn't, not for her sake,' he said, sounding rueful. *'I suppose you want to find out about those bloody Morrison videos? I've been thinking about them myself actually.'*

'Oh really?' she said, smiling.

'Aye, I have. What I've been thinking is, I can't call her, but you can. You went to her wedding and that's a day you're never going to forget, is it?' He paused for a second, evidently savouring that amazing occasion. *'So that qualifies you as friends. Ask her how married life's going - and give yourself at least half-an-hour for the answer - and then you can just drop it casually into the conversation. I mean, she'll know what's going on, but I think she'll be fine with it. I'll text you her number in a minute. And don't worry, she's not on the cops' watch list. Although even if she was, she would have come up with some techie magic so she couldn't get caught.'*

She nodded. 'Brilliant, I'll call her straight away. By the way, have you got an umbrella? I don't want you coming down with pneumonia before the wedding.'

She heard him laugh. *'Nah, remember I'm Scottish. We're inoculated against wind and rain from birth. Anyway, must go now. But I can't wait to see you again. Bye-bye.'*

***

Surprisingly, Eleanor had sounded pleased to hear from her, and the scientist's demeanour had remained agreeable all through the call, which was in stark contrast to her feisty manner on any other occasion Maggie had met with her. Now she was pretty sure of what she had long suspected, that the young woman's Mrs Grump persona was, if not an act, at least heavily exaggerated when she was in the presence of dear Frank. Today, perfectly pleasantly, Eleanor gave a full-fat update on the first year of married life - not all it's cracked up to be was the summary, though it took her close on forty minutes to say it - and then, an equally full-fat account of her hands-on experience with Carrie-Anne Fisher's Langley Virginia Labs and their truly awesome next-generation memory-resident de-compilation software engine. The gist of which was, after another twenty minutes or so of highly-technical and unfathomable explanation, that, *yes*, she had been able to discover some strong clues to the national identity of the coders behind the deep fake videos. And *no*, of course she was not allowed to tell Maggie or especially Frank what that precise identity was, given their current outlaw status. But *yes*, she had passed on to her bosses that it could only be the work of a highly-resourced hostile state, given the sophistication of the code, and the fact that the comments were typed in the Cyrillic alphabet pointed rather strongly to a particular culprit. And then with a knowing *that's like all I can tell you*, Eleanor had rung off.

So it was Russia who was behind the Donnie Morrison honey-trap affair. Despite Frank's mockery of the likelihood of such forces working undercover in stupid little Scotland, as he colourfully would have put it, it seemed that, unbelievably, it was indeed true. Two or three times a year you read stories in the newspapers about Russian agents being unmasked and expelled, so much so that they barely caught your attention. But happening *here*, in *Scotland*? It seemed totally crazy for only one reason. *It bloody was.*

Now she couldn't wait for her mid-afternoon catch-ups with Frank, Jimmy and Lori, to tell them what she had discovered and to hear in turn what they had found out on their missions. After that, she calculated there would be just three remaining pieces of the jigsaw to be put in place in this massive super-complicated thousand-piece puzzle. The first would be when Frank completed his digging into the background of Sienna Taggart stroke Agnes Lomond. The second would be achieved when Jimmy and Lori had completed their investigative visit to the Royal Mile Grampian hotel. And the third? Right now, she had no idea *exactly* what the third was, other than it vaguely had something to do with that classy soap actress Paige and her bonkathon with the murdered but evidently not-gay Johnny Pallas. The significance of that she could not say at this precise moment, but she had little doubt that with a bit of power thinking, it would all become clear.

Yeah, no doubt about it, they were getting bloody close.

Chapter 23

It wasn't exactly the most enticing of missions, that was Jimmy's definite opinion, but after ten years in the army, taking orders came as naturally as brushing his teeth in the morning, so he wasn't given to complain. Besides, he would do anything it took to get Maggie out of the mess she was in, and if this meant being basically a babysitter to her young and inexperienced assistant, then so be it. The drive down from Braemar was as uneventful as it was beautiful, and he arrived in Edinburgh nicely on schedule at around one o'clock, dumped the car in an exorbitantly expensive underground car-park, then made straight for the Royal Mile Grampian, where they'd arranged to meet in the entrance lobby. Lori was already there when he arrived, which he'd fully expected because even in the short time she'd worked for the agency, her punctuality and diligence had been exemplary. But what he hadn't expected was the way she looked today. On every other occasion he had met with her, she had been wearing black jeans, T-shirt and scruffy trainers. But today she was in an elegant navy short-sleeved dress that reached just below the knee, with flesh-coloured tights and heels. Her hair was held back from one side of her face with a silver clasp, and that face was made up as if she was on a night out. He had to admit it, she looked rather fetching.

'Miss Logan,' he said admiringly. 'Who's the lucky guy?'

'You are,' she said, unblinking. 'I've booked us a double room and I've asked for the fifth floor. In your name.' And then, to his surprise, she put his arm around his waist, drew him close to her and kissed him on the cheek. 'We're having an affair. You're the boss and I'm the hot young office assistant that you're bonking. And we're so loved-up we can't keep our hands off one another.'

'Excuse me?' he said, slightly flummoxed but laughing at the same time.

'Not in real life,' she said, frowning. 'Like *obviously*. It's just our cover story. We need to get a room to be able to get onto that fifth-floor corridor. Because we need a swipe-card key for the lifts to work.'

'Ah, I get it,' he said, relieved. 'And that kissing thing just then....?'

She nodded towards the reception desk. 'They watch everyone coming in. I wanted to make it look realistic.'

'Well it was *that* alright,' he said wryly. 'So, what's the plan?'

'We check in, then head up to the room and have sex,' she said, grinning mischievously. 'No, only joking, sadly. Actually, we dump your bag and then just wander about the corridors until we bump into one of the housekeeping team. They're always scooting about with these wee trolleys so we should have no bother in finding somebody to talk to.'

The plan agreed, they wandered over to the reception desk to complete the check-in formalities, Lori staying resolutely in character by clinging to him and whispering disturbingly raunchy - and audible - endearments in his ear, whilst he held his credit card against the payment terminal. The male receptionist gave him a faintly disapproving look and said pointedly, 'I don't suppose you will want a receipt sir?' Jimmy looked back at him, smiled and said, quite loudly, 'Oh aye I do. Miss Smith here's going on my expense account as usual,' causing her to give a noisy giggle. The unsmiling receptionist was silent for a moment, then said, 'Enjoy your stay at the Royal Mile Grampian, Mr *Stewart*, Miss *Logan*.'

'Shit,' Lori exclaimed as they made their way to the lift. 'He knew who we were.'

Jimmy gave her a rueful look. 'Aye, we were in the papers, remember? The dangerous associates of the fugitive Magdalene Bainbridge.' He tried to make light of it, but there was no doubt that it had momentarily discomforted him, and he wondered for a moment whether the reception guy might have twigged what they were up to. Up in the room, he asked. 'Did we ever get a name for this supposed witness?'

She nodded. 'Frank did. Maja Jankowski, she's Polish I think. That's all he was able to find out.'

'Well aye, he's not exactly flavour of the month at New Gorbals nick so he did well to even get that,' Jimmy said. 'So we best get started I guess. What are we going to do, take a floor each? I do this one and you go down a floor?'

'No, I've just had a better idea,' she said, her eyes lighting up. 'Let's pretend we're having a scene because you've booked me into a room where some guy's been killed. I storm out, you chase after me, and we kick up a racket. That's bound to attract the attention of the maids or housekeepers or whatever they call themselves. Then when they ask what's up, I can naturally go straight to the subject of the murder.'

He laughed, shaking his head in admiration. 'You love this stuff don't you? You should have been a bloody actress, you really should. Only trouble is, I'm no actor. I'll be absolutely rubbish.'

'I know you will,' she said, omitting to soften the blow with a smile. 'But I'll be doing all of the acting. You just need to kinda stand around.'

He laughed again. 'I can do that alright. So when does this diva performance start?'

'Right now. Starting with me stomping out into the corridor and slamming the door behind me. Don't forget to come after me, and all you have to do then is call out my name in a sort of pathetic pleading voice. You know, *Lori, Lori, please darling, don't,* or something like that.'

'So you're writing my script too now are you?' he said, suppressing another laugh.

'You can ad-lib if you want,' she said, shrugging. 'So, you ready? Because I am.' Without waiting for an answer, she jumped over to the door, flinging it open then stepping out into the corridor before turning to slam it behind her, tugging the handle with both hands for maximum effectiveness. And then, as promised, she started to shout, the volume turned up to eleven, such that he could comfortably hear every word even through the closed door.

'You are like *so stupid* and selfish, expecting me to have sex with you in *that* room. All *I* can think about is all that blood, and *you* expect me to take all my clothes off and lie in that bed where he was horribly stabbed to death. It's like *totally* gross.' Struggling once again not to laugh, he pulled open the door and followed her into the corridor. He saw she had already set off in the direction of the lifts, continuing her performance as she went, presumably so she passed by as many room doors as possible and thus attracted the attention of any staff working therein.

'Look Lori, don't do this,' he shouted, feeling slightly self-conscious, whilst taking advantage of her invitation to improvise. 'How the hell was *I* to know it was the same room. They don't exactly advertise it, do they? Please, come back here. *Darling.*' She had already reached the double doors that led to the stairs and lifts, and she stopped and turned around when she heard his pleadings. And then started again.

'You wouldn't bring your precious little *wife* here, would you? Oh no, she would be far too good for *that*.'

'But darling...,' he started to respond, but then suddenly she flew at him, arms flailing, forcing him to grab her wrists in an attempt to restrain her during this admittedly impressive demonstration of method acting.

'Calm down, *please*,' he said, warming to the part. 'You're making a scene.' Which of course was the general idea.

'Calm down?' she screamed, struggling to break free from his grasp. 'Don't you tell *me* to calm down you *bastard*.'

At that moment, he heard the creaking of an opening door. A woman emerged, smoothing down a pale blue overall that was emblazoned with the hotel's logo. Pinned to the garment was a badge that read *Aleksandra, Housekeeping Team.*

'What happens?' she asked, looking confused. 'Is man attacking you?' she added, the question obviously directed at Lori. 'I call security right away.' She looked about mid-forties, Jimmy reckoned, of careworn appearance and with a distinct Eastern European accent. He was about to protest when Lori jumped in. 'He took me to *that* room, can you believe it? Where that man was *murdered*. I mean, I could *smell* death in the air. It was everywhere, even in the bathroom. *Especially* in the bathroom.'

The maid shook her head. 'No, no, room not available. Management not allow bookings since horrible murder.'

'See, I *told* you,' Jimmy said, weirdly realising he was actually enjoying the opportunity to put one over on his colleague.

'Oh my God I'm *so* sorry,' Lori blurted out, covering her mouth with her hands. She paused for a moment, then said. 'But Aleksandra, it must have been you that discovered the body, since it's your floor. How *totally* gross. Poor you.'

The woman shook her head again. 'No, I worked on fourth floor that day. Maya discovered body.'

'Poor Maya,' Lori said. 'Is she a friend of yours? And is she okay?'

'She not friend. She work through same agency as me, but only for one week. She saw murderer too. I think she very upset about everything. Then she did not come back after police spoke to her.'

'So she just left?' Lori asked. 'And she was only here for a week. Is that normal?'

'No,' Aleksandra said. 'All girls work here long time. It is good job in nice hotel and we get very good tips.'

'Except Maya,' Lori said, evidently thinking out loud. *'Except Maya.'* She was silent for a moment then asked, 'This Maya. What did she look like? What I mean is was she young or old, attractive or plain, that sort of thing?'

The maid looked at her suspiciously. 'Why you want to know?'

'She's just a really nosey girl,' Jimmy said, cottoning on to where Lori was going with this. 'We sort of... well, we come here quite a lot, and last time there was a maid still in our room when we checked in. And Lori went mad when I started staring at her.' He gave what he hoped was an embarrassed laugh. 'You know what us men are like. But she was bloody sexy and I couldn't help myself.'

'She was whore, that is what girls thought,' Aleksandra said suddenly. 'And not Polish, even though she said she was. She spoke language but she did not have accent.'

'So where *was* she from?' Jimmy asked.

The woman shrugged. 'Maybe Czech, maybe Bulgaria, maybe Russia even, I don't know. I spoke only two times to her I think.'

'And now she's gone,' Lori said. The woman gave a single nod, but didn't look her in the eye. Then suddenly she said, 'But now maybe I should not speak again. Have nice stay in hotel.' And with that, she returned to the room she had been cleaning and quietly closed the door behind her.

'Well that was bloody interesting,' Jimmy said. 'But I bet she's in there phoning someone, so we'd better disappear I think. Which is a shame, because I quite fancied staying here tonight.'

Lori gave him a wistful look, and it seemed as if she was going to make some comment, before thinking better of it. Instead she sighed, then after a moment's silence said, 'Yeah, *suppose*.' But her evident disappointment didn't last long. 'This is like *mental,*' she said, wide-eyed. 'I mean, I had this crazy idea that it might be Jade Niven, but I didn't actually expect it to be *true*.'

'It's no more crazy than *both* of them being Sienna Taggart,' he said, frowning. 'The whole thing is just off-the-charts mental. If it was a plot in a TV detective show it would make you laugh out loud with the improbability of it all. And yet, it's happening, here in bonnie Scotland.' He took a quick glance at his watch. 'We're due on a conference call with Maggie and Frank in what, about an hour and a half? I might as well come back to Glasgow with you and stay overnight at their house, and that will give us plenty of time on the journey back to chew it over. But as I said, I think we'd best get out of here quick as we can. And I don't think we'll bother checking out either.'

They opted to stroll back down Cowgate, heading for the South Bridge which led directly to the entrance of Waverly

Station. Being summer, the Mile was packed with tourists, and within a few hundred feet Jimmy reckoned he'd heard the dulcet tones of at least a dozen-and-a-half different nationalities. But as they turned the corner into South Bridge, a black Mercedes taxi-van suddenly drew up alongside them, the door sliding open as it came to a complete stop. *'Hey youse, are youse Bainbridge Associates?'* an enquiring voice shouted from inside the cab, and Jimmy had no difficulty in recognising *this* accent, a rough Glasgow rasp that immediately put him on the alert. And then he spun round to better see its owner. The guy was huge, built like a nightclub bouncer, with a shaven head and wearing a short-sleeved Scotland football shirt that displayed massive tattooed arms. But it wasn't the guy's physique that was the focus of his attention, it was what the thug was holding in his hand.

The fact was, Jimmy had never been tasered before, but he was absolutely bloody certain he wasn't going to like it.

Chapter 24

'I've tried both of them independently now and I'm getting no response,' Maggie said, her voice betraying her mounting concern. 'And I've checked on Find My Phone and it looks like both of them are switched off. I don't know why they would do that, do you?'

It was four-fifteen in the afternoon, and she'd not long before clicked the link through to their scheduled video call. Frank had already been online when the call connected, and they'd chatted and joked whilst they waited for the other two to join. But after a few minutes they had begun to get worried, and now, ten minutes beyond that, they struggled for an explanation as to their colleagues' continuing non-appearance.

'Might be that the mobile service is down again,' Frank speculated. *'We've had two or three of these cyber attacks over spring and summer remember, and it could be another one of them I suppose.'*

'Yeah maybe,' she said. 'But I was kinda expecting them to have arrived back in Glasgow by now, and you're there and you're connected okay.'

'Aye true,' he said. *'But listen, I'm sure they'll turn up in a bit, so whilst we're waiting, let me give you an update on the Agnes Lomond story. I've been down at Renton talking to her old school. Not particularly illuminating, I have to say, but it's got me thinking.'*

'Yes okay,' she said, although in truth she doubted whether she would be able to concentrate on Frank's story given her growing concern for the whereabouts of Jimmy and Lori.

'So I spoke to the head teacher, a Mrs Boyd. Nice lady and she's been at the school for nearly twenty years, first as a teacher, then deputy head and then the head, not that her career history is all that important. The key thing is she was there for Agnes's school-days, and described her as a poor wee thing. Her dad legged it when she was a baby and then her mother had a massive breakdown, which resulted in her daughter being taken into care. Agnes wasn't academic or particularly pretty either is how Mrs Boyd remembers her, but she said the school had a really good careers service and they managed to get her a traineeship with Global Holidays, you know, the big package holiday outfit. She became a rep and moved to Cyprus, where she stayed for a number of years. More than ten actually.'

Maggie smiled. 'Before making a triumphant return to Scotland.'

'Aye,' he said, *'and looking nothing like she did before, according to Mrs Boyd. And that, as I said, got me thinking. I mean it seems bloody obvious now, but what if Sienna isn't Agnes Lomond at all? Let's face it, there's just so much that's mental about this bloody case that another bit of craziness wouldn't make it any worse.'*

'So who is she?' Maggie said, furrowing her brow, 'and what happened to the real Agnes?'

Frank shrugged. *'Who she is, I can't answer. What happened to Agnes, I can't answer either...'*

Involuntarily, Maggie found herself laughing. 'That's brilliant work darling.'

He grinned. *'I was just going to say except, before you so rudely interrupted. So if you don't mind...'*

She laughed again. 'No please, go ahead.'

'Okay. So I was going on to say that I phoned Global Holidays and asked them when Agnes Lomond had left them. It was a nightmare by the way, getting to the right department, but I eventually found one of those human resources manager types who was prepared to talk to a Chief Inspector of the Metropolitan Police.'

'Frank...', she began to protest.

'I know, I know,' he said jumping in before she could finish, *'I'm suspended. But anyway, I sweet-talked her a bit. Said it was just a quick two-minute call, and I knew that employee information was all totally confidential and that we would in due course be coming to them with a proper official warrant, but that it would help us enormously if I could just get a rough idea when Agnes Lomond had left their employment. I said I didn't want a date or even a month, just something to the nearest quarter or so that would give us a fast start in an important murder enquiry. And then I said that she shouldn't feel obliged and if she was uncomfortable giving even that information over the phone I would totally understand.'*

'And did all this impressive schmoozing work?' Maggie asked, although she suspected it must have had, otherwise Frank wouldn't have been telling her the story.

'End of Quarter 3, 2017,' Frank said, with a distinct air of triumph. *'Which, I find, is about six bloody months after Sienna Taggart first pops up on the radar back in Scotland.'*

'Bloody hell,' she said, surprised. 'So the question is, what does this mean?'

He shrugged again. '*Who knows? But what I'm suggesting is that our Sienna Taggart meets the real Agnes Lomond out in Cyprus, finds out about her background and specifically - and this is very important I think- finds out that she has no family, so our Sienna is able to take over the identity of Lomond and head back to Scotland to carry out her dastardly scheme.* '

'What dastardly scheme?'

He paused for a moment then sighed. *'No bloody idea. But that's for us all to try and figure out, because when we do, we'll crack this case wide open, and make no mistake.'*

'So the original Agnes Lomond is still out in Cyprus?' Maggie asked.

He gave another sigh. *'Maybe. I'm guessing some money changed hands such that the original Agnes keeps schtum about the whole arrangement and goes off to live a quiet life on the island. But I think we're dealing with some really bad guys here, and the best way to ensure someone stays schtum is to silence them permanently. So no, I don't fancy her chances much.'*

Suddenly something came to her. 'I went there on holiday about ten years ago. With Philip. Before we had Ollie.' Even now, more than three years after his death, she found it almost impossible to say her ex-husband's name without a feeling of revulsion threatening to overcome her, and in truth, it was a holiday she would have been quite happy to forget forever. Taking a breath, she continued. 'And what was massively noticeable was that the place was absolutely *awash* with Russians and Russian money too. But you know what was even more noticeable?'

'Tell me,' Frank said.

'It was the women. They all dressed like whores, all these Svetlanas with their high heels, short tight dresses and showing off their breasts.' She paused for a moment before continuing. *'Exactly* like Sienna Taggart in fact.' And, when she reflected some more, exactly like Dominique Tremblay too.

'That's it,' Frank exclaimed suddenly. *'That's bloody it.'*

'What is?' Maggie asked, her voice urgent with expectation.

*'I **knew** there was something bloody strange about the way Mrs Taggart spoke one of the times I met her. It was just one phrase, what was it now? Aye, that's it. **I have big list to get on with**. You see? Not **a big list** like we would say, just **big list.** It's been bugging me all this time. But now I know.'*

'Know what?' she said, still puzzled.

He gave a triumphant smile. *'Sienna Taggart's a bloody Russian. A bloody Russian. I guarantee it. See, I told you it would be something crazy. And now it all adds up, with the Cyprus thing and what you said about the women out there. And all that bloody deep-fake stuff that's being going on too.'*

She was just about to agree when her phone buzzed in her hand, signifying another video call was coming in. Her heart missed a beat as she saw it was Jimmy. 'Frank, I'll need to put you on hold for a minute. It's Jimmy.'

'Where have you been?' she said, giving a smile of relief as she swiped onto the call. And then, as she looked at him properly, she stopped smiling. 'God, what the hell's happening?' she exclaimed, aghast. His eyes were puffy and bloodshot, and a stream of what she could only assume was dried blood made a wide track down one cheek. But it wasn't that which made her gasp in horror. It was the fact that he was naked from the waist up, sitting facing her on a wooden chair, his arms stretched out behind him, his wrists almost certainly bound. Being Jimmy though, he tried to crack a joke. 'What's happening? We're just having a party here, that's all. I've made some new friends. Nice lads, but a bit rough.'

'Shut the f**k up,' a Glasgow-accented voice from off-camera said. 'Just get to the f**king point.'

Jimmy smiled. 'Aye, the point. So it seems, Miss Bainbridge, that you've upset some folks and they want to have a chat with you. They're saying you need to be back at your office tomorrow at nine o'clock prompt, otherwise they're going to perform some crude plastic surgery on Lori's lovely face.'

'God no,' Maggie said, covering her face with her hands. 'Look, of course, I'll be there. Of course.'

'I wouldn't, ' Jimmy said, speaking quickly. 'Because I think me and Lori are in trouble whether you do or whether you don't.' And then, to her absolute horror, a fist smashed into

Jimmy's face, knocking him off balance and causing the chair to totter uncertainly. And this time a figure came into shot, a gorilla of a man, shaven-headed and tattooed. And wearing what she recognised as a replica Scotland football shirt. He pointed at the phone and said, 'You'd better be in Byers Road tomorrow morning lady, or your pals are f**king dead. But right now your pretty boy's going off to have a night of fun with my gaffer. See you tomorrow. Tatty-bye.' And then she saw him stretch out a finger towards the *End Call* button, and a second later, they were gone.

'Shit shit shit,' she cried, as she switched back to Frank's call, her mind in total turmoil. In a torrent of garbled words, she tried to explain what had just happened. And then the truth hit her like a sledgehammer, plunging her mood even further into despair.

'Oh God, this is my fault Frank, isn't it?' she said, struggling to hold back tears. 'My stupid call to Dominique set it all off, didn't it? What a bloody fool I've been.'

He didn't answer immediately, and she couldn't work out of it was because of the shock, or whether he was silently angry with her for being so impetuous.

'It was bound to come out eventually,' he said finally, with a softness of tone that she hoped was for her benefit. 'But this is serious shit Maggie, and I'm certain we're dealing with some very very scary forces. And to be honest, I've no idea what we're going to do, because this is a hundred percent no-win situation.'

She didn't need to ask him what he meant, because the bleakness of their predicament was as plain as the nose on her face. She, Maggie Bainbridge of Bainbridge Associates, had information that could expose the truth about Dominique Tremblay and her co-conspirators, and so she, and by implication, her colleagues, had to be silenced. The horrible fact was, Jimmy and Lori were dead whether she went to the Byers Road office the next day or not. She looked at her watch. *Twenty minutes to five.* Which meant they had little more than sixteen hours to work out where the hell they were being held and to come up with some crazy plan to rescue them. Not that *she* was going to be able to do much, marooned as she was in the middle of bloody nowhere.

Other than *think* of course. And usually, that was enough.

***

They'd stayed on the line for almost an hour, desperately trying to figure out what they should do, she with her scribbled notes in front of her, Frank relying on his slightly-fallible memory. But then she had quite brusquely told him that she needed to be on her own, to be able to think properly, a proposal to which, she judged, he had taken no offence, having simply told her he loved her, wished her luck, then rung off. For almost half an hour since she had just sat on the sofa, chewing her pen and calmly reviewing the jumbled pile of facts that she knew would in time be assembled into a coherent whole. The only problem was, time was the one thing they didn't have.

The breaking news was, at least according to Frank, that Sienna Taggart was Russian, causing Maggie once again to think about that unhappy Cyprus holiday and the tarty Russian women that were everywhere. What was startlingly obvious was that the men they had been attached to were generally old and unattractive, some grotesquely so, but they were all *very* rich. Fabulously rich in fact, with Ferraris and Lamborghinis and superyachts and amazing villas and dozens of white-uniformed flunkies attending to their every whim. These powerful men liked to parade their success to the world, and a critical part of that success was the possession of a beautiful and sexy wife, the sort of wife that other men would lust over and envy. She remembered thinking at the time that for these women, it was a perfectly logical life and career choice, even if it was one Maggie herself would have shunned. These were women who were using their sexual power to get what they wanted. Which, she realised, was *exactly* what Dominique Tremblay and Sienna Taggart had done, using their allure to snare two of the most important men in Scottish politics. The difference was, these women in Cyprus had done it for their own financial gain, whereas Tremblay and Taggart had done it for.... well, that was the question, wasn't it? *Why exactly?* That surely had to be important in figuring out this whole mess, yet for some reason, she found herself coming back again and again to the tabloid story about that classy soap actress Paige and her all-night sessions with Johnny Pallas. In her bones she knew it had some important significance, but no matter how much she wracked her brain, she just couldn't see how.

Setting that aside for the moment, she decided to focus her attention on the bizarre fact that Sienna Taggart had also been Jade Niven. She'd made a one-line entry in her notes. *Jade Niven, the honey-trapper*. It dawned on her that such women, unlike the Cyprus trophy wives, weren't doing it for their own personal gain. The seduction was simply the point of entry to a grander scheme, as yet unknown, and unlike the Cyprus women, they had back-up - money, almost certainly, muscle, where necessary, and, as demonstrated by the dodgy Donnie Morrison videos, sophisticated technical resources too. Crazy as this all seemed, it pointed squarely at one of these so-called bad actors that Carrie-Anne Fisher suspected were operating in Frank's homeland. She could just imagine the ecstatic reaction of Yash Patel if he ever managed to get a hold of the story. *Exposed: Russian agents operating undercover in Scotland.* But still, the Paige and Pallas thing just wouldn't go away. *Where the hell did that fit in?*

As she thought some more about the *modus operandi* of the generic honey-trapper, it brought to mind a phrase she had heard in some American cop show a while back, a phrase she had found intensely distasteful yet had stuck with her. *Men will do anything for a sniff of pussy.* That, surely, was the central premise on which the success of the trapper depended. And then out of the blue, it came to her, and as it did, her face instantly turned a vivid crimson and she felt an explosion of elation. *'That's bloody it!'* she screamed at the top of her voice, momentarily forgetting about little Ollie sleeping soundly in the next room. The question, the huge, off-the-scale *critical* question, was staring her in the face, as it probably had been *weeks* ago if only she had thought about it properly. But now she *knew*. She picked up her notebook and, smiling with a smug satisfaction, wrote it down.

What if they don't like pussy?

Chapter 25

The call from Maggie had been close-on unintelligible, she excitedly firing a staccato of facts at him like lurid-coloured pellets from a paintball gun. At one point, he'd had to move the phone away from his ear, such was the volume of the torrent that was coming at him. Struggling to keep up, he'd gently suggested she slow down a bit, to no avail, but eventually he got the gist of it, and it wasn't good news. *The two of them are being held at that Harley-Dee's club, and Jimmy's going to suffer unimaginable horrors and then he and Lori are going to be killed. You need to get there, and quick.* And then she had abruptly hung up, he guessing so that he didn't hear her crying.

Without pausing to think, he had grabbed his car keys and ran for the door, and two minutes later he was swinging onto the Glasgow Road, thick with traffic even on this midweek early-evening. Cursing, he thought of the drive ahead, threading through the city's congested urban motorway network before hitting the car-park nightmare that was the main M8 to Edinburgh. Impulsively, he punched at his phone. DC Lexy McDonald answered on the second ring.

'Great to hear from you sir,' she said brightly. *'We've all been worried sick about you. Me, Eleanor and Ronnie I mean.'*

It was a nice sentiment, but he didn't have time to acknowledge it. 'Look Lexy,' he said quickly. 'I'm in deep shit and I could really do with your help.' *And I'll probably be landing you in the shit too* was what he should have said, but didn't. 'Where are you right now?' he asked, hoping he'd get the answer he wanted.

'I'm at home sir. They've got me on a big warehouse robbery at the moment and I'm just sitting at my laptop trawling through the CCTV. Dead thrilling,' she added, sounding anything but thrilled. *'So what is it you want me to do?'*

'Are you still allocated that wee blue Vauxhall pool car?'

He heard her laugh. *'It's sitting outside sir. But I'm hope we're not wanting to do a car chase, it's not exactly fast.'*

He smiled. 'No worries, all I need is the blue light and the siren. Listen, any chance you can meet me at that big petrol station on the way down to the Clyde tunnel, you know the one that doubles as a convenience store? There's something I need to pick up there before I go. We'll swap over and you can drive my car back to your flat. You're only ten minutes away I think.'

'What do you mean, drive your car back?' she said. *'I'm coming with you, aren't I? Whatever it is you've got planned.'*

'Actually you're not,' he shot back. 'You'll be in enough trouble just doing this for me.'

'You're not getting the car unless I get to come,' she said, adding a delayed *'sir'* in a voice that suggested she found the situation rather amusing.

'This isn't funny,' he said, it coming out sharper than he meant it to, and immediately regretting it. 'Sorry Lexy, I'm in a bit of a state at the moment. And I don't want screwing up your glittering career adding to my woes. Besides, this could all get a bit exciting.'

'What, more exciting than looking at CCTV?' she said. *'Sir, if you let me come on whatever it is your doing, I'll do exactly as you tell me, I promise. Girl Guides honour.'*

'You were never in the Girl Guides,' he said wryly. 'Listen, some really bad guys have captured Jimmy and Lori and I think we've got no more than a few hours before they get killed.'

'Shit,' she exclaimed. *'God, sorry sir, I didn't realise. Otherwise...'*

'I didn't tell you,' he interrupted. 'But you can see why I'm a bit agitated.' He glanced at the clock on the dashboard. 'Look, I'm just a mile or two from Anniesland. If you set off now, we should be at the petrol station at about the same time. I'll talk to you then, bye.'

She pulled in just ahead of him, selecting one of the parking bays reserved for convenience-store shoppers who were not requiring fuel. He parked up at the slot alongside her, jumped out of his car and half-sprinted to the automatic sliding door of the shop. 'Just give me a minute Lexy,' he shouted over to her, giving her a thumbs-up. Two minutes later, he emerged with a green plastic petrol-can then jogged over to the nearest free pump, slotted in his credit card to authorise the payment, and filled it up. Back at the parking space, he saw that Lexy had slid over to the passenger seat of her Vauxhall Corsa.

He yanked open the rear door and placed the can on the floor. 'I thought I told you you weren't coming,' he said, closing the door and simultaneously placing a hand on the handle of the front door. 'Not optional I'm afraid,' he finished, as he slipped into the driver's seat. 'Here, I'll give you my keys and you can tootle off back home.'

She turned to look at him. 'Sir, you'll do anything to save your brother and his colleague,' she said earnestly, 'and you don't give a stuff how it affects your career. I'm right, aren't I sir?'

'Aye, but...' he started, but she interrupted before he could finish.

'So I've just found out that two members of the public are in desperate danger sir. As a serving police officer, I just can't ignore that. It's my duty sir, and I have to put that before any selfish career considerations.'

He paused for moment, gave a deep sigh, then shook his head. 'DC McDonald, I wish you weren't so *bloody* damn smart,' he said, failing to suppress a laugh. 'That's why you're going to be Chief Constable one day, I bloody guarantee it.'

'I don't know about that sir,' she said, grinning, 'but I *am* coming to Edinburgh with you this evening. Although could I just say sir, it would be a lot better if an armed response team could come along with us too.'

He gave a bitter laugh. 'Aye, can you imagine how *that* conversation would go? *Hello ma'am, it's DCI Frank Stewart here, aye that's right, that Met bloke who's been suspended for helping a prime murder suspect to do a runner. What it is, my brother and his colleague have been kidnapped by a bunch of guys who we think might be Russian agents, and they're being held in a gay club just off the Royal Mile and they're going to be murdered in the morning. So, would you mind sending in an armed response unit as soon as you can?'*

'Yeah, I see what you mean sir. So it's just us then, is it?'

'Just me actually,' he corrected. 'You're not going anywhere near that place.' Although, he thought ruefully, that might be easier to say than to enforce.

Contrary to his expectations, the eastbound traffic was lighter than he'd anticipated, with only the occasional need to resort to the blue light or siren to clear dawdling drivers from their path. En-route, he did his best to update Lexy on the situation and explain Maggie's theory as to how it all fitted together, although if truth be told, he didn't really understand it himself. All he was really concentrating on was what he was going to do when he reached that Harley Dee's club, where according to Maggie's conjecture, his brother and their colleague Lorilynn Logan were being held against their will. However that was all it was, conjecture, and if he went ahead with his plan - and the fact was, it wasn't much of a plan - and they weren't there, then the consequences would be unthinkable. But less than forty-five minutes after leaving the garage, they were passing Edinburgh airport, with just a few miles to run until they reached the city centre. He looked over to Lexy and shot her a smile.

'Thank God for bus lanes, eh? As long as there's no bloody buses blocking our way. Should be a doddle from here on in.'

She gave him a doubtful smile. 'Yeah, but they've got the trams some of the way I think sir, and they hold up everybody. Maybe you could use their tracks too.'

'Aye that would be a laugh, wouldn't it?' he said. And the fact was, if it eased their passage, he wouldn't be ruling it out. But now Lexy had punched Harley Dee's address into her phone's sat nav and was staring at it anxiously as they approached the western end of Princes Street, having run through three straight red lights in a row. 'It's a nightmare around here, with all these one-way streets everywhere sir. The club's on Cockburn Street, and that's one-way too. There's about a two-mile round trip to get to it, according to this.'

He grinned. 'That's why I wanted your motor. Normal rules don't apply to us cops.' Switching on both flashing light and siren, he floored the accelerator and gave a loud whoop. 'Tally-ho, off we go. Oh and Lexy?'

'Yes sir?'

'Dial nine-nine-nine right now and tell them you're a barmaid at Harley Dee's and you're witnessing a big stooshy kicking off. Tell them there's guys fighting and one of them's got a knife and it looks like someone's already been stabbed. Oh aye, and say someone's set fire to the curtains so you need the fire brigade as well. And don't worry about getting done afterwards for raising a false alarm, because it's all going to come *absolutely* true when I get there.'

She laughed. 'So that's your plan is it sir?'

'Well, have you got a better one?' he said, simultaneously slamming his fist on the horn as an unsuspecting pedestrian stepped out in front of him, quite reasonably not expecting a car to be travelling the wrong way down a one-way street. 'The thing is, there's more than one type of rapid-response squad. The fire brigade boys and girls hardly ever get to attend any real fires, they spend all their time rescuing cats up trees. They'll be so excited by this one that they'll probably get there before we do, and they'll send everything they've got.'

It took another few minutes of weaving in and out of the traffic, but at last they arrived. Frank screeched the car up on to the pavement and said, 'Right Lexy, you wait here, and that's a bloody order.' She looked as if she was about to protest, but he held up a hand to silence her. 'Look, it's part of the plan. You need to keep the motor running so that if I succeed in springing Jimmy and Lori we're ready for a quick getaway. Because these guys will probably come after us all guns blazing, and I mean that literally.'

Jumping out of the driver's seat, he yanked open the rear door and grabbed the petrol can, at the same time fumbling in a side-pocket to make sure the disposable lighter he'd also purchased hadn't fallen out, and then to his back pocket to make sure he had a supply of cable-ties and his trusty penknife. All good, so now it was time to see if his plan survived its first encounter with real life. He sprinted up the three steps that led to the front door of the club and shoved it open, finding himself in a large dark room with a full-length bar down one side. Disco lights strobed overhead and a sound system was pumping out a hi-tempo dance beat of the type he hated with a passion. Being just eight o'clock, the place was sparsely populated, no more than a dozen or so punters sprinkled around the tables enjoying a drink. Looking over, he saw the bar was being tended by just one barman. And then, doing a surprised double-take, he realised he recognised who it was.

'Well well well,' he said as he reached the bar, 'If it's not the Taggart's flunky. Jimmy Petrie isn't it? Remember me? I'm the cops, and I want to talk to your gaffers. Are they here?'

Caught by surprise, the boy stammered, 'Eh... Mr and Mrs Taggart don't normally see visitors.'

'So they're here are they?' Frank said. 'That's good. So I suggest you toddle off backstage and bloody well find them, okay son? Because I'm one-hundred-percent sure they'll want to see me.'

Frank could see the fear in the boy's eyes. 'No, I'm no' doing that,' the barman said. 'No way.'

'Okay then,' Frank said, smiling, 'Let's go immediately to Plan B.' Ostentatiously, he held out the petrol can, removed the cap, then began to slosh petrol over the floor. 'That should do nicely,' he said, sniffing the air. 'And I just *love* that smell, don't you? Beautiful.' He took the lighter from his pocket, shook it in front of the barman's face and said, 'Do you know what this is pal?'

By the look of him, he thought the boy was going to faint with fright. 'You're f**king mental,' he screamed, wide-eyed. 'F**king mental.'

'Lots of people say that. I take it as a compliment.' He clicked the lighter, sending up a flickering blue flame which he held so close to the boy that it risked setting his hair on fire. 'And don't you forget it.' He paused for a moment as he thought through his options. Then he gave a shrug, and with an audible *what the hell,* he bent down, the lighter still aflame. There was a loud *woof* as the petrol vapour caught alight, instantly spreading across the floor and shooting up several feet of orange flames. Seconds later, and as he had calculated, the smoke detection system kicked into action, switching on bright overhead lighting whilst triggering a deafening alarm that filled the room with an unbearable cacophony of sound. He was expecting a sprinkler system to start dowsing the fire, but after a few seconds it was clear that the place either didn't have one or it was out of action. *Shit.* Amongst the few customers, panic had already set in, with screams of fear just about audible above the din of the alarm. 'Come on guys, out you get,' Frank shouted, ushering a quartet of drinkers towards the door. 'Go go go, get a bloody move on!' Nobody needed telling twice, and within a minute the room was empty, the young barman amongst the first to leg it, ignoring any *what to do in the event of fire* training he might have received.

Suddenly, a door at the back of the room marked *Staff Only* burst open and Tommy Taggart stepped out, shielding his eyes against the blinding light as he scanned the room. And with a stomach-turning feeling of revulsion, Frank saw that Taggart was dressed only in a towel. Knowing he had seconds to exploit the element of surprise he had earned, he leapt over to the politician and thrust the man's arm up his back, at the same time forcing him violently to the ground. As he did so, Frank heard Taggart's nose crack against the hard floor. He grabbed a handful of hair and hauled it back up with a brutal jerk.

'Where are they Taggart?' he shouted, his face just inches from the man's. 'Where's my brother and Lori? *Tell me*!' Getting no answer, he smashed Taggart's face back into the floor with a force that this time had probably broken his nose. But now reinforcements had arrived, as a pair of the football-shirted goons he'd seen at the Glasgow Green rally stood framed in the doorway. 'Hello boys,' Frank said, looking up at them and not liking what he saw. But evidently, like the barman before them, the goons' credo was to put self-preservation above loyalty to their boss, their sole concession to duty being to land a forceful boot in Frank's face as they charged through the flames on their way to the exit.

'Nice guys,' Frank said, gingerly feeling his burst lip. 'Right then Taggart,' he said, returning his attention to his quarry, 'you're nicked and I'll work out the charges when I get back to you.' He pulled out two cable-ties from his pocket and yanked them tight around the politician's wrists. And then, as an afterthought, he ripped off the towel, leaving him sprawled stark-naked on the floor. 'Head for the door if you like,' he shouted, grinning. 'That'll make a nice picture for the papers. Stick it on your campaign leaflets.'

Jumping up, he ran through the doors into a corridor that he assumed led to storerooms and the office area. It was evidently equipped with a repeater alarm because here the noise was no quieter, and already it was filling up with smoke from the fire. Looking down, he saw there were three doors leading off it, as well as, pleasingly, a fire exit which was located at the opposite end. He kicked open the first door he came to and peered in. An office, with two silent desktop computers on two empty desks. The next door got the same treatment, this one disappointingly opening into a tiny broom cupboard containing some cleaning equipment. Which meant there was only one more room where they could be, if they were in fact here at all. He paused for a moment to catch his breath and to gather his thoughts. If they were in there, they would probably be guarded, and there might be guns too, not exactly an appetising prospect. But then, he thought back to the very first meeting he and Lexy had had with the Taggarts. *And smiled.*

The alarm was still going off ten to the dozen, so he knew it would be hard to recognise anyone's voice over the din. Still, despite being no mimic, he did his best to adopt the rough-arsed accent that had become so familiar across Scottish airwaves in the last year. He wrapped on the door then shouted, *'Hey Sienna doll, get your arse out here. I need your help with this bastard.'* A few seconds later, the door swung inward, and Sienna Taggart stepped out into the corridor, wielding a pistol. Frank, pressed hard against one wall, had made a bet with himself as to which way she would look first, a bet with unpleasant fifty-fifty odds, but a bet which he had just won. He took one step towards her and chopped down hard on the gun-carrying arm, sending the weapon spinning down the corridor. Taken by surprise, she spun round, just in time to catch the full force of his fist smashing into her face. 'Sorry Sienna doll,' he mouthed as she crumpled to the floor, 'I don't like to hit a woman, but I've already used all my cable-ties.'

As Maggie had so brilliantly deduced, Jimmy and Lori were there, he with his eyes closed and lying spread-eagled and naked on a king-sized bed, his wrists attached to the metal head-board with rope. Lori sat in one corner, gagged and cable-tied to a wooden chair. 'Christ,' he exclaimed. 'Bloody hell!' He ripped off Lori's gag and shouted, 'Come on, we've got to get you two out of here before Sienna wakes up.' He fumbled in his pocket, brought out the tiny penknife and gave it a doubtful look. Still, it was sharp enough so should be up to the job, he hoped.

'Jimmy's been drugged,' Lori said, her eyes wide with fear. 'I don't know what they used but it's as if he's drunk a whole bottle of whisky. It was an injection, I saw them do it.'

'Shit,' Frank said. 'But let's get *you* free first Lori, then you can help me.' Swiftly he slashed her cable-ties, she shaking off the stiffness from her arms as she got unsteadily to her feet. Giving her a supportive smile, he handed her the little knife and said, 'Any chance you can cut his wrists free whilst I try to wake him up?' She nodded, taking a couple of steps over to the bed then kneeling alongside it. Frank went round the other side, and grabbing his brother by the shoulders, began to shake him vigorously. 'Come on Jimmy-boy,' he said. 'You need to wake up pal. Come on, wake up.' This having failed to make him stir, he repeated the process, but this time added half-a-dozen slaps on the face.

'What?' Jimmy said groggily, raising his head trying to sit up. 'Where am I?'

'That's not important right now,' Frank said, slipping an arm under Jimmy's armpit in a bid to help him up. 'What's important is that you're not here very much longer. Do you think you can stand up mate?'

'I'll try,' Jimmy said, his voice shaking. 'I'll try.'

'You'd bloody better,' Frank said, 'because you weigh about fifteen stone, even in your birthday suit and I'm not bloody carrying you.' Then he realised he was still holding Tommy Taggart's towel. 'Here, let's get this round you, we don't want you frightening the horses. Lori, turn left out the door and you'll see the fire exit. Give the metal bar a good shove and let's get out of this dump PDQ.'

***

Outside had been a modern re-imagining of bedlam, Frank counting at least a dozen emergency service vehicles outside the club with lights flashing and sirens blazing, and nearly as many incident commanders trying to look masterful whilst bellowing importantly into their walkie-talkies. Courtesy of a convenient side passageway, they'd managed to slip away unobserved and into the waiting Vauxhall, parked anonymously a hundred feet down the hill from where he had left it, and from where DC McDonald had whisked them back to the Milngavie bungalow and a waiting bottle of fifteen-year-old Glenfiddich. Back at the scene, word had got round that rebel-rouser Tommy Taggart had been found on the premises, naked and trussed up, whilst his wife, suffering from an apparent assault which the police suspected had been administered by her husband, was found in possession of an illegal handgun, with which, it was alleged, she meant to enact revenge on her spouse. Naturally this information had instantly leaked to the press, and specifically to the *Chronicle's* Scottish editor Jimani Shah, who was presently debating with herself whether she would share this sensational breaking news with her lover Yash Patel, and deciding that she probably wouldn't. The next day, there had been a lot of complicated explaining to do, a task that had taken Frank the best part of two hours whilst locked in the stuffy office of Assistant Chief Constable Natalie Young. But eventually the ACC had been convinced, and urgent calls had gone out to Special Branch and MI6 and to CIA secondee Carrie-Anne Fisher, causing well-rehearsed but seldom-used counter-espionage plans to kick into action. Frank of course, had had his suspension immediately rescinded, for which he was naturally most grateful.

But best of all, he was able to make a phone call to that isolated little love-nest up in the Highlands, conveying the news to his beloved that finally, she could come in from the cold.

Chapter 26

It was, by general public consensus, the most sensational happening that the United Kingdom had experienced in a generation, and in fact some of the more excitable commentators were contending that nothing quite like it had occurred since the start of the Cold War. Accordingly, it had caused a media storm, a frenzied bidding war breaking out to get the exclusive inside story from Maggie Bainbridge, the modest private investigator who had exposed the outrageous conspiracy. Six figure sums had been mentioned, and Lorilynn Logan, the agency's most recent recruit, had spent the last week urging her boss to accept a ridiculously lucrative offer from a US media powerhouse. But Maggie, loyal to the last, had determined from the start that if the story had to be sold, it could only go to Yash Patel at the Chronicle. Which explained why they were assembled here on a Friday evening in what the Royal Mile Grampian hotel called their premier event space. An army of tartan-clad waiting stuff circulated discreetly, offering expensive champagne and mouth-watering canapés to the invited guests. The Chronicle was picking up the bill, which was expected to be significant, but to the newspaper's syndicating team, it was small beer, salivating as they were on the enormous sums that would come flooding in when the story was licensed around the globe. These glossy media shindigs were becoming almost a tradition for the agency, Maggie reflected, a consequence of the high-profile cases they seemed to be attracting these days. But for her lovely assistant Lori, it was evidently another matter that was exercising her, and that was the fact that her boss had inexplicably turned down the opportunity to be the cover star of the next edition of the country's glossiest fashion magazine.

'It would be bloody amazing Maggie,' she was pleading. 'They spend a fortune on hair and makeup and everything and then they use fancy lighting and filters and photo-shopping to make you look like a movie star. Why wouldn't you want to do that?'

Maggie gave her a look of wry amusement. 'It's just not *me* Lori. Besides, we're getting enough publicity as it is. I don't think we need any more.' But it was more than that of course. It just wouldn't have been right, she thought, given the devastating sting in the tail this already horrible case had delivered just yesterday. 'And it would be terribly disrespectful to the Morrisons, now that we know what happened to their son Rory.'

The girl paused for a moment, evidently weighing up whether to say what had obviously been on her mind for some time.

'Well, can I do it instead?' she said coyly. 'They could run a feature on me, and I could be the beautiful young aide of rock-star private-eye Maggie Bainbridge.'

'Who's a rock star?' Frank asked, arriving on the scene with a mouth full of upmarket sausage roll. He nodded in the direction of a group who were tucked in a far corner of the room. 'See that lot?'

'You mean with your lovely Carrie-Anne Fisher?' Maggie said, the tone a tad sharper than she intended.

'Aye, but I'm talking about the ones with her. See that fifty-something woman? Patel thinks that's Dame Celia Carrington, although no-one's ever seen her picture.'

'What, the head of MI5?' Maggie asked, surprised.

He nodded. 'And MI6 too, I think. And the goons in the suits are her head honchos. You can tell they're all spooks because they never stand near a window in case of snipers.'

She wasn't sure if he was joking or not. 'Interesting,' she said. 'But why are they all here?'

'National security. They're here to make sure the Chronicle, and more specifically you and me, young Maggie, keep to the script.'

'Which is?'

He shrugged. 'Which is that only the government understands *realpolitik*, and whilst public outrage at the current situation is understandable, they're elected to look at the bigger picture.'

'Bollocks, in other words,' she said, and once again, the thought of what was likely to be the fate of the two women at the centre of the affair left her feeling deflated.

'Realpolitik,' Frank repeated, 'but aye, it amounts to the same thing. Anyway, let's go and have a chat to the gang before we get started on our big speech.'

The gang in question was standing next to a large serving table laden with food and drink, evidently provided for those guests unwilling to wait for a circulating waiter or waitress. Ronnie French and Jimmy were taking full advantage, availing themselves generously of the comestibles thereon, both solid and liquid. Lexy, Lori and Eleanor were in a huddle, clutching untouched champagne glasses and deep in conversation. A few feet away, Yash Patel stood wearing a faintly smug expression, staring across the room as if in silent meditation. Maggie wondered wryly if he might be mentally rehearsing the speech for his next major award.

'Hey guys,' Frank said, raising his glass as he approached them. 'We've done some bloody important work here, so congratulations to you all. The usual technical wizardry from you Eleanor, which was amazing, and as far as I know DC McDonald, you've not been sacked, which I consider a result.'

Eleanor, characteristically, gave a scowl but it was mild by her standards. Lexy smiled and said, 'Not so far sir. I think I'm safe for a while yet.'

'Good good. And what about you, Jimmy-boy? Still having nightmares about that close escape you had? Tommy Taggart must have thought Christmas had come early when he saw you lying on that bed with your kit off.'

Jimmy gave him a dry smile. 'Do you think so? But you're right bruv, I dodged one there right enough.' He smiled at them. 'So I guess we're about ready for your big speech are we?'

Maggie nodded, an apprehensive expression momentarily crossing her face. 'Yes, we're just about to start. Although I can't say I'm exactly looking forward to it. I'm just glad Frank will be up there with me.'

'Yeah, it's a bit like them football manager post-match interviews, ain't it?' Ronnie French interjected. 'They don't like doing them, but it's part of the deal with the TV companies. Suppose you're in the same boat Maggie,' he added. 'I'm thinking about young Yash here and the wad of cash his paper handed over for your exclusive story. They've dished out the mullah, and now they want to hear from the main woman.'

'Unfortunately Ronnie, you're right,' she said, laughing, 'but it has to be done.' Turning to Yash she asked. 'So Mr Patel, are we ready?'

He smiled. 'Yeah. Let's go.' Resting his hand on her shoulder, he gently steered her towards the podium that had been set up at one end of the room. She stood to one side of him as he mounted the wide single step of the rostrum, Frank one pace behind.

'Good evening ladies and gentlemen,' Yash said, speaking slowly then pausing to wait for the hubbub of conversation around the room to stop. 'And thank you for coming along this evening. There's press packs circulating for the media representatives and just remember, if you want to publish or broadcast anything, you need to sign one of our syndicate agreements. Otherwise our legal sharks will hunt you down and bite your balls off.' It was evidently meant as a joke, but gathered only a muted reaction from the gathered hacks, probably still smarting from missing out on the story themselves. 'So without further ado, give a big hand for the stars of our show. Miss Maggie Bainbridge of Bainbridge Associates and DCI Frank Stewart of the Metropolitan Police.'

They stepped onto the wide podium to a ripple of polite applause, Frank raising a hand in acknowledgement. Taking a deep breath Maggie said, 'Thank you. Let me apologise in advance, but this probably won't be the smoothest of talks you have ever heard, and given the terrible news yesterday about Rory Morrison, it might be one of the saddest. So please, bear with us as we stumble through.' She paused again, then began.

'It seems beyond implausible, but, we now know, it is indeed true. Two undercover Russian agents were operating in little old Scotland. Irina Antonov and Olga Lebedev, or as we better knew them, Dominique Tremblay and Sienna Taggart, were part of a vast network of agents operating across the western democracies, many patiently lying silent and undetected for years, waiting for the right opportunity to arise. And in Scotland, it was the 2014 Independence Referendum that provided that opportunity, causing a rift in society that split friends and family, young and old, left and right. Afterwards, Scottish politics took a nasty turn, with, in particular, a rise in overt anti-English sentiment that many detractors described as racist in nature. Not that I've ever experienced any of that myself. In fact...' She paused to smile at Frank. 'So much so, I'm actually marrying one of them.' A wave of laughter extended across the room. 'But it was this polarisation that allowed a nasty piece of work like Tommy Taggart to gain an audience.'

'And so the sleepers were awakened,' Frank commented. 'And got to work.'

'Exactly,' Maggie said. 'They were awakened. First to be called into action was Irina Antonov, who a couple of years earlier had surfaced in Scotland masquerading as Dominique Tremblay, a Canadian journalist with an impressive CV earned at Montreal's leading French-language newspaper, impressive enough to land her a job with the Globe. It was all fake of course, because the real Dominique Tremblay was killed in a skiing accident back in 2004. Our second agent, Olga Lebedev, had been stationed in Cyprus, a place thousands of Brits visit every year and where the UK military forces maintain a number of bases. Anyway, back in Moscow, the orders went out for Olga aka Sienna to target Taggart whilst Irina aka Dominique was targeted at Jack Urquhart. But more of *her* later.' She paused again for a moment and smiled. 'Everyone still with me?'

'Not got a bloody clue,' a familiar voice from the audience shouted. The accent was central-casting Cockney and loud enough for the whole room to hear, causing an outbreak of laughter. 'As usual. But I'm still enjoying the story. And I'm on my third glass of pop too.'

Maggie laughed. 'I'm glad you're having a nice time DC French. So of course,' she continued, 'the primary weapon these agents use to snare their prey is *sex*. Irina Antonov and Olga Lebedev are very alluring women, the sort of women who most men would find irresistible, and they would have been specifically recruited because of that, before being subjected to years of intense training. Olga's mission was to seduce Tommy Taggart and place the enormous financial and technical resources of the Russian espionage machine at the disposal of him and his Scottish

Freedom Party, the objective being to cause maximum mayhem in Scotland, and by extension, the UK. Their ultimate aim was nothing less than the breakdown of the democratic order.'

'Bloody hell,' someone shouted from the audience.

'Exactly,' Maggie agreed. 'So over in Cyprus, the real Agnes Lomond was paid off, Olga adopted her identity, then flew back to Scotland and went to work.'

'Only to discover that our Tommy didn't like girls,' Frank said.

'No, he didn't. But it wasn't *just* that he was gay. The fact was, Tommy Taggart had a veracious appetite for hard-core sex, and when Sienna discovered that, she realised it was something she would be able to exploit. A deal was done, wherein Tommy and Sienna would portray themselves as Scotland's new power couple, whilst she arranged that he got all the hot gay sex he wanted in return for doing exactly as she told him.'

'Bloody clever but bloody horrible too,' Frank said. 'But before all of that, they had to get him a seat in parliament.'

'That's right. And by good fortune, the Reverend Dr Donnie Morrison happened to occupy the ideal seat, in Paisley. It's predominately working-class and pretty deprived, exactly the sort of folks who were already out on the streets marching for Taggart's SFP. It was well known that Morrison had a reputation for being a creep around women, and so with a ginger wig and a ton of mascara, the fictional Jade Niven was born.'

'And he fell for it,' he said. 'Except, that when they met up in the pub on the evening in question, he didn't actually make a pass at her. Which sort of squared with the view we heard from his wife, that he was all mouth and no trousers, so to speak. But that wasn't a problem, not when you've got a couple of hundred deep-fake geeks beavering away for you in a big coding factory in Moscow. Probably only took a few hours of work to knock up these videos, and that was the end of Morrison's political career. And then after a bit of polling station intimidation by SFP goons and the destruction of a couple of thousand postal votes - and well done to DC Ronnie French for uncovering that last bit of dirty work by the way....' Frank smiled as French raised a hand in acknowledgement. '...Taggart got himself elected.'

'That's right,' Maggie said. 'So now Sienna had to deliver on her side of the bargain, which was to deliver all the hard-core gay sex that Tommy Taggart demanded. She knew he was a patron of the Harley-Dee's club, and so that became the base of her operation.'

Frank nodded. 'Aye, I got Eleanor Campbell to dig in to the ownership of the place and it turns out it's owned by a shell company which bought out the original owner a couple of years back. We've not completed our investigations yet, but we're pretty sure we'll find it's Russian money behind that firm.'

'For Tommy Taggart, the club was like a supermarket for sex,' Maggie said. 'All he had to do was pick out the men he wanted and help himself. We imagine some of the sex was consensual - and we think that was probably the case with the pole dancers Andy and Rab McVie. The police have since looked at their social media, and it's pretty clear they were into some wild stuff, with a particular penchant for threesomes.'

'Classy,' Frank said, raising an ironic eyebrow. 'But some *wasn't* consensual. And just to make it clear, I'm talking about rape here, nothing less than that. And that's what pointed you in the direction of the club, wasn't it Maggie?'

She nodded. 'There were two things really. Firstly, it was the fact that the Taggarts employed an obviously gay house-boy or whatever you would call him, which made me wonder about Tommy's sexuality. Secondly, it was what that actress Paige said in the press about her boyfriend Johnny Pallas.'

Frank laughed. 'The all-night bonking stuff?'

She nodded again. 'That's right. Pallas wasn't gay, but he was a patron of the club, and I figured that was only because of his association with Taggart's politics. But he was incredibly good-looking, and we can imagine that Tommy Taggart must have been *desperate* to bed him, whether he was gay or not.'

'So he was forcefully dragged into that bedroom and raped.' Frank paused for a moment, then said gravely. 'And then he was murdered. Just as the McVies were. Two o'clock in the morning, on the Royal Mile, just round the corner from the club. Tasered, stabbed and dumped.'

Maggie gave a sad look. 'And that too, sadly, was the fate of Rory Morrison.' She too paused, allowing the audience a moment of quiet reflection, before continuing. 'The police found evidence on Taggart's laptop. Pictures....' She felt herself welling up, reaching out to take a sip from a glass of water. 'They had to be silenced you see, whether the sex was consensual or not. The Taggarts couldn't take the chance that any of his conquests would talk, shattering the image of the big macho man. It's heartbreaking, the whole thing.'

'And bloody evil too,' Frank said.

'Yes it was,' she agreed. 'After Taggart's goons murdered Rory, it was Dominique who orchestrated the elaborate cover-up. Remember she told me that he had talked for months about starting a new life in Ibiza? Well that was of course a lie, and all the supposed social media postings from Ibiza were fakes. But when his friend Nathan Duke told me that Rory had never mentioned going to the island to him, that's when I started to get suspicious.'

'But we've got Taggart banged up now and he's going to spend the rest of his life in prison,' Frank said. 'We won't hear anything of him or his stupid party again.'

Maggie nodded. 'And good riddance too. So now we come back to the role of Irina Antonov, otherwise known as Dominique Tremblay. Her job was more subtle, a kind of insurance if you will, in case the main plan to back Tommy Taggart didn't turn out to be as successful as they hoped it would.' She paused for a moment, taking a sip from her glass of water. 'Dominique had two main tasks. The first was the seduction of Jack Urquhart, whom the Russians had identified as the up-and-coming star of the Nationalist party, and who had a track-record of infidelity that suggested he might fall for Dominique's ample charms.'

'Which he did,' Frank said, grinning. 'Men eh?'

She returned a knowing smile. 'Yes exactly. Her second role, in her job as journalist with the Globe, was to discredit the ruling Nationalist party by engineering a series of scandals, thereby giving the impression that this was a tired and corrupt administration whose time was up. The Russians are masters of this kind of disinformation campaign, and they put all their resources at Dominique's disposal to make it happen.' She turned and smiled at Yash. 'But I think Yash, you had kind of figured that out, hadn't you?'

He nodded. 'Yeah, it was just too... actually, I don't know the word, but there was that *drip drip drip* of scandal, and it was always bloody Dominique Tremblay who had the scoop on the story. Yeah, too neat, that's what it was. Too bloody neat.'

'But she made a mistake, a big mistake,' Frank continued. 'And it was one of timing. Because when it became clear that the Tommy Taggart plan was going to work out, there was no need for the plan B, making Jack Urquhart suddenly surplus to requirements. And from that point onwards, Dominique had no need to keep her lover sweet, so she became less keen on delivering on what we might call the conjugal side of the relationship.'

'Which made him suspect she might be having an affair, and which led him to my agency,' Maggie said.

Frank smiled. 'And the rest is history as they say. And that *is* true, because this bloody saga's going to be talked about for years.' He paused and took a drink from his own glass, then pointed at the audience. 'But *you* folks,' he continued, 'you want to know the inside scoop on Maggie's murder rap, don't you?'

'Yes please,' a voice shouted out.

'Right, well here it is. So with Urquhart no longer part of the plan, he had to be eliminated. And aye, I know it will shock you greatly, but that's the way these Russians operate. Life is cheap to them, and it was going to be much more neat and tidy if our boy Jack was murdered, just in case he'd harboured any suspicions about his lovely Canadian girlfriend during their time together and opened his big mouth. And as luck would have it - I mean, lucky for them, not us - along comes the perfect patsy in the shape of Miss Maggie Bainbridge. Dominique is routinely spying on her partner and knows about his meetings with Maggie. So she engineers a meeting at the Bikini Barista cafe, with two main purposes. First, to take a look at this woman in the flesh to assess if she is the type Jack Urquhart would make a play for.' He paused for a moment then smiled. 'Well, we know the answer to that one, don't we?' he said fondly. 'Because she's very lovely.'

Maggie could feel her face turning red in response to Frank's public flattery. Jumping in, she said, 'And the second purpose was to set me up for a bloody murder charge. When I met Dominique, she did this really creepy thing, running her hand through my hair and down my cheek. And that, I subsequently found out, was to get a strand of my hair she could plant on the pillow in this very hotel.'

'Aye, the frame-up,' Frank said, the thrusting his arms out in front of him as he surveyed the room. 'This place is popular with the politicians on account of its proximity to the parliament, and Dominique of course knew that Jack particularly favoured it. She was hacking his phone remember, so she knew about his lunch date with Maggie, and she guessed that if he operated true to form, he would try to get her to go to bed with him in the afternoon.'

'Which he did,' Maggie said ruefully. 'But I told him to get stuffed.'

Frank nodded. 'The thing is, even if he hadn't, they had booked another room in his name, because with these guys, there's always a plan B. So anyway, for one day only, Sienna Taggart, who we now know just *loves* dressing up, becomes the Polish agency maid Maja Jankowski, who swears that she saw Maggie and Jack Urquhart hand-in-hand and heading for some afternoon delight, if I can call it that. The Russian hackers have caused cyber chaos all over the capital, including buggering up the hotel's CCTV system. Urquhart's obviously disappointed that Maggie has turned him down, and decides he might as well head back down the hill to the parliament. Before he goes, he pays a quick visit to the loo, where he's confronted by a couple of Taggart's goons armed with a top-of-the-range Russian-made taser. A quick blast from that, then the dazed Urquhart is bundled into the lift, with no CCTV to evidence it, taken up to the fifth floor, then dumped in the room he's booked in his own name. A few seconds later, one of the goons plunges the knife into his gut, and then Maggie's hair is left on the pillow to be found by the forensic guys. To put the final icing on the cake, there's some What's App deep-fakery conjured up to make it look like Maggie and Urquhart had been desperately looking forward to the assignation.' He paused for a moment. 'You have to hand it to them, it was damn clever.'

'So me and my little boy became fugitives,' Maggie said, giving a wry grin. 'Actually, *he* absolutely loved it. He wants us to do it again sometime.' She paused for a moment. 'I said no, especially if I have to be accused of murder first.' A burst of laughter swept around the room. 'But at least it gave me time to think.'

Frank gave her a sardonic look. 'Aye, enough time to think it would be a good idea to dust down your schoolgirl French and give Dominique a surprise phone-call.'

She looked sheepish. 'Yes, perhaps not my brightest move, because Dominique unfortunately recognised my voice and realised we were onto them. I really put Lori and Jimmy in terrible danger, didn't I?'

He laughed. 'Aye, you did, especially Jimmy. God knows what my poor brother had in store for him at the hands of Tommy Taggart. But I suppose all's well that ends well eh? At least, as long as they don't send me the bill for burning down that Harley-Dee's place.'

'They won't be making you an honorary member, that's for sure,' Maggie said. She was silent for a moment, and then she spoke, her voice taking on a grave tone. 'But of course the most disturbing thing about this whole affair is that the perpetrators are quite likely to get off scot-free. In fact, as I understand it, right now they're at an RAF base in the south of England where an unmarked plane is poised to fly them back to Moscow.' She shook her head sadly. 'Yes, I know all about *Realpolitik* and all that, but it's still bloody ridiculous.'

Unexpectedly, Yash Patel spoke up. 'Don't worry Maggie, the Chronicle isn't going to be silenced on this one, no matter what *they* say.' He nodded his head in the direction of the assembled senior spooks. 'Tomorrow we'll be running a front-pager demanding that the UK Prime Minister shows some backbone and puts Irina Antonov and Olga Lebedev in front of a jury on a charge of murder. And believe me, we won't be giving up on this one. No way.'

Frank gave a wry smile. 'Well good luck with that Yash, that's all I'll say. But what do you think Maggie? Are we done now?'

She sighed. 'We're done. *Finally*. And thank *goodness* for that.'

***

Words were said afterwards of course, stern words directed by super-spook Dame Celia Carrington at both Maggie and Yash, reinforced by the hovering menace of her coterie of smooth-suited deputies. Stupid and naive just about summed up the message she wished to convey, although her words were sugar-coated in the oblique language of international spook-dom. At this very moment, she had said, with an air of superior world-weariness, the Kremlin was just deciding which prominent Western journalists they were going to arrest and accuse of spying. Innocents of course, but that would be no consolation to their families, facing the prospects of their loved ones being banged up in some Russian hell-hole prison for an indefinite period. *That* was the actuality of Realpolitik, and if it conflicted with everyone's idea of justice, then that was just the way it was. So Irina and Olga would be going home, but hardly to a hero's reception, which was some small consolation in a general unsatisfactory outcome. Carrie-Anne Fisher of the CIA had also added to the rhetoric, with a sly little speech to Frank about how easy it was for provincial police forces like his to get out of their depth when dealing with sophisticated matters of national security, a speech that, to Maggie's immense pleasure, had seriously pissed him off.

But now the media were beginning to disperse, surreptitiously slugging down a last glass of fizz before sloping off to their newsrooms to file their stories. Jimmy wandered over to declare the canapés insufficiently nourishing for his needs, a view shared *fortissimo* by Ronnie French, both resolving to set off in search of a burger. Lori would very much liked to have joined them, but instead, after some indecision, opted to join the shopping trip to Princes Street proposed by Lexy and Eleanor. Yash Patel had evidently made a proposal of a different kind to Jimani Shah, Maggie watching with amusement as they slid off in the direction of the elevator. Frank too had spotted their move, smirking and nodding in the direction of the couple.

'Actually, I thought about booking a room myself,' he said, deadpan. 'But then I thought again, given the circumstances.'

She gave him a wicked grin. 'Actually, so did I. The difference is, I actually did it. But don't worry, we're not in 507.' She reached up and kissed him on the cheek. *'Follow me.'*

A BIG THANK YOU FROM AUTHOR ROB WYLLIE

Dear Reader,

A huge thank you for reading *The Royal Mile Murders* and I do hope you enjoyed it! For indie authors like myself, reviews are our lifeblood so it would be great if you could take the trouble to post a star rating on Amazon.

If you did enjoy this book, I'm sure you would also like the other books in the series -you can find them all (at very reasonable prices!) on Amazon. Also, take a look at my webpage - that's robwyllie.com, where you can find bonus material which you might find enjoyable.

Thank you for your support!

Regards
Rob

Printed in Great Britain
by Amazon

28927393R00185